'Does it still pain you?'

'Would it give you pleasure to know that it does?' Rob asked, and his hand went to his face, for he knew that she must be revolted by its ugliness. 'Your brother told me that I had insulted you—and this was my punishment. I bear it with pride, for it is a constant reminder of the perfidy of women.'

Her hand crept to her throat. She was wearing the trinket he had once given her, hung from a ribbon around her neck. His eyes followed her movement and she saw him frown as he looked at the jade heart.

She raised her head proudly, meeting his eyes as anger bolstered her courage. 'Believe what you will. It makes little difference now.'

Rob came towards her, his expression stern, unforgiving. 'I came to inform you that you are now my prisoner, lady,' he said.

Anne Herries lives in Cambridgeshire, where she is fond of watching wildlife and spoils the birds and squirrels that are frequent visitors to her garden. Anne loves to write about the beauty of nature, and sometimes puts a little into her books—although they are mostly about love and romance. She writes for her own enjoyment, and to give pleasure to her readers. She is a winner of the Romantic Novelists' Association Romance Prize.

Previous novels by the same author:

MARRYING CAPTAIN JACK
THE UNKNOWN HEIR
THE HOMELESS HEIRESS
THE RAKE'S REBELLIOUS LADY
A COUNTRY MISS IN HANOVER SQUARE*
AN INNOCENT DEBUTANTE IN
   HANOVER SQUARE*
THE MISTRESS OF HANOVER SQUARE*
THE PIRATE'S WILLING CAPTIVE

A Season in Town trilogy

And in the Regency series
The Steepwood Scandal:

LORD RAVENSDEN'S MARRIAGE
COUNTERFEIT EARL

And in *The Hellfire Mysteries*:

AN IMPROPER COMPANION
A WEALTHY WIDOW
A WORTHY GENTLEMAN

FORBIDDEN LADY

Anne Herries

MILLS & BOON

First published in Great Britain 2010
Harlequin Mills & Boon Limited,
Eton House, 18-24 Paradise Road, Richmond, Surrey TW9 1SR

© Anne Herries 2007

ISBN: 978 0 263 21451 2

Harlequin Mills & Boon policy is to use papers that are natural, renewable and recyclable products and made from wood grown in sustainable forests. The logging and manufacturing process conform to the legal environmental regulations of the country of origin.

Printed and bound in Great Britain
by CPI Antony Rowe, Chippenham, Wiltshire

FORBIDDEN LADY

Prologue

'Melissa!' Rob cried, shock and despair in his face as he looked at the girl he loved and found her cold and remote, her eyes seeming to look straight through him. 'You cannot mean it. I beg you, tell me it is not true!'

Melissa stared at a point somewhere beyond his shoulder as she answered, 'Your suit is unwelcome to me, Robert of Melford. I do not wish to wed you.'

'Only yesterday you swore that you loved me,' Rob said, a flash of accusation in his eyes now. 'You laughed and kissed me and begged me to come here today and speak to your father…' He took her by the upper arms, his fingers digging into her soft flesh. 'Now you say you do not wish to be my wife? What has changed you? Tell me!' In his passion he was so magnificent that she almost broke, but somehow…somehow she kept her body stiff and straight and raised her eyes to his.

'I was merely playing a game,' she told him, deliberately making her voice cold and toneless. 'You are a fool to believe that I would truly wish to marry a man of your order. I am the daughter of a rich and powerful lord—and you are merely the son of a knight.' Her laughter was false and shrill. 'How could you think that I loved you? Leave this house now and never return!'

Rob stared at her for a moment longer, hardly able to credit that she was saying these words. Had her father been in the room with them he might have wondered if she was being forced, but they were alone and he had been welcomed to the castle by Lord Whitbread's steward before being brought here to speak with Melissa. Looking at her now, he saw how proud she was and realised that he had been mistaken about her nature.

'You laugh, lady,' he said, his voice harsh as he looked down into her lovely face. She had flawless skin, eyes that reminded him of a clear, mountain pool and red-gold hair that clustered about her face and fell to the small of her back in soft waves—but her words showed she was a heartless witch. 'But do not forget me—for I shall not forget you and one day…'

He left the threat in the air, turning to stride from the chamber. Melissa remained standing until the door closed and then she sagged, falling to her knees, her hands covering her face as the sobs broke from her. And then the tapestry behind her moved and a tall, heavily built man with a pockmarked face came out from the alcove behind it. Melissa rose to her feet and turned to look at him.

'Are you satisfied, Father?' she asked, her heart breaking. Yet pride returned as she met his stern gaze. 'You will keep your promise to me now that I have sent him away as you demanded?'

'He shall live, yes.' Lord Whitbread grunted. 'I doubt that puppy will come sniffing 'round here again in a hurry. You did well, Melissa.'

'And now you will send me to my aunt? You will allow me to live with her in the Abbey—and take my vows?'

Lord Whitbread's thin lips drew back in a sneer. 'No, you may not. Take the veil you shall not. For this you would need my permission and I do not give it. In time I shall arrange a marriage for you. One that will bring credit to our family.'

'But you promised…' Melissa looked into his eyes and knew that he had lied to her. She had done what he demanded of her but he did not intend to keep his word. She moved towards him as the fear started up in her. 'Father, you promised that *he* should be safe if I did what you want!'

'I promised that he shall live,' Lord Whitbread told her, his eyes glittering. 'His life shall be spared, though I do not think he will thank you for it.'

'What will you do to him?'

'I have told Harold to have some sport,' Lord Whitbread said, and his mouth curved in a cruel sneer. 'You know your brother, Melissa.'

'He is not my brother!' Melissa cried. 'That oafish brute is a bastard and no true…' She gave a little scream as Lord Whitbread struck her across the mouth and she tasted blood.

'Get to your room, girl, and stay there until I give you leave to come down,' he ordered. He moved nearer to her, his face close to hers. 'Remember that I own you, Melissa. I can do what I like to you—and if you displease me I might give *you* to your brother for his amusement.'

Melissa shuddered, for she knew that her father loved Harold but despised her. 'Why do you hate me so much?'

'Leave me!' Lord Whitbread thundered. 'You are lucky that I do not have you flogged for bringing Robert of Melford to my house. Remember, girl, if I ever discover that you have seen him again you will suffer.'

Melissa looked into his face and turned away. As she walked up the twisting stair that led to her solar she knew that she had made a terrible mistake. Her father had been so angry when he learned that she had promised herself to Rob, and he had warned her that if she did not send him away he would kill him. Melissa had obeyed him for she knew that he was a cruel hard man and would have carried out his threat. Now she knew that she ought to have run away and met Rob. She should have begged him to take her away…somewhere that her father and half brother would never find her.

But it was too late. She had seen the pain and anger in Rob's eyes when she denied her love. She had known that she must be harsh to make him leave her, and for his sake she had used words she knew would cut him to the heart. And now *her* heart was bleeding for she had lost the man she loved, her only chance of happiness denied her. Her father had promised that she would be allowed to visit her aunt at the Abbey, but now he had decided to keep her a prisoner in her chamber. He meant her to marry a man of his choosing but how could she marry another when she loved Rob?

But he must hate her now. She knew that it was too late to go back and that he would never forgive her for her cruel words. She had played her part well to protect him from her father, who had warned her Rob would die a slow and painful death. So she had done her father's bidding, and now she had lost the only man she had ever loved.

She took a tiny jade heart from inside her gown, holding it in the palm of her hand, and then she raised it to her lips and kissed it. Rob had given it to her on the day he had taken her to a fair. It was but a cheap trinket, but it meant more to her than all the gold and jewels in the world. She would keep it close to her as a reminder that once she had been loved.

Melissa raised her head proudly. Lord Whitbread had banished her to her chamber and ordered her to stay there until sent for, but one day she would leave this hateful place, though what would become of her she did not know. It did not matter, for it would be better if she had died rather than see the hurt her cruel words had inflicted on the man she loved more than her life.

Rob strode from the manor house, which was a later addition to the castle at Meresham and meant to make life more comfortable, his expression one of anger. How could Melissa's smiles and sweet kisses have fooled him so? She was beautiful and the scent of her drove his senses wild, but she was as false as she was attractive—and he was well rid of her!

It was as he approached the ancient Keep that several men fell on him. Rob was taken by surprise, but he struggled against them valiantly, knocking two to the ground and winding another before they finally subdued him.

'What is the meaning of this?' he cried out. 'I came here in good faith to ask for the hand of the lady Melissa. I demand that you unhand me now.'

'And you shall be repaid for your insolence,' a voice said. 'My father wishes you to have a token of his esteem. Harris— tie his hands behind him. I want to teach this dog a lesson.'

Rob gazed into the face of the man who had spoken. He knew Harold of Meresham only slightly by sight, but his reputation was common knowledge. He was an oafish lout who took pleasure in the lusts of the flesh and indulged his tastes by inflicting himself on village wenches. However, his most dangerous vice was bullying and he had been known to beat a man near to death for amusement when under the influence of wine.

'You may do your worst, Harold of Meresham,' Rob said, meeting his eyes fearlessly. 'I have done your family no wrong.'

'Be quiet, dog!' Harold said, and struck him across the face with a metal bar he had in his hand. It was sharp and cut into his flesh, making the blood spurt. Rob recoiled from the pain of it but could do nothing with his hands tied behind his back. 'That was for my sister! She told me that you had insulted her and she wanted nothing more to do with you. You are too low for her, Robert of Melford. She will marry into one of the best families in England. How dare you imagine that you were fit to be her husband?' He was raging now, his eyes staring and spittle upon his lips as he raised his arm and brought his weapon crashing down against Rob's skull, sending him to his knees. Rob was almost unconscious but he heard the words that decided his fate. 'Take him out and kill him, Harris. Let it be away from the castle for my father wanted him to live with the knowledge of his humiliation, but I prefer him dead.'

'Yes, sir. It shall be as you wish.'

Harris grabbed Rob by the arm, making him stand upright even though the faintness was washing over him and he barely knew what was going on. He was dragged away, the pain so overwhelming that he could not think clearly.

'Come on, fool. You deserve all that you get for thinking that you could insult the lady Melissa!'

Rob's wits were reeling. He hardly knew what the man was saying. Blood was running down his face, into his mouth and his eyes. He could see nothing as he was hustled away. Harris barked some orders and a horse was brought. Rob was hoisted over its back, his head hanging down to one side as if he were a sack of wheat. Dimly, as from a distance, he heard the drawbridge being lowered and the horse moved forward. Everything was becoming hazy and he felt as if he were falling into a black pit, the sounds of voices fading as he lost his senses.

It was a long time before the blackness began to get lighter. He gradually became aware of a throbbing in his head. He could not see clearly but he knew that he was being carried, not thrown across the horse as before but in a sling between two horses. His mouth was dry and he was feeling very ill, but he was alive—and he should not be alive.

He moaned aloud and a man came to his side, looking down at him. A water flask was put to his lips and he swallowed as a few drops trickled into his mouth.

'Do not try to talk, sir,' the man said. 'They meant to kill you, but I found help and beat them off. There were three of them but they did not know I followed. We shall soon have you home— though I fear that you will never be as handsome as you were.'

'Who are you?' Rob asked through cracked lips. 'Why…'

The man smiled. 'All you need to know for now is that I am a friend—and that you are safe…'

Rob closed his eyes again. He was alive. The pain was almost unbearable but he would bear it…as he would bear the agony of *her* betrayal. She had led him on, making him believe that she loved him as he loved her. Oh, God, how he had loved her! But she had betrayed him.

He saw again the triumphant sneer of Harold's mouth as he struck him across the face, laying the flesh open to the bone.

That was for Melissa. She told me that you had insulted her.

Rob groaned, knowing that the pain of those words and her false laughter would live on long after his wounds had healed.

Chapter One

'I do not think it wise for you to make the journey alone,' Owain Davies said. 'There are many lawless bands roaming the country, my lady, and they would not hesitate to take you prisoner and hold you to ransom. I do not think that Lord Whitbread would be pleased if that happened—do you?'

'He would be very angry,' the lady Melissa of Whitbread said. 'But it will not happen if you are with us, Owain. I must get to the Abbey, because I may never have another chance. You know that I have been kept almost a prisoner for the past several months since…' Her voice broke and she lifted her head, hiding her pain. She didn't want anyone to guess how she had suffered these past months, not even the man she trusted most. 'My father is determined that I shall marry a man of his choosing and I would rather die.'

'That is foolish talk, my lady.' Owain's eyes narrowed. He had not been in the castle when Robert of Melford had been sent away and he did not know her true feelings on the matter for she had not confided in him.

'Foolish or not it is how I feel. I have decided to beg my aunt for sanctuary. If she grants it, I may live at the Abbey in safety and perhaps take the veil.'

'You should do so only if you have a calling,' Owain replied, his eyes thoughtful as he looked at her face. He knew that her life had been hard these past years, and sometimes it was as much as he could bear to stand by and watch as she was ill-treated.

'Are you willing to risk your father's anger, knowing that he may punish you again?'

'Yes, because there is no other way. Besides, she is my aunt and the only link to my mother,' Melissa said, her eyes dark with sorrow for a mother's love she had never known. 'I would speak with her, ask her about my mother if she will tell me. She has always refused to talk of her sister, but she may relent this time if she understands how unhappy I have been…'

Her look was so wistful that Owain could not refuse her request, though he knew he ought not to allow this madcap idea. Lord Whitbread's anger would know no bounds when he returned to find her gone.

'If you wish it so much, I shall escort you,' Owain said. 'But we must return on the morrow. If we are gone no more than a day, it may be that your father will never know.'

Melissa smiled at him. She had known he would help her as never in the years that he had served her had he failed her. He had been the father she lacked, helping her in so many small ways that she had lost count. Yet she felt a little guilty for not having told him the whole truth. It was true that she wanted to ask her aunt about her mother, but it was not the only reason for her flight from Lord Whitbread's manor.

It was a warm afternoon, but the canopy of ancient trees sheltered the traveller from the fierce heat, the stillness broken only by the heavy pounding of the destrier's hooves and the sound of a thrush trilling from its secret hiding place. Suddenly, a woman's screams rent the air; shrill and desperate, they sent a flock of birds winging into the sky, destroying the peace of the forest.

Robert Melford was riding hard, leaving his train lagging behind in his anxiety to reach his home on the borders of England

and Wales. He had lately been at the Castle of Angers in France, where he had pledged his father's affinity to Henry Tudor, Earl Richmond. Descended from the great John of Gaunt and Katherine Swynford, through Margaret Beaufort, Henry Tudor had a slender but legitimate claim to the English throne, and was even now gathering an army. Rob had gone to Richmond's court with his father's good wishes, for the wars that had plagued the country for nigh on thirty years were not yet done. The English crown sat uneasily on the head of King Richard III, who had seized it, in the opinion of many, from King Edward IV's heir by treachery.

Now Rob was returning ahead of Henry Tudor's army in order to gather support in the lush valleys and lowlands of the Marches. Even as he had prepared to leave Angers, a message had reached him that his father had been struck down with a dread illness and Rob's haste was not so much on behalf of his promise to Richmond as his fear that he might be too late.

However, despite his impatience to be home, Rob was too much the chivalrous knight to ignore a woman's cries for help. When he came to the clearing and saw the three ladies being attacked by a band of brigands, his first thought was to aid them. Drawing the trusty sword that he carried slung across his body, always at the ready, Rob rode directly at the brigand attempting to subdue a young woman. She was fighting for all she was worth, struggling against the superior strength of the great brute that had his hands on her, but it was the other two women who were screaming.

Rob leaned down from the saddle of his mighty steed, swinging the heavy sword and delivering a blow that cut deeply into the shoulder of the brigand, sending him staggering away to fall bleeding to the ground. Wheeling about, his destrier snorting with the lust of battle, Rob rode down another of the brutes and sent him flying, trampled beneath his horse's hooves. Seeing that they were facing a powerful knight, who was trained for war, the other three robbers fled in panic.

Rob laughed in triumph as they disappeared into the forest, dismounted and turned to the woman who had fought so valiantly against her attackers, sweeping her a courtly bow.

'I hope you are not harmed, lady,' he said, and turned to her, smiling at her in a way that had charmed many a lady at Angers despite the disfiguring scar that marred one side of his face. Robert Melford was well formed, his shoulders broad, his legs long and powerful. He was also handsome, with his dark hair worn long, and his eyes as blue as the cloudless sky above their heads in this sunlit clearing. However, the humour left his eyes as he stared down into the face of the woman he had sworn to forget. 'You!' he exclaimed, his gaze fixed on her like a hungry wolf, ravenous and menacing.

'Rob…' Melissa said, the colour draining from her cheeks as she looked at him. His was a strong face with well-defined bones and, despite his stern expression, a soft mouth—but she could see only the terrible scar on his left cheek. 'I… What happened to your face?'

Rob reached up to stroke the scar. It was no longer a source of terrible agony, though it had given him weeks of sleepless nights. The thick welt of red flesh was unsightly, for it had been crudely sewn and had never quite healed as it ought, though the blow to his head had recovered well and there was only a thin scar beneath his thick hair. Her question made him angry and he could barely restrain himself, his hands clenching at his sides.

'You dare to ask?' he said harshly. 'This was your parting gift to me, lady. Your brother laid my cheek open to the bone to remind me not to look above my station in the matter of a wife.'

'No…' Melissa felt the sickness in her throat as she stared at Harold's work. 'I knew that my father had told him…but that is so cruel…' She closed her eyes for the realisation of what he must have suffered had washed over her, making her faint. 'I feared the worst and wondered if you were dead….'

Although a wimple covered her head, a few strands of red-gold hair had escaped to curl waywardly about her face. Her complexion was fair, her eyes more green than blue. Rob's eyes dwelled on her beauty, anger stirring as he understood that she still had the power to move him.

'As you see, I am not,' Rob said coldly. 'I am sorry to disappoint you, lady, but your brother did not finish his work and I live still.'

Melissa opened her eyes and looked at him. 'You think that I wished for…' She turned away from him, fighting her tears. She must not give way to weakness. 'No matter. I am innocent of the sin you would place on me, sir—but I shall not beg for your understanding. You have come to my aid, though perhaps you wish now that you had not?'

'I have not said it,' Rob growled. 'You may be faithless, lady, but your women deserved my help.' He looked around him. 'Where are your men? Why has your father allowed you to ride out unprotected in these uncertain times?' His gaze narrowed. 'Or does he know that you are here?'

Melissa raised her head proudly. 'I go to the Abbey to visit my aunt who is Abbess there. She wrote some weeks ago to say that she was unwell…and I took the opportunity to visit her while my father was away.'

'As I thought,' Rob said, looking down at her. What was it about her that affected him so? He had every reason to distrust and hate her, and he had made up his mind to put her from his thoughts—but seeing her had brought the pain and anguish of her betrayal rushing back.

She affected him as no other ever had. She was surely the most beautiful woman he had ever seen! He experienced a surge of fierce desire that made him long to sweep her up in his arms and ride off with her. But he fought it, listening to her explanation in silence.

'My groom accompanied us, but he lies dreadfully wounded a little back there....' She pointed in the direction she had come from, which was opposite to that Rob had taken to reach this clearing. 'I believe he may well be dead.' A little sob escaped her. 'Owain was loyal and kind and I will blame myself for his death…as you say, I ought not to have come without men-at-arms to guard me. It will be my fault if he dies because he was against this journey.'

'Your will prevailed as always,' Rob said scornfully as the memory of her scorn stilled the surging desire. She was false and not to be trusted, so even if his body still burned for her, his mind rejected all that she was. 'Show me where you left the man…we should go and see whether his wound is fatal. You have been foolish and wilful, lady, and we must hope that the loss of your serf is the worst that befalls you.'

'Owain is not a serf,' Melissa said, and her eyes flashed with fire as she was aware of his scorn. 'He is his own man but chooses to give his affinity to me.'

Rob knew that he was right to distrust her, for plainly she was as haughty and proud as she was beautiful. 'To you, lady?' he asked, raising his brows. 'It is more usual for a man to offer his affinity to a nobleman for his good lordship.'

'Owain was my mother's kinsman,' Melissa said. 'When she died in childbed, he gave his loyalty to me. He asks for nothing more than a roof over his head and the food he eats.'

'And wears your father's livery no doubt?' Rob said, mocking her in the hope of some reaction. She did not fail him, her eyes sparking as she raised a hand to strike him a blow. He was too quick for her, seizing her wrist and holding it in an iron grip. Against the fairness of her skin, his was dark toned and bronzed by the sun of France.

'Let me go, you devil!' Melissa blazed at him, feeling angry now. He hated her for what had been done to him, and perhaps he had the right—but his scorn pricked her and her anxiety for Owain had brought her close to tears.

'Let you go?' Rob asked, wild thoughts of revenge in his mind. He could take her now, ride off with her to his home and teach her what it felt like to know despair, and yet her beauty moved him and he smiled oddly. 'No, no, lady, let us not come to blows. I shall take you up with me since your horse has been lost. If your ladies wait here my men will arrive at any moment and they may follow us to the Abbey, bringing your horses if they can be found nearby. If your faithful kinsman still lives we shall take him there for the monks to nurse. If he is slain my men will bury him and a candle shall be lit in the house of our Lord and the priest paid to say a mass for his soul.'

'You are kind, sir,' Melissa said, her manner proud and re-served, for she had seen the mockery in his eyes. 'I do not know why, because you have been served ill by my family.'

'The cruellest blow of all was yours, Melissa,' he told her. 'Yet I shall not take foul advantage for it would not set well with my honour.'

Melissa stared at him for a moment and the look in her eyes gave him pause for thought. It was almost as if she were accusing him of something, though he could not imagine what—she was the one who had betrayed him.

'I will help you because my father was once, long ago, your father's friend,' Rob said. As young men, Rob's father had pledged his affinity to Lord Whitbread, as many did to the most powerful lord in their district. But they had quarrelled years ago, and of late the divide had grown wider because they were now on opposite sides.

After King Edward died and the throne fell to Richard, Duke of Gloucester, Sir Oswald Melford had changed his allegiance to another powerful lord. The rumours that King Richard III had ordered the murders of King Edward's sons in the Tower of London had caused Sir Oswald, like many more freemen of England, to become disaffected. Lord Whitbread remained loyal to King Richard, but Sir Oswald had sent his son to the Earl of Richmond.

'Why does my father hate yours?' Melissa asked. 'What is between them that…' she choked back the words and shook her head. If she once faltered, if she gave way to the emotions swirling inside her she would weep—but she must not.

'An old quarrel, I do not know. We waste time, lady,' Rob said, a note of impatience in his voice. 'Come, I am in a hurry. I must return home in all haste for my father is ill, but I shall see you safe to the Abbey before I continue my journey.'

Without more ado, he brought his horse forward, swept her up upon its back and leaped up behind her. Even as the great horse began to move ahead, his retainers were pouring into the sunlit clearing.

'Follow to the Abbey and bring the women with you,' Rob cried to his squire and urged his mount into the forest. He turned his attention back to the lady he was holding lightly against his chest, clamping down on his senses though her perfume was a bittersweet memory that hurt him still. 'How far did you travel after your kinsman was struck down?'

'It cannot be far for they pursued us and soon fell upon us,' Melissa said as they moved on to the track that wound between the trees. After a few moments she pointed to a figure that lay sprawled upon the ground just ahead of them. 'See! There lies my faithful Owain…' As Rob drew his horse to a standstill once more, she slipped from its back without assistance and ran to where her servant lay. A little cry escaped her as she saw that his eyelids fluttered when she touched him. 'I think he lives. The saints be praised, he is not dead!'

Rob dismounted and went to her side. He saw at once that although the man had received a blow to his head that ought by rights to have slain him, he clung stubbornly to life. Turning him over to look at his face, Rob knew at once that this was the man who had saved him and carried him back to his home, departing the next day before he was well enough to thank him.

'This man is your kinsman?'

'Yes, his name is Owain Davies.'

'I am glad to tell you that God has seen fit to spare him, lady,' Rob said, bending down to examine the wound. 'He lives yet, though for how long I know not. We shall carry him with us to the Abbey.' He was glad that he had not given way to his baser nature because this man needed his help, and he owed him his life.

Some of his men had followed hard upon their heels and he summoned them to his side, giving orders that a sling was to be fashioned so that the man might be carried between two of the baggage horses—just as Owain had carried him home that night. He stood up, taking hold of Melissa's arm, tearing her from her weeping examination of her faithful kinsman. For some reason her tears made him angry. She wept for Owain Davies, but she had cried none for him!

'Come, lady. I have no time for this. I must see you to the Abbey and be on my way.'

Melissa looked at him. 'I owe you my life and that of my ladies,' she admitted. 'Since you are in haste to be on your way, I must not detain you. Perhaps if you were to give us horses and the escort of three of your men it would suffice?' She felt that she could hardly bear to be near him and know that he despised and hated her.

'Perhaps,' Rob said. It would be convenient for he was impatient to continue his journey, and yet something held him. He knew he could not rest easy in his mind if he abandoned her to his men. 'But it is not my way to desert a lady in trouble. I shall see you safe to the Abbey for those robbers are not the only danger a lady of your standing might face. You were foolish to venture out without at least ten of Lord Whitbread's men to protect you.'

'We do not live in the days of poor mad King Henry,' Melissa said, becoming proud and haughty once more, though she knew he spoke truly. 'My father has told me that the kingdom was indeed lawless in those days, but it is not thus now.'

If she believed that then she was indeed a fool! King Edward had managed to subdue some of the lawless nobles for a while but they had too much power and would never be brought into line while they were allowed to continue the custom of livery and all that that implied. Many of the earls and barons had set up a court to rival that of the King himself with hundreds of followers through various affinities, and were likely to take the law into their own hands. Only strong rule would break their power, which had grown so strong during King Henry VI's reign.

Rob was tempted to tell her that England was once more on the brink of war. Yet it was best to keep a still tongue whilst nothing was absolutely certain. Henry Tudor had promised to bring an army to these shores soon, but until he actually arrived it might be unwise to speak of these things—especially to the daughter of a man who was the King's stalwart and his enemy.

'I shall not argue with you, lady. Come, your kinsman is being attended. We shall ride on.' He held out his hand to her, his manner imperious, brooking no refusal.

For a moment she hesitated, but then gave him her hand and once again he threw her up on the great warhorse. She said nothing as he mounted behind her, though he felt her body stiffen when he put his arms about her.

'You have no need to fear me, lady,' he whispered, as her warmth and the delicious scent of her roused forbidden feelings in his loins. 'I swear by all that I hold sacrosanct that I shall not harm you. There may come a time when I shall take revenge on you and yours—but it is not yet. I do not prey on vulnerable women.'

'I do not fear you,' she replied, and yet she knew it was a lie.

To be with him like this would bring back the sleepless nights and the terrible pain she had endured for months.

'I have always admired your courage,' he said.

Melissa relaxed slightly against the hardness of his chest. For this little time, she would let herself believe that the bad things that stood between them had never been. She would let herself remember a young man who smiled at her with love in his eyes and the sweetness of his kisses. For a few short weeks, while her father was absent from the castle, they had met in secret, wandering through the woods hand in hand or riding together on his horse as now. Once he had taken her to a fair, buying her sweetmeats and ribbons from the peddlers...so few memories, but each one precious. If only her father had not forbidden the marriage...if only she had run away with him before it was too late! She held back the sob, which rose to her lips, because she must not give way to the overwhelming longing, the desire to tell Rob the truth...but would he even care or believe her? After seeing scorn and anger in his eyes, she thought that it would only shame her to confess her love.

They rode in silence for some time, covering a distance of no more than five leagues when the forbidding shadow of the great Abbey fell across their path. It was a thirteenth-century building with arches, narrow windows, little bigger than arrow slits, and a massive undercroft, built to house both monks and nuns in separate quarters. At the huge gates of iron-studded oak, Rob dismounted and lifted Melissa down, placing her gently on her feet before turning to tug at the rope, which rang the bell above the arch.

Moments later, a nun came to answer the summons, and looked out through a little peephole in the gate. Melissa gave her name and the nun recognised it, beginning to draw back the huge bolts that kept the gate secure to admit her.

'I must leave you now.' Rob made his bow to Melissa. His expression was cold and hard, his manner reserved. 'If I were you, lady. I should send word to your home. It would be folly to attempt the return without an escort.'

'Yes, perhaps…' Melissa raised her head, then, her expression a little hesitant. 'Thank you, sir. You have done more than I could have expected.'

'I did what any decent man would do for any lady in distress, no more and no less.'

Melissa inclined her head, regretting the coldness between them. Once he had smiled at her, his bold eyes challenging her but with warmth…with love. He had loved her once, she knew, but she had killed his love—and her brother had humbled his pride, making him cold and bitter. How could she expect more from him? She raised her eyes to his, her own pride making her seem haughty, though inside she was weeping for what had been lost and would not come again.

Rob left her as she was admitted to the Abbey, remounting and riding on even as his men brought in her kinsman. He had wasted precious hours and must ride all the harder if he were to reach his home in time.

Melissa lingered a moment to watch the knight ride away. She knew that he had saved her from a fate worse than death for the men who had attacked her would hardly have been satisfied to take her purse. Yet to leave secretly, without an escort, had been her only chance of escaping her father's tyranny.

Lord Whitbread had been visiting someone of importance and she had been informed that he might bring a guest with him when he came home. She knew that he was thinking of finding a husband for her and she believed that his guest might be the man he was considering giving her to in marriage.

However, the letter from her aunt telling her that she was unwell had made up her mind. She had seized it as her excuse and taken the chance to escape the domination of her father.

Lord Whitbread had never been kind to his daughter. Melissa's mother had died in childbed and for some reason

Lord Whitbread had chosen never to marry again. He had acknowledged Harold his bastard son as his heir. Harold might be a great brute of a man, coarse and strong with the manners of an oaf, but he was clever in his own way and had found favour with his father.

Melissa did not know why her half brother should be so favoured by their father, while she, his legitimate child, was scorned. She knew that he hated her and she feared him, though his habit of cuffing her about the head had ceased since her fifteenth birthday. He had suddenly realised that she was a beautiful young woman, and that her beauty might be an asset. In the time since then Melissa had lived in dread of the marriage he would make for her. She knew that he would not take her feelings into account and that she would be sold for position or power.

Sometimes she wished that she was not an heiress, for then she might have been allowed to live in obscurity and peace. However, her mother's father had been the Earl of Somersham and his lands had been left in trust for her when he died earlier that year because he had no other heir. Melissa had begged to be allowed to retire to her lands, but her father had refused her. Until she married she was under his domain, and he meant to use her beauty and wealth to his advantage.

Melissa was sure that had he been able to snatch her lands from her—her father would have done so without compunction. However, the earl had made King Richard the steward of her fortune, and her death would have brought no gain to her father with the estate then becoming the property of the Crown. Even now, her father would have to gain the consent of the King to her marriage. Melissa was praying that if her aunt recovered her health, which she prayed she would, she might petition His Majesty to allow her to retire to the Abbey. She was recalled to the present, as she became aware that the nun was speaking.

'It is good that you have come, my lady,' the nun was saying. 'Mother Abbess has asked for you many times.'

'I would have come before if I could,' Melissa said, and glanced at the men who were bringing Owain in. 'But we were attacked and my kinsman has been injured. Will you tend him, sister? Forgive me, I do not know your name?'

'I am Sister Cecile,' the nun told her. 'The monks will tend to your servant as in this order we are not allowed to care for men, only women, unless given special dispensation by the Bishop—but your kinsman may be admitted and taken to the infirmary. However, the rest of your men must stay outside the gates.'

'They are the men of...a gallant knight who came to my rescue,' Melissa said. 'They will depart once they have done their duty—but I do not intend to leave just yet. How is the Abbess? It is some weeks since I had her letter, but I was not able to make the journey here until now.'

'A little better this morning,' Sister Cecile told her with a smile. She waited until Melissa's women and the men carrying the injured Owain were inside the gates before addressing them. 'You must take him to the infirmary and leave by that gate. The monks will attend you, good sirs.'

Rob's men inclined their heads and went off in the direction of the outbuilding she had indicated. Cecile led the way towards the building used by the nuns. A high wall and another heavy gate separated the living quarters of the nuns and the monks, though the chapel was used by both for worship.

'I thank God that He has spared her,' Melissa said as Sister Cecile led the way. 'I feared that I might be too late as she said that she had been gravely ill.'

'Indeed, when you were sent for we thought she might not last the night,' Sister Cecile said. 'But come, lady. I shall take you to her quarters. Your women will be cared for by my sisters and you may see them later.'

Melissa turned to her women, telling them that she would see them in a little while, and then followed Sister Cecile inside the living quarters provided for the Sisters of Mercy. Although it was a warm day in June, Melissa shivered as she went inside the stone building. It had only tiny windows and the sun was shut out by the thickness of the walls. Even wearing her cloak over her silk tunic and surcote, she still felt chilled. Glancing at Sister Cecile, she saw that the nun did not seem to notice the cold, and realised that she was accustomed to the discomfort.

For a moment Melissa was discouraged. Did she truly wish to devote her life to God? Once she had thought that happiness, love and children were her future—but now she knew that all that was at an end. Melissa realised that she had secretly hoped to meet Rob again and that he would declare his love for her and beg her to ride off with him—and she would have gone. His coldness, the scorn in his eyes combined to tell her that he no longer loved her. It was foolish to dream though, because even if he had spirited her away, Lord Whitbread would have taken retribution. Melissa could not live with so many deaths on her conscience, knowing that it had been no idle threat.

The nun had stopped outside a closed door. She knocked and waited for a moment, then looked inside. Putting a finger to her lips, she beckoned Melissa to enter.

'Are you sleeping, Mother?' she said softly.

The Abbess opened her eyes, looking at Sister Cecile for a moment and then her gaze transferred to Melissa. Her lips moved and her hands fluttered as if she were in some distress.

'Melissa, my child,' she said. 'I was not sure that your father would let you come.'

'I could not stay away from you when I knew you were ill,' Melissa said. 'My dearest aunt. I have seen you all too seldom these past years, but you are often in my thoughts.'

'My child…' The Abbess held out her hand as Melissa approached. 'I do not know how long I may be spared to this life and I wished to see you once more before I die.'

'Please do not speak of dying, Aunt.'

'If my time has come I must accept it,' the Abbess said. 'When I entered this place I put away worldly things, but I have loved you from afar, Melissa. I wished to tell you something…' She glanced at the nun still standing near the door. 'Thank you, Sister Cecile. You may leave us.'

'Yes, Mother. You will ring when I am needed?'

'Of course.' The Abbess waited until the door closed behind Cecile and then reached beneath her pillow, taking out a paper sealed with wax. She put it into Melissa's hands. 'No, do not read it yet, child. It tells you a secret that I vowed never to reveal in life. When I am gone you may read it and take what action you will, but until then promise me that you will abide by my wishes in this matter.'

'Yes, dearest aunt,' Melissa said, taking the letter and placing it in the leather pouch that she wore attached to a braided belt at her waist. 'I shall remember and respect your wish.'

'I promised that I would never reveal the secret,' the Abbess said, and her eyes held an expression of distress. 'But I have feared for you, Melissa. I know…' She drew in a sucking breath. 'I must not reveal what I know while I live for I gave my sacred promise. Yet I would not have you at the mercy of that…' She shook her head and fell back against the pillows, closing her eyes.

'Aunt!' Melissa cried, frightened that it was her aunt's last moment, but after a few seconds the Abbess opened her eyes once more. 'I love you, Aunt Beatrice.'

'I am Mother Abbess,' her aunt reminded her gently. 'I am not allowed to care for you as I would wish—but I think God will forgive my final sin.'

Melissa looked at her, feeling bewildered and uncertain. If her aunt had guarded her secret for so long it must be important—and yet it seemed to concern her.

'Is there something I may fetch for you?' she asked. 'Some water perhaps?'

'Sister Cecile will return soon,' the Abbess said. 'She will give me my medicine which needs to be measured carefully. Though it heals, it also kills, as do many of the herbs we use in our cures. You have travelled a long way and should rest. Leave me now and we shall meet again tomorrow.'

'I wish that I could do something for you,' Melissa said, her throat catching with emotion. 'But I shall leave you to rest, dearest aunt.' She turned away from the bed. As she opened the door, she discovered Sister Cecile about to knock. 'I believe that Mother Abbess wishes to rest,' she said. 'Perhaps you would show me to my cell and then return to her?'

'Yes, of course,' Sister Cecile said, glancing past her at her superior. 'She seems to be resting now. I shall return and tend her later.'

Melissa nodded, following the nun from the room. She had not mentioned her mother, nor yet her wish to remain at the Abbey, to her aunt, and she was not sure why. Perhaps she had not wished to distress the sick woman at such a time, and yet she knew that she must do so unless she wished to return to her father's house. Only the sanctuary of the Abbey could save her from the fate he was planning for her.

Reaching his home, Rob lost no time in entering the house. David, his father's faithful steward, a man of advanced years, grey in his beard but honest and generous of nature, came hurriedly to greet him and the look in his eyes told him that he was too late.

'My father?'

'He died two days ago, Rob,' David said. 'Forgive me. I would have sent for you sooner, but he would have it that nothing was wrong.'

Rob felt an overwhelming surge of grief. 'I should have been here! I should have been with him!'

'He bid me give you his blessing,' David said. 'He told me that he was proud of you because he knew that you would choose the right path in life—and he asked your pardon.'

'My pardon—for what?'

David's eyes went to the scar on his face. 'He blamed himself for what was done to you, because of the quarrel between him and Lord Whitbread.'

'I have told him that it was none of his doing,' Rob said. 'What kind of a man would do this over a piece of land?'

'I do not believe it was just the land,' David said. 'It began long ago, when they were both young…'

Rob frowned, his gaze narrowing. 'What is this? I have heard nothing of it before. I believed it was that woodland Whitbread coveted?'

'That came later,' David said. 'Do not ask me to tell you what was the source of their anger because I do not know but I believe it may have been a woman.'

'My mother?'

David shook his head. 'I can tell you no more. Will you go up and see your father now, Rob? Megan has cared for him, but we waited to bury him until you returned.'

'You did as you ought,' Rob said. 'I shall go up to him now.'

He was thoughtful as he walked up the stairs. What was this quarrel that had led to such hatred between his father and Lord Whitbread? If his father had lived he might have told him. Rob had been young and foolish when he fell in love with the beautiful girl he had seen walking in the meadows by her home. For some weeks he had gone every day to meet her, and their courtship had been sweet—but he had been blinded by his passion and her beauty, for Melissa was obviously as cold and proud as her father.

He would put her from his mind…but what of his heart?

This was no time to be thinking of such things! Rob was angry at himself. He must keep a vigil by his father this night and in the morning Sir Oswald would be laid to rest with all the honour due to the honest, decent man he had been.

Melissa was thoughtful as she walked in the Abbey gardens that evening before it grew dark. It was peaceful here, with the birds singing from the branches of ancient apple trees and a scent of lavender on the air. She had requested another interview with her aunt, but had been told that the Abbess was sleeping.

Would she be content to spend her life here? Melissa wondered. It had been her intention to ask for a dispensation when she left her home that morning, but now she was uncertain. She did not wish to admit it but she had not been able to forget the sweet feeling that had swept through her as she rode through the forest with Robert of Melford's arms about her. But that was foolish because he hated her! He had loved her once, but she had sent him away and her half brother had done terrible things to him. He must hate her very name!

She was a fool to think of him, but he would not be dismissed from her thoughts. She could not help wondering what he was doing now, and if he had been in time to see his father alive.

A hand shaking her shoulder awakened Melissa. She was deep in sleep, dreaming of a time when she had been happy, walking barefoot in a meadow, and she awoke with a smile on her lips, but the smile left her swiftly as she saw her serving woman's expression.

'What is it, Rhona?'

'Sister Cecile told me to wake you,' Rhona said. 'She fears that your aunt has taken a turn for the worse and asks that you join her immediately. The priest has given her the last rites.'

Melissa needed no further bidding as she sprang up from her pallet. Her serving woman had her cloak waiting, slipping it about her shoulders over her flimsy shift. Melissa slid her feet into leather shoes and tossed her hair back from her face. It had tangled as she slept but there was no time to dress it. Her heart was thudding as she left the small cell where she had spent the past few hours in repose, knowing that the nun would not have sent for her if it were not urgent.

She prayed silently that her aunt would be spared as she hurried down the cold and narrow passage, which was only dimly lit by a torch at the far end. By the time she reached her aunt's chamber, she was shivering, the fear striking deep into her heart. She hesitated outside the door for a moment, and then went in. Tallow candles were burning in their sconces, the smell pungent and adding to the unpleasant odour in the room. Melissa realised that her aunt must have been sick, and she saw Sister Cecile wiping vomit and blood from the lips of the Abbess.

'Dearest Aunt Beatrice,' Melissa said, going to her side. The stricken woman held out her hand and she grasped it, but she could see the colour fading from her aunt's face. 'God give you peace....'

'May God bless and keep you, child,' the Abbess whispered, and then gave a little cry, her head falling back against the pillows. Her eyes were open and staring, and Sister Cecile closed them, making the sign of the cross on her forehead.

Melissa felt the tears welling inside her as she came forward and bent to kiss her aunt's cheek. The stench of the vomit was vile and made her gasp and draw back swiftly.

'What made her be sick like that?' she asked the nun. 'Has she done so before?'

'No, my lady, she has not,' Cecile said, and looked upset. 'I had thought she was rallying before you arrived—but this came upon her suddenly. It is not natural...'

'What do you mean?' Melissa was startled. 'Do you suspect...' She lowered her voice to a hushed whisper. 'It is not poison?'

'I do not know,' the nun said. 'I say only that I think the manner of her death suspicious.'

'But who would do such a thing and how?' Melissa saw the nun's look and shook her head. 'You do not suspect me? I swear before God that I did no such thing. I loved her and wished her to live.'

'I know that you loved her,' Sister Cecile said. 'She has spoken of you with fondness and I hold you blameless in this—but your women and you are the only strangers in our midst at this time. No one else has been admitted—and none of the sisters would harm one hair of Mother Abbess's head for we all love her dearly.'

'You think that one of my women...' Melissa shook her head. 'You must be wrong. Both Rhona and Agnes have served me faithfully all my life. Why would either of them betray me by taking her life? They knew that I hoped...' Melissa sighed as she realised that she could not stay here now. She had hoped that the Abbess would petition for her inheritance to be released so that she might offer at least a part of it to the Abbey in return for sanctuary. She shook her head, because the idea no longer appealed now that her aunt was dead. 'I do not believe that either of them would have done anything so wicked.'

'Well, perhaps it was not poison,' Sister Cecile said, clearly uncertain. 'I must write a letter to the Bishop and he will send a brother versed in these things to investigate. I shall not lay the blame at your door whatever his decision—but do not trust Agnes.'

'Why do you suspect her?' Melissa asked, her fine brows raised.

'I found her coming from Mother Abbess's room not an hour ago. When I asked her why she was not in the cell she had been given, she said that she had gone out to the privy and lost her way—but that would be hard to do unless she is blind or a fool.'

'Agnes is neither,' Melissa said. 'Say nothing of this to anyone but the Bishop and his representative when he comes. I shall watch Agnes and if she betrays herself in any way I shall send word to the Bishop myself.'

'Then we are in agreement,' the nun said. 'I do not wish to distress my sisters at this time. Perhaps I am wrong to suspect foul play.' She was thoughtful, then said, 'May I ask why the Abbess wished to speak to you in private? Did it concern matters here?'

'No, it was merely a family matter,' Melissa said. 'I am sure that it had nothing to do with her death.' And yet the letter she had given Melissa contained a secret that she had not wanted to reveal until after she was dead.

'Very well,' Cecile said. 'Her body will be displayed in the chapel once I have made her clean and sweet. You may pay your respects to her in the morning before you leave.'

'May I not stay until she is buried?'

'You are not one of us. Unless you need nursing—or receive a dispensation from Mother Abbess or the Bishop—you may not stay here more than one night. I am sorry but I did not make the rules, though I must abide by them.'

'Yes, I understand,' Melissa said. She had hoped that her aunt would grant that dispensation, but it was too late.

'What of my kinsman Owain?'

'The monks care for him,' the nun said. 'I will inquire in the morning how he does—but if you wish to remain nearby you must find lodgings. I believe there is a decent hostel in the village of Melford, which is some five leagues distant.'

'I thank you for your kindness—and your devotion to my aunt,' Melissa said. 'We shall leave you in the morning.'

'Yes, you must go. We need to grieve for Mother,' Cecile said, and her eyes were bright with unshed tears. 'I am sorry that you must leave, but you may not remain at such a time—and I would remind you to be wary of the woman Agnes.'

'Yes, I shall watch her,' Melissa promised. 'I can find my own way back to my cell, thank you.'

Sister Cecile inclined her head. Melissa walked to the door.

There she glanced back and saw the nun on her knees beside the bed, her head bent in prayer. Closing the door softly behind her, Melissa was thoughtful as she walked back to her tiny cell. Was it possible that one of her women had administered a poison to the Abbess—and if so, why had she done it? She could hardly believe it was so for why would anyone wish to harm that good woman?

Melissa felt the beginning of a deep anger inside her. If she discovered that Agnes had murdered the Abbess she would make sure that she was justly punished. Yet there remained the mystery of why a woman who had always seemed loyal should do such a thing.

Rhona was waiting for her when Melissa returned to her chamber. She greeted her mistress with an anxious look.

'You look distressed, my lady,' she said. 'Is your aunt no better?'

'My aunt died,' Melissa said, a catch in her voice. She was keeping her tears at bay for she needed to be alert. 'Where is Agnes?'

'I do not know, my lady. She said that she needed to visit the privy and she has not returned, though it was more than an hour since. Would you wish me to look for her?'

'No, stay here with me,' Melissa said. 'And light one of the wax candles we brought with us. I cannot bear the stench of tallow.' She did not think she would ever forget the smell of burning tallow mixed with the foul bile that her aunt had vomited. 'There is something I wish to read.' Melissa knew that she was fortunate that she had been taught to read, because many women were not. It was not always thought necessary, but in this at least, Lord Whitbread had been generous.

'As you wish, my lady.' Rhona took a thick candle from their saddlebag and brought it near, striking tinder. As it flared to life, she lit the candle and set it upon the stool for the only pieces of furniture the cell contained were a stool and the straw pallet. 'Is there light enough or shall I bring another?'

'I can see if I kneel on the pallet,' Melissa said, and took the letter from her pouch, breaking the seal. She read the words her aunt had written, gasping as she realised what they meant. 'No, it cannot be…'

'Is something wrong, my lady?'

'Go to your own bed, Rhona,' Melissa said. 'I would be alone.'

As the woman left her, Melissa held the letter closer to the candle, reading it once more. She had thought that she must have imagined its contents, but the words had not changed.

The Abbess had accused Lord Whitbread of murdering his wife!

It is certain that your mother did not die in childbed. I received a letter from her to say that you were born and asking me to be your godmother. I could not give that promise, but as you know I have always taken an interest in you, my dearest child. When I heard that your mother had died I believed it from a fever, for your father wrote that it was so—but some weeks later your mother's kinswoman, Alanna Davies, came to see me.

She swore to me that her cousin had been well when she was sent on an errand and when she returned she was not allowed to see her. For some days she was barred from Lady Whitbread's chamber and then she was told that her cousin had died, but she says it is a lie. She heard screaming in the night and she believes that Lord Whitbread killed his wife for she saw him coming from her chamber and there was blood on his clothes.

I made discreet inquiries but nothing could be proved, though I incurred your father's lifelong hatred for it. I can tell you no more, Melissa, but if you are in danger go to Alanna Davies for she would help you. She resides with Morgan of Hywell and has influential relatives or I doubt not that she too would have met her death.

If you are reading this then I am dead. Know that I have loved you beyond what was permitted me. I have revealed my secret only because I wish you to be aware of Lord Whitbread's nature. If you should cross him I dare not think what he might do. Live well and kindly, my dear child, and think only that I loved you. Your Aunt Beatrice— Abbess of the Church of Saint Mark and the order of the Sisters of Mercy.

Melissa folded the paper and returned it to her pouch. Her hands were trembling and for some minutes she could only sit and stare at the shadows on the wall. Her father had not been kind to her but she could never have imagined that he could be guilty of the murder of his own wife. It was a wicked crime, yet she could not be certain of his guilt for there was no proof against him. He had sworn that his wife had died of a fever that came upon her after the birth of her child, and Melissa had seen her mother's tomb in the family crypt.

There was only the word of her mother's kinswoman to give the lie to his story. Melissa began to pace the confines of her cell, her mind reeling with the horror of what had been revealed to her. She had no doubt that her aunt had believed it true for she had not wished to reveal her secret until after her death.

Had she been threatened with dire consequences if she revealed what she knew? Or was it merely that she had given a promise to someone? Melissa would never be sure. She could not even know whether Alanna Davies had lied to the Abbess, but she was certain of one thing—she did not wish to live beneath her father's roof again.

Yet where could she go? Melissa raised her head, pride and anger raising her spirit as she realised the truth. There was no one she could turn to for help. She had no alternative but to return to her father's home, but she would refuse to marry the man he had chosen for her—and she would demand the truth of him!

Chapter Two

Rob turned away from the graveside, walking back through the peace of the old churchyard, the song of a missel thrush bringing some joy to a sorrowing heart.

Seeing David anxiously waiting for him, he brought his mind to the business in hand. He had given his word that he would rouse as many men in the Earl of Richmond's cause as he could, and he must begin immediately.

'We have work to do, David,' he told his father's steward. 'I have promised there will be at least two hundred men ready to join Henry Tudor when he comes to wrest the Crown from King Richard.'

'I know that the Stourtons will come in when you give the word. The Davies of Wroxham have pledged their affinity to your cause, Rob. As for their cousins, the Davies of Shorely, I have no word of their intentions, but if they come they will bring in twenty others.'

'Then I think I must make them my first call,' Rob said. 'If I can win them to our side we shall have others flocking to our standard.'

'Aye, Rob,' David said. 'These Plantagenets are a quarrel-some brood. It would be good to see the throne of England under stable rule again, though I like not war. We have seen too much bloodshed these past thirty years.'

Rob touched the old man's shoulder in sympathy. 'There are times when a man must stand for what he believes in. No matter what it may cost.'

Melissa visited Owain in the infirmary the next morning. He had recovered his senses, but was deep in a fever, tossing restlessly from side to side. She bent over him, laying a hand on his brow, which was hot and damp to the touch.

'My dearest friend,' she said. 'Forgive me for what I have done to you. You were right, I should not have come for it has all come to nothing.' She turned anxiously to the monk who was hovering nearby. 'Will he recover?'

'It is in God's hands,' the man said. 'We shall tend him and pray for his soul—there is no more we can do.'

'Thank you for what you have done,' Melissa said, and bent over Owain again. He opened his eyes and looked at her and for a moment he smiled.

'Elspeth…' he said. 'You have come.…'

'No, Owain, it is her daughter,' Melissa said, and bent to kiss his forehead. 'Rest now, my dear friend. I shall add my prayers to those of the good monks.'

'My lady,' one of the brothers had come up to her. 'I have been asked if I will send someone to escort you to your home. Are you ready to leave?'

'Yes, thank you,' Melissa said. 'It was kind of you to offer to send one of your servants to accompany us, sir.'

'We are simple people and serve God,' the monk told her. 'You came here at a sad time and I am sorry that you have not been offered better hospitality.'

'It is no matter,' Melissa said. 'Sister Cecile has her reasons for asking us to leave.' It was obvious to her that the nun believed one of their party was responsible for the Abbess's death and wanted them gone.

She followed the monk to the gates of the Abbey, where

Rhona was waiting together with the horses and a tall, burly-looking servant who worked in the stables and was not one of the order. The monks employed only a handful of such men and it was good of them to spare him to her. She smiled at him, but he did not respond, merely giving her his hand to help her mount her palfrey.

'Do you know the path we must follow through the forest, sir?'

He inclined his head but still spoke no word to her. Melissa sat her horse proudly and glanced at her serving woman.

'Is there still no sign of Agnes?'

'No, my lady. It is strange, is it not?'

'Very strange,' Melissa agreed. 'Unless…' She shook her head. It was difficult to believe that Agnes was responsible for her aunt's death no matter what Cecile had told her. 'Come, we must leave. I hope to be home before my father returns to the castle.…'

Her face was pale but she gave no other sign of the turmoil inside her. She wanted to run away and hide somewhere, but there was nowhere she could go—no one who would dare to stand up against her father. She thought that perhaps Robert of Melford might have done so if she asked, but her pride forbade it.

She had no alternative but to return to her father's house.

How many of the promises given could he truly rely on? Rob had spent the past five days riding the Marches, talking with men who could bring in trained fighters if they cast their affinity with Richmond's cause. Some had smiled to his face but he had thought them false behind his back, for he was aware that the King was also hoping to raise support in the border country. Yet if even half the promises made were kept, Rob would be able to take between two and three hundred men with him when Henry Tudor set up his standard. At least half of them would be skilled fighters. And he was sure that there would be a rising in Wales in support of Henry.

He was feeling weary and in need of a cooling drink when

he gave the reins of his horse to a groom and went into the house. It felt strange to hear himself addressed as master or my lord, for he still thought of his father as the master here. It would take some getting used to, he thought, and sighed as his steward came to greet him.

'What news, David? Have any messages come for me?'

'None, sir,' David said, and looked anxious. 'But there is something I think I should tell you…concerning your father's illness.'

'You said nothing of this before?' Rob walked into the room that had been his father's place of business. 'What troubles you?'

'Before the seizure that laid him low, there was a visitor.'

'A visitor?'

'He claimed to have brought a message from Lord Whitbread. Your father was closeted with him privately for some minutes and they quarrelled—for we heard shouting. I hurried there when the man left and found him lying on the floor. He recovered after a moment or two—but it was that night he was taken ill.'

'Can you name this messenger?' Rob frowned for he did not like this tale. 'You have no idea what was said between them?'

'The messenger is known as Harold of Meresham—the bastard son of Lord Whitbread.'

Rob's mouth thinned into a grim line. 'Then I hold Harold of Meresham responsible for my father's death—and one day there shall be a reckoning between us.'

Rob touched the scar on his cheek, his thoughts swept back to the day of his humiliation at Harold of Meresham's hands and the pain he had endured.

In those first dark nights, when the pain made him cry out and weep like a child he had vowed to be revenged on the man who had done this to him—and the witch who had cast her spell over him. He must have been mad to believe her…and to help her when she was attacked in the forest. She had aroused a heated desire when he held her to him as they rode through the forest

but he had forced himself to behave as an honourable knight—
he should have taken his revenge while he had the chance! In
his anger at the news of what had happened to his father, he was
tempted to take as many men as he could muster and attack the
castle. He would like to burn it to the ground with those devils
in it! And yet he knew that there was more important work—
work that prevented him seeking personal revenge.

His bitterness knew no bounds as he paced the room and
thought of his father at the mercy of that oafish brute. It seemed
that there was an evil curse on all that that family touched or
did—and one day they would suffer for what they had done!

'Be careful, Rob,' David said, looking at him sadly, for he
could guess what was in his mind. 'The bastard was only obey-
ing his father's orders—and Lord Whitbread is a powerful
man. If you cross him, he will destroy you.'

'He may do his worst!' Rob said, and scowled. 'I have
given my word to Henry Tudor and must keep it—but one day
my chance will come.'

Melissa's heart sank as she and Rhona rode into the castle.
Seeing her father's flag flying at full mast, she had known that
he was home, and she had given the monks' servant leave to
go as soon as they were in sight of it. As she and Rhona rode
over the drawbridge, she saw her half brother, Harold, standing in the courtyard, and her heart caught as he turned to look
at her. His expression was triumphant, and she knew that that
meant her father was angry with her.

Harold came to help her down. She shook off his hands, giving him a look of dislike, for she hated it when he touched her.

'Where have you been, little sister?' he asked, his thick lips
curving in a sneer. 'Father was in a rage when he discovered
that you had gone. I hope he orders the thrashing you deserve—
and allows me to do it.'

Melissa gave him a haughty look. 'You would enjoy that, my

dear brother, I have no doubt, but my father has more sense than to allow it. I am an heiress and the King is my guardian....'

'If it were not so, I should have had my pleasure with you before this,' Harold said, his mean eyes glittering. 'If Father did not fear that the King would seize your lands, you would have died long ago.'

Melissa walked away from him, her heart hammering. She had always known that her father hated her, but he held his counsel and she had not guessed that her life was in danger. She wished that there was somewhere she might find sanctuary, but all hope had gone with her aunt's death. No other Abbey would take her for they might suffer a terrible retribution at Lord Whitbread's hands. Her only hope lay in a petition to the King—but who would stand up for her?

Owain would have done it had he been able, though his word would carry little weight for he was not a noble, merely a freeman of England. Surely there must be someone who would help her? Yet try as she might, she could think of no one.

She went into the house, walking up the curved stone stair to her chamber. For the moment she must wait and see what her father had in mind for her.

Rob had been training with his men all the morning. He had been working hard and was wiping the sweat from his body in the courtyard. He doused himself with cold water drawn from the well, and then dried his body on a coarse cloth. He shook his head, the water flying from his long, dark hair as it would the coat of a shaggy dog. The sun was in his eyes and it was a moment or two before he realised that the man approaching him was Owain Davies.

'You are better,' he said, greeting him with a smile. 'I must thank you for what you did for me that night, sir. Had I known your name I should have done so long ago.'

'No thanks were necessary. I could not stand by and see

murder done by those villains— Besides, from what I have been told, you have since repaid the favour.'

'I did what any decent man would have done,' Rob said, but his smile had gone for the bitterness was deep in him and grew stronger as the days passed. 'Is there something I may do for you?'

Owain was dressed plainly in leather doublet and hose, his shirt of wool and dark in colour. The monks had cropped his hair short so best to tend his hurts, and there was a livid scar across his head. Yet he was a handsome man, who held himself with pride, his eyes green and bolder than many a man in his position. Something about him seemed oddly familiar, though Rob was not sure what made him think it.

'I came to offer you my affinity,' Owain told him. 'I know that my lady has returned to her father's house, for the monks told me it was so—and I can no longer wear the livery of Lord Whitbread. He stands for the King and I am for Henry Tudor. I have heard that you are also of this mind—and I would fight with you, if you will have me?'

'Yes, and right gladly,' Rob said, offering his hand. 'Indeed, I am proud to call you my friend.'

'Thank you,' Owain said, and smiled. 'But I would have you know that I shall return to the service of my lady when this conflict is done—she has my loyalty, no matter what she may have done....'

Rob touched the scar on his cheek. 'What do you know of this?'

'I know what I saw and no more,' Owain said. 'I have been told that she sent you away—and that she knew of her father's intent, but I do not believe it. If you knew her as I do, sir...'

'No more,' Rob said. 'I accept your friendship and honour you for your loyalty to the lady of Whitbread, but nothing beyond. She betrayed me, and her brother punished me for daring to look above my station. I have since learned that he caused my father to suffer a seizure that later killed him. I have sworn revenge on them.'

'Harold of Meresham is no true brother to her,' Owain said. 'And her…father is a brute who treats her ill. I would help you kill them both and gladly—but she is innocent.'

'Perhaps…' Rob's expression did not ease. 'We shall not speak of this again, Owain. For now we must prepare for war. I expect the summons any day.'

'You will obey me, daughter.' Lord Whitbread's fleshy face was dark with anger, a deep red colour seeping up from his neck. He wore a long, rich blue gown bordered with gold braid, a chain of heavy gold about his neck, and looked every bit the powerful and rich lord he was. His eyes were filled with loathing, undisguised now for he no longer kept even the pretence of care or understanding. She had shamed him by running from his house and he would not forgive her. 'I have promised you to Leominster and you shall marry him if he will have you, though you do not now deserve the honour.'

'No, Father,' Melissa cried. 'I shall never marry a man I neither know nor care for. I have heard of the marquis's reputation and he is not a man that my mother would have wished me to marry.'

'Your mother is dead,' Lord Whitbread growled. 'Even if she lived my wish would be paramount. You are my property and I shall dispose of you as I please. You leave for the north in the morning. You will go to my cousin, the Earl of Gifford, who will keep you safe until I have time to arrange your marriage.'

'Father, I beg you, do not do this,' Melissa said. 'For the memory of my mother, spare me. Let me marry as I wish…'

'What is this? You speak as if you favour another…' His hand snaked out, gripping her wrist. 'Down on your knees, girl. Tell me the truth or it will go hard with you. Have you shamed me even more? Have you given yourself to a man? If you think still of Melford it will be the worse for you!'

'No, Father,' Melissa said. She tried to resist but the pressure on her arm was so painful that she was forced to her knees. She refused to bow her head, her expression defiant as she looked at him. 'I would never forget my honour. I sent Rob away…and I have never ceased to regret it.'

'Have you seen him again?' Lord Whitbread demanded. 'If he has dared to lay a finger on you he shall die. I warned you what would happen if you disobeyed me.' Melissa shook her head. 'Speak, girl, or it will be the worse for you!'

Melissa gave him a stubborn look. Nothing would make her betray what Rob had done for her that day in the forest. She felt her father's hands on her shoulders, dragging her to her feet, shaking her like a rag doll. He held her by one arm, drawing back the other to strike her hard across the face. Melissa cried out with the pain, but still she was defiant. She raised her eyes, gazing at him with hatred in her eyes.

'Is this how you killed my mother?' she asked, all caution lost. 'You suspected her of having a lover. Did you try to beat the truth out of her, too? Is that how she died?'

'Damn you!' Lord Whitbread let go of her, still in a rage but thoughtful now. 'I suppose that damned sister of hers told you. I had hoped she might take the secret to her grave, for I warned her that if she did not I would punish you in her stead.' His eyes narrowed. 'If you think to beg the King for help you are too late. He has given his permission for your marriage in return for pledges of support from Leominster and myself. Leominster will have control of your fortune, and in return a part of your lands become mine. The deal is done, Melissa. You go north to my kinsman in the morning, and when the traitor Henry Tudor has been dealt with, you will marry the Marquis of Leominster.'

Lord Whitbread left the room, locking the door behind him. Melissa looked about her in despair. She was a prisoner in the small circular chamber at the top of the Keep, and she knew there was no way she could escape.

'Oh, Rob,' she whispered, tears trickling down her cheeks. 'If only I had not let you go when you took me to the Abbey. I was so proud, so foolish! You are the only one who could have helped me—but you hate me now.' She should have taken the risk and told him the truth, but it was too late now.

Melissa felt that her heart would break. It seemed that there was no hope for her, because she could not escape her fate—and yet if she could not wed the man she loved, she would rather die.

She had hoped that perhaps she might plead her case with the King, but there was to be a war and she was but an insignificant woman to be traded for the promise of men and arms.

If they married her to the Marquis of Leominster, she would die by her own hand rather than let him take her to his bed.

She sank to her knees, praying that something or someone would help her, but she knew that she was alone and friendless. Even Owain had deserted her—she had had no word from him in all this time.

Melissa's head was aching as she was led across the courtyard the next morning and taken to her own rooms. The guards who had escorted her thrust her inside and the door was locked behind her. They were taking good care that she should not escape, though there was little likelihood of that, for where could she go?

Rhona had been packing a trunk with Melissa's clothes, but she smiled and came towards her. 'You need food and fresh clothes, my lady,' Rhona said. 'I dare say you did not sleep last night.'

'No, I could not,' Melissa agreed. 'You know what my father has planned for me?'

'Yes, my lady,' Rhona said. 'Is there no one who would help you?'

Melissa shook her head. 'My mother's kinswoman, Alanna Davies, might have helped me if she could—but I do not know how to reach her. Besides, what could she do now that the King has given his permission for my marriage?'

'Is there no one else—Robert of Melford? Would he not come if you asked?'

'He hates me now,' Melissa said sadly. 'If I had not sent him away… But you know that I had no choice. Nothing has changed.'

'I am not sure,' Rhona said. 'I have heard that he has become a powerful knight with many followers since he returned from Angers—and he saved us in the forest. He took you to the Abbey. If he truly hated you, he might have held you captive and demanded a ransom for your return.'

'Perhaps…' Melissa sighed. 'He is brave enough to stand up to my father, I know that—and if he has followers he might be victorious, but why should he help me?'

'Will you not send him word?'

'It would do no good,' Melissa said. She saw that Rhona was doubtful. 'There is something else you would say?'

'Agnes is here. She begs that you will see her, my lady. She swears that she did nothing to harm the Abbess. She says that she ran away because she heard that she had been accused and was afraid.'

'Do you believe her?'

'I am not sure,' Rhona said. 'Until that night we had no reason to doubt her—and you have only Sister Cecile's word that she saw her near your aunt's chamber.'

'Yes, that is true.' Melissa was uncertain. 'Very well, I shall see her—but we must be careful, Rhona. We should watch her and see what she does. Do not trust her too much.'

'Shall I ask her to come in?'

'Yes, please.'

Melissa walked to her bed and sat down, taking off her wimple to let her hair cascade down her back. She had thought that Agnes was gone for good, and she was not sure how to greet her.

Agnes came into the room looking nervous. She stood just

inside the door, her hands clasped in front of her. 'Forgive me for deserting you. I was afraid that I should be accused of murder and…'

'Did you give the Abbess poison, Agnes?'

'No, I swear I did not,' the girl said. 'I did not mean to harm the Abbess. She begged me for her medicine, because she was in pain. I poured some into a cup and she drank it. I did nothing more.'

'Do you swear it on the Body of Christ?'

'On my honour I gave her only what she asked of me.'

'But what were you doing in her chamber?'

'I lost my way and heard her cry out in pain. I tried only to help her.' Agnes was white, the fear in her eyes as she fell on her knees before Melissa. 'Forgive me. I did not know what I did.'

'Did you not know that some medicines can kill as well as heal?' Melissa saw that the woman was frightened and wondered if after all it had been an accident, and yet the doubt was still there. 'I should write to the Bishop and tell him of your sin. Do you know what they would do to a woman who murdered the Abbess who had given her shelter for the night? I think that if you came before the church courts they would show you no mercy. They would say you were a witch and you would hang and afterwards they would burn your body.'

'I beg you, do not denounce me.'

Melissa hesitated. She was minded to dismiss the woman, but knew that if she did Agnes would be forced to work in the kitchens for she would not easily find work elsewhere. And she did not know for certain that she was guilty of anything, other than ignorance.

'Very well, I shall not send you away for the moment—though you will not serve me again. You may take your instructions from Rhona, but I do not want you near me. You may go now.'

'Yes, my lady.' Agnes kept her eyes downcast, but once she had left the room they blazed with anger and she placed her ear to the door, listening.

'She is not to serve me,' Melissa said to Rhona. 'She may wash and mend—but I do not want her in my chamber.'

Rhona nodded, pleased that she was to be her mistress's chief attendant. 'Do you not think it might be worth sending word to Robert of Melford?'

'I do not think he would care what becomes of me,' Melissa said. 'But I shall send word to Owain and ask him to come to me. He may know where Alanna lives—or someone else who would take me in.'

'I am watched,' Rhona said. 'We need someone we can trust to take your message....'

'Then ask the priest to come to me. I wish for his blessing—but do it secretly for I do not want anyone else to know.'

'Yes, my lady. I shall go at once.'

Outside the door, Agnes darted away before it could open. She had known full well what she did when she gave the Abbess her medicine, and she would report everything to her master. He had paid her generously on her return from the Abbey—and would give her a dowry if she continued to serve him.

Rob was sitting in his father's chair, which he had brought downstairs to his chamber. His head was bent over his work as he honed the edge of his sword to a fine sharpness that would cut through bone like butter. For some reason, his cheek was throbbing as it did at times, though the skin had long since healed over, due to the care lavished on him by the faithful Megan. She had laid poultices of herbs and cures on his tortured flesh, nursing him through his fever but her herbs had not healed the deep-seated pain that was eating away inside him.

Melissa would not be banished from his mind. She had haunted him these past few nights, and he had an odd feeling that she was in some kind of trouble. Yet what could it matter to him? She was a deceiver and faithless and he was well rid of her...but sometimes in the dark of night, it seemed that she came to him in his dreams and it was as before when they loved each other.

'You know that I would never betray you,' she had cried in his dream the previous night. 'I need you…I need you…' But he was a fool and the dream was only that. He was nothing to her and she could be nothing more to him.

He looked up from his work as David entered the room. Seeing that his steward carried a sealed letter, he reached for it with impatience thinking it some unimportant estate matter. However, when he broke the seal and read the contents, he gave a great shout of joy. It was the summons he had been waiting for since his return to the Marches.

'It has come,' he cried. 'Henry Tudor has landed with a force of two thousand men and bids me meet him with all the fighters I have raised. God be praised! At last we shall have some action.'

'It is what you need, Rob,' his steward said. 'You have been brooding too much of late…' He raised his eyes looking at the man he loved as a son. 'She has bewitched you! You have not been the same since she sent you away. No woman is worth the agony you have endured because of her!'

'You have not seen her,' Rob said, and for a moment the old smile was there in his eyes. 'Besides, she did not do this—my wound was courtesy of her brother. She was distressed when she saw it.'

'You would be a fool to forgive her. She is the daughter of your father's enemy. I do not like to see you brought so low by a woman's treachery.'

'Perhaps it was my own fault,' Rob said with a shrug of his shoulders. 'Have you seen Owain Davies? He was to ride with us, but I have not seen him for some days.'

'I think he had some business of his own,' David said. 'A message came for him from the Abbey and he left at once. He said that if the summons came before he returned he would meet you on the field of battle.'

'Then he will keep his word,' Rob said. 'I shall leave today for Shrewsbury for I wish to speak with Morgan of Hywell. He would not give his promise until he was sure that Henry really meant to come—but now I am certain he will agree.'

'As you wish, sir,' David said. 'Forgive me if I spoke out of turn, Rob—but I know she made you suffer.'

'I could never be angry with you,' Rob said. 'Besides, you were right—she is not worth the pain she has caused.'

Rob tested the blade of his sword. Melissa was false and it was foolish to lie in torment each night thinking of her. Yet the scent of her was imprinted into his senses, and he could not forget how it had felt to hold her in his arms. He still wanted her, burned for her, even though she might be a proud witch who had merely played with his emotions.

He left the chamber, shouting orders to his servants. He must ride with all haste to Shrewsbury and give Morgan of Hywell the news that Henry Tudor was to come. At last he had something to do and could forget his own problems for the moment.

Melissa rode in stony silence. Her father had sent Harold in his place to see her wed, for he was too busy to accompany her to his cousin's fortress. She had been told that she was to be betrothed to the Marquis of Leominster when she reached the stronghold in the north of England. The marriage would take place almost at once after the betrothal, and she would leave the Earl of Gifford's home to travel to that of her new husband not far from the city of Nottingham. What was more, she had been denied Rhona's company and given Agnes as her only attendant.

'You think that I do not know you plotted with Rhona to escape me again,' Lord Whitbread had told her. 'Well, I am not a fool, daughter—and you shall have Agnes to serve you. I know that she is loyal to me and will guard you well until you are safely wed—as for the other, your maid may think herself lucky if I do not give her to Harold for his sport.'

'Do that, Father, and I shall never reach the earl's house alive.'

'You defy me still?' Whitbread took her arm. 'The girl is safe—but if I hear that you have somehow escaped from your brother's care, she will die. Do you hear me?'

Melissa had not answered him, but she knew that he would carry out his threat if she escaped or took her own life before she was the Marquis of Leominster's wife. She had no choice but to make the journey to the earl's house and see what presented itself then. Perhaps there was some way out of her dilemma, though she did not know what it might be, for her freedom might mean Rhona's death.

Melissa had met the Earl of Gifford only once. He was her father's cousin and a tall, thin man with a long nose. She recalled that she had not liked him when he visited with her father some years previously—but she had not disliked his wife, who was a pretty woman with pale hair and limpid blue eyes. She would not have minded the visit so much had it not been for the shadow that hung over her—the fear that they would force her to marry a man she did not know and could not like.

All she had heard of the Marquis of Leominster was that he was a hard, cold man and twice her age. She had learned from the casual talk of the men who rode with her that he was known for his brutality. He had, it was said, taken the wife of one of his neighbours after a dispute between them, keeping her a prisoner and using her as his mistress until he had tired of her. He then turned her out, but when she returned to her husband he would not have her back for she had dishonoured his name. Friendless and broken, she had walked into a river and drowned herself.

What kind of a father would sell his daughter to a man like that? Melissa shuddered at the thought of her likely fate if she became Leominster's wife. She would rather die by her own hand! It was a sin to take your own life, but Melissa thought that she would risk eternal damnation rather than live in the hell that such a marriage would bring—but had she the right to condemn Rhona to a cruel death?

'We shall break our journey at the next inn, sister.' Harold's voice brought her back from her reverie. 'We have made good time and you must be weary.'

Melissa flashed him a look of dislike. 'Do not pretend to consider my needs, Harold. I am not hungry. I would prefer to continue until we reach our resting place for the night.'

'Well, I am hungry if you are not,' Harold told her, a sulky expression in his eyes. 'I swear I know not why Leominster wants a sharp-tongued witch like you for a bride. Give me a woman with a merry laugh and a warm heart, anytime.' She was too thin for his tastes, for he was used to seeking his pleasures in the arms of a plump tavern wench. His father had taught him to fight and given him a hunger for good living, though he lacked all the qualities and refinements of a true knight.

Melissa had tried to feel affection for him, but his coarseness and his surly manner had killed any feeling she might have had for him. She lifted her head, a look of scorn in her eyes.

'I am sorry that I do not find favour in your eyes, brother. I wish that you might allow me to slip away to an Abbey and save yourself the trouble of this journey.'

'If it were up to me, I would slit your throat and be done with it,' Harold said, an evil leer on his lips. 'I cannot see why we may not just take your lands for ourselves, but Father says it must be done within the law.'

'I thank you for your kind words, brother,' Melissa said. She turned her head from him. 'I care not what becomes of me.'

'And I care even less,' her brother snarled. 'Because of you I may miss all the excitement. Father has heard that Henry Tudor is bringing an army from France. That is why he could not spare the time to escort you himself. He has received a summons to join the King. And I might have gone with him if it had not been for you.'

'I am sorry to be such a trouble to you—but let me go to an Abbey and you may ride to join the King's army.'

'And earn my father's displeasure? You would love that, sister.' He glared at her. 'Just remember that I do not have Father's scruples concerning you, Melissa. If you were dead it would suit me very well....'

'Yes, I know,' Melissa replied. 'But you have no need to fear me, Harold. Father would never disinherit you for me.'

'Not for you,' Harold said, eyes cold as they rested on her face. 'But you might have a son...'

'But my son would not bear his name,' Melissa reminded him. 'You are safe unless Father has a legitimate son, which he cannot unless he marries again.'

Harold shot a startled look at her. 'You do not think he intends to take another wife?'

'I have no idea, brother,' Melissa said. 'For your sake I hope not—but you can never be sure. Father is still a strong man and capable of giving his wife a son.'

'What do you know?' Harold demanded his eyes narrowed. 'Have you heard something?'

'Father would not tell me,' Melissa said. 'But it is a thought...'

'He would not marry without telling me,' Harold declared, but there was a frown on his face as they rode into the inn courtyard.

Melissa smiled inwardly. She had given her brother something else to think about, and perhaps he would forget about her...but even if she had the chance, she could not in all conscience run away.

Rob gave his horse to the young lad who came running, tossing him a small coin for his trouble. He was at the outskirts of Shrewsbury and meant only to eat something while his horse was rested. He had come alone, giving his men orders to meet him at the appointed place the following day, for he would pass the night at the house of Morgan of Hywell.

It was as he was crossing the inn yard that he saw the woman lingering at the edge of the woods he had just left. She had not seen him, but seemed furtive, as if she wanted to slip away and did not quite dare. For a moment he hesitated, and then walked swiftly towards her. It was dangerous in those woods for there were armed men everywhere.

'Melissa? What are you doing here?' he demanded, his voice harsh.

Melissa turned, her startled gaze on his face. 'Oh, it is you,' she said, and caught her breath on a sob. 'I thought it was Harold.…'

'Your half brother is here?'

'Yes, he is taking me to the north to my kinsman's house. I…am to be married…' Her eyes were wide, dark with longing as she looked at him. To be so close to him and yet unable to speak from her heart! If only Rhona were safe, she would beg him to take her away, now, before her brother could stop them!

'I see…' Rob's expression hardened, ignoring the look of appeal in her eyes. 'Then I wish you every happiness, lady.' His mouth curled with bitterness and he was about to turn away, but she caught his sleeve, making him turn to look at her again. 'What more would you have of me?'

'I shall not be happy in this marriage for I can never love my husband. Surely you know that I shall only ever love one man?'

'Indeed? How should I know that?'

She hesitated, 'Sir…are you here alone?'

'Yes, why do you ask?' His eyes narrowed in suspicion. 'I am armed even if alone and your brother would not have the advantage of me now. They tied my arms that day I came to ask for you for I brought no weapons.' He touched the sword that hung across his chest. 'I am more than a match for Harold of Meresham!'

'But he is not alone, for he has ten armed men.' Melissa stopped because she had seen Harold come to the door of the inn to look for her. Her chance of escape had gone, if she had ever had one. She gave a little sob of fear, because alone Rob had no chance against her half brother and his men. Besides, if she went with Rob, her father would carry out his threat against her serving woman. She was bound as surely as if Harold had her in chains. 'No, you are right—how should you know that I loved you? Except that had you loved me, you would not have believed me capable of what they did to you. Forget me, I will not be the cause of your death. My brother looks for me. I must go.'

She ran away from him. Rob turned to look and saw that Harold of Meresham was at the inn door. He saw him take a rough hold of her arm and give her a shake and frowned. For a moment he was tempted to go after him and challenge him. He would like to plunge his sword deep into the blaggard's heart, but Melissa's words had warned him. He was alone and it was unlikely that Harold would meet him in single combat— and he could not afford to be wounded now. Nigh on two hundred men had promised to follow him, and Henry would need every man if he were to win his cause.

He turned away. He would walk into the town and seek out Morgan of Hywell. It was for this he had come—and Melissa was promised to marry another. She had gone to her brother willingly and therefore must be happy with the marriage, despite the way she had looked at him.

'Who were you talking to?' Harold asked as he hustled her inside the inn, his fingers digging into her soft upper arm. 'And what were you doing outside the inn?'

'I went out for some air, because my head aches,' Melissa said. 'I am feeling unwell…' She gave a little sigh and sagged against him, knowing that she must hold his attention until Rob had time to leave. If Harold had seen him he would undoubtedly have killed him. 'I think I must rest here for a few hours, Harold. I may be sickening for something.'

'If this is one of your tricks…' Harold glared at her. 'Do not try my patience too far, Melissa. I would as soon break your neck as look at you!'

Melissa smiled. 'I know that you have no love for me, brother—but my father wants this alliance with Leominster. I should take care if I were you.'

She did not know why, but the brief encounter with Rob had lifted her spirits. He was still angry, she had sensed that, but while she lived there was still hope that she might see him again—and perhaps one day she could tell him the truth and he would no longer hate her.

'I am glad to see you, Robert of Melford,' Morgan Hywell said, and took his hand. 'Now that Henry has set foot on Welsh soil I shall give you my affinity. I was doubtful that he would come, but he has and I shall give him my support. You will stay with us this night?'

'Yes, thank you,' Rob said. 'It is good of you to offer, sir. I rode here in all haste as soon as the news arrived.'

'I am glad to be with you at last,' Morgan Hywell said. 'And now, I would like you to meet the lady who orders my house for me—Mistress Alanna Davies. She is cousin to Owain Davies and was kinsman to the wife of Lord Whitbread.'

Alanna was a tall lady, quite stout and no longer young. She dressed in dark clothes and wore only a wimple to cover her hair—but Rob saw something in her face that seemed familiar, though he could not place it.

'You are Owain Davies' cousin, lady,' he said. 'He is with us in the cause and we are friends, for he once saved my life.'

'I have not seen Owain for some years,' Alanna said. 'I was living then with my lady—but after she died I left the castle and came here.…'

'Whitbread threatened her and she was in fear of her life for some time,' Morgan Hywell said. 'But the years have passed and I daresay he has forgotten her.'

'I have not forgot him or what he did to my lady,' Alanna said. 'But I must say no more for if he should hear gossip…' She shook her head. 'Come, I shall show you to your chamber, sir, because you will want to refresh yourself before we eat.'

Rob followed her upstairs. It was a substantial house, for Morgan of Hywell was a rich merchant and an important man in his town, which was why he had not been prepared to offer his support until he was sure that Henry Tudor had come. Now that he had, he would bring at least thirty men to their cause.

'I trust you will be comfortable here, sir?'

'I thank you yes.' Rob detained her as she would have left. 'You may trust me, lady. What did Lord Whitbread do to Melissa's mother?'

'You know her?' Alanna's face was wistful. 'I have oft wished to see her—but it was impossible. You see, he knew that I had seen him leave my lady's chamber—and that I suspected what he had done.' Her eyes were dark with remembered horror. 'He beat her so badly that she died of her injuries. He told everyone that she died of a childbed fever, but it was not so—he murdered her.'

'May he rot in hell!' Rob was angry. He knew that Melissa had often wished that she had known her mother, for she had told him as they walked together in the meadows: it had been a source of great grief to her. 'One day he will pay for his many crimes, lady. I promise you that…'

'I have often prayed that he might suffer for what he did,' she said. 'But I could do nothing…he would have killed me had I not run away. Perhaps I should have taken the child? I have often wished it, but then he would never have let me be.'

'I thank you for telling me,' Rob said. 'I can tell you that your lady's child is to be married, though I am not sure that is of her own choosing…' He could not shake the look he had seen in her eyes from his mind; it had begun to haunt him, for he had sensed that she was in distress.

Alanna nodded and went out, leaving him alone. He was thoughtful for he had remembered Melissa's words. He had been too angry to listen to her at the time, but now they had come back to him.

You should know that I shall only ever love one man.

Had she meant to say that she loved him? Rob frowned as he thought it over. If she meant that…but he would be a fool to believe her. She had sworn that she loved him and would marry him—but then she had driven him away with words intended to cut him to the heart, as they had. Her father had not been in the room. If he had forbidden the marriage there had been nothing to stop her telling him so. He could recall her every word, remember the proud way she held her head, the coldness in her eyes as she told him that she did not wish to see him again.

Why would she have done that if she loved him?

'Wait one moment, sir,' Alanna came to him as he was about to mount his horse the next morning. 'I have something I must tell you…'

'Something you wish me to tell Owain perhaps?'

'Yes. It would be best if he knew what I saw—though it is only a suspicion. I cannot swear to the truth of it, but I have thought…' She raised her head, looking at Rob. 'I know that I told you my lady was murdered—and it is true that he beat her. She sent me on an errand the next day, and when I returned he told me she was dead…but I think I may have seen her since then.'

'Where?'

'In the Isle of Ely, at the shrine of Saint Ethelreda,' Alanna said. 'It was Ethelreda who began the great Cathedral there and they say she has the power to work miracles. I went there with Morgan who made the pilgrimage to pray for his son…

and a woman came up to me. She pressed a lily into my hand and then walked quickly away.'

'Did you see her face? Did you know her?'

'I did not notice her until she gave me the lily, but I recall that her head was clothed in shawls that covered her face and she was dressed shabbily. I thought nothing of it until later, and by that time she had disappeared—but that particular lily was always Elspeth's favourite.'

'And you thought it was her because of the lily?'

'Yes, I began to believe so as I thought about it. I asked Morgan to make inquiries in the Isle of Ely and he has, but nothing has come of it.'

'The evidence is slight.' Rob frowned for it was unlikely that the woman could have been Melissa's mother.

'Yes. I have done nothing more for I thought I must have been mistaken—but I think Owain should know.'

'Then I shall tell him,' Rob said, and smiled at her. 'This has lain on your conscience for years, has it not?' She nodded. 'Very well, you may rest easy, for I am sure that Owain will do what he can. He is very loyal to Melissa.'

'And not only Melissa,' Alanna said, standing back as Rob mounted his horse.

As he rode away, Rob wondered what she had meant by her last remark.

Melissa awoke from her dream. It had been so pleasant, for it was of the time when she had first met Rob. In those early days she had not thought of anything but the pleasure that came from seeing him smile at her.

He was so handsome, his eyes so bold and filled with laughter. She had never been teased and had hardly known how to respond to him, but she had loved him…she had loved him from the first.

She was sure that he had loved her then. They had walked

together hand in hand, often saying nothing but just content to be together. Sometimes he had taken her up on his great horse and they had ridden for hours at a time, his arms about her, her head back against his chest…just as they had after he had saved her from those rogues.

A sob rose in her throat for she had felt his anger that day, and known that the gentle loving knight she had known was gone forever. In his place was a man with cold eyes who looked at her as if he hated her.

Yet she would still have begged for his help at Shrewsbury if she had not feared for his life and that of Rhona. And despite his anger, she believed that he would have given it—as he had that day in the forest.

The tears trickled slowly down her cheeks, because she had loved him so much, so very much…and now he hated her. She touched the small jade heart he had bought her at the fair, which she had hidden inside her gown next to her own heart. It was all she had left of the happiness that might have been hers…a trinket and her memories.

They were approaching their destination and unless she could think of some way to delay their journey, she would soon be the Marquis of Leominster's wife!

Chapter Three

Henry Tudor had brought a force of more than two thousand men with him when he landed at Milford Haven on the 7th of August 1485. He sent out his messengers from the town of Haverford-west, which he had occupied, appealing to the men of Wales on claim of descent from Cadwaller the one-time King of the Welsh.

Rob had raised a force of nearly two hundred strong, including archers, miners and men-at-arms. A few had failed but most came in in answer to his summons. They rode to greet Henry Tudor, Earl of Richmond, as he marched across the borders of Wales into England, his army swelling with growing numbers of men who flocked to his banner.

When he greeted Henry Tudor, the earls greeted him warmly. Robert of Melford had brought in a strong body of men and was therefore doubly welcome. Henry Tudor's army was reinforced by the arrival of Gilbert Talbot with a force of five hundred men, which raised the numbers beyond four thousand. The struggle for the throne of England had begun.

Watching the huge body of men assemble, Rob was aware of a growing feeling of excitement. While Henry Tudor remained in France it had been merely been a dream, but now it had become a reality. War was imminent, for reports had reached them of the King's efforts to raise men in his cause, but as yet many of the powerful lords had decided to sit on the fence and wait until they saw who seemed likely to win the coming struggle.

Owain found Rob when they were camped in the country-side around Leicester.

'I have come as I promised.'

'I had given you up,' Rob said. 'Where did you go?'

'I had to discover what had happened to my lady,' Owain replied. 'She sent word by the priest that she was being forced to marry against her will. He left her message at the Abbey, and it was by chance that I went there to ask them something.'

'Against her will?' Rob's eyes narrowed. 'You are sure that it was against her will?'

'They have taken her north to Whitbread's kinsman. She will be kept a prisoner at the home of the Earl of Gifford until she is wed to the Marquis of Leominster. But he will have brought his forces south to meet Richard and the wedding must be delayed until his return.'

'Good grief! What kind of a man would give his daughter to that monster?' Rob was horrified at the news for he knew of Leominster's reputation.

'A man who would let his bastard split your cheek to the bone and send you to your death with your hands bound behind your back.' Owain answered him straight, his look unflinching even though such plain speech might cause offence.

Rob's gaze narrowed. 'Did she go willingly?' She must have! For if she had not, why had she not begged him for help? She must have known that he would give it, despite all that had happened between them. He had helped her in the forest, and though he had been cold to her, he had delivered her safely to the Abbey. She had no reason not to trust him.

'What choice had she?' Owain said. 'Do not blame her, sir. Whatever her father said to you, whatever her brother did, she had no hand in the punishment they inflicted on you.'

Rob's expression did not change, his mouth set in a grim line. 'You plead her case well, sir. I know you are loyal to her—but you saved my life. We shall not quarrel over this, for now is not the time for personal grudges.'

'You speak truly, Robert of Melford,' Owain said. 'And I know that there is nothing either of us can do to save Melissa from her fate at this time—but when the war is won and Henry Tudor has his crown, I shall seek revenge for what has happened to her. At that time I shall ask for your help, though whether you will give it is for you to judge.'

Rob nodded, his expression harsh. Despite all the activity and preparation for war, there had hardly been a moment when he had not thought of Melissa and the revenge he would take against her father. He put a finger to the scar on his cheek, tracing the hard welt that had formed. He would be a fool to let down his guard, and yet the idea that Melissa had gone reluctantly to her wedding lingered in his mind. But if she had not wanted the marriage, why had she not asked him for his help at Shrewsbury? She had run to her brother when he came to look for her—why?

It puzzled him, for the pieces of the puzzle did not seem to fit any pattern. She had been proud and cold that day in the forest when she might—if she had wished—have told him that the beating her brother had given him had been none of her doing. And why had she run to her brother in such haste at that inn if she did not want to be wed to the man her father had chosen? Besides, he had it from her own lips that she desired a marriage of consequence to a rich and titled man.

'If we both live through the coming battle, we shall speak of this again, Owain. I intend to seek revenge for what was done, but as yet I do not know what part of that concerns your lady.'

Owain inclined his head. 'You are angry, but I know you for an honest man. I shall serve you well and fight by your side.'

Rob nodded but said nothing more as he turned away to go about his business. He had no time to dwell on thoughts of Melissa or what was happening to her, and yet the thought of her being forced to the bed of a monster like Leominster made the bile rise in his throat.

He could do nothing to help her even if he would. His promise was given to Henry and the battle was imminent. If he lived he would think again of Melissa and what he might do about her situation, though if she had become the wife of another man there would be little he could do—unless he murdered her husband and took her back! The thought brought a smile to his lips, though he dismissed it in an instant—if she was wed to another it must be her choice for she could refuse if she wished.

'You look pale, my lady,' Agnes said. They had reached their destination that night after several delays on their journey, for Melissa had been sick and Harold had been forced to let her rest. 'Shall I tell Lady Gifford that you are not well enough to leave your chamber?'

'My head aches dreadfully,' Melissa said.

'Lie down and try to sleep. I shall go to Lady Gifford and tell her that you are ill.'

'Thank you,' Melissa said. She waited until her serving woman had left the room, and then drank from the flask she had filled with brackish water from a stream they had camped beside on the way here. She had been warned not to drink from it, but she had already done so twice and it had made her feel truly ill. Her headache was genuine and she had been sick several times. Even Harold had realised that she could not travel. He had stayed longer than he intended on the journey and they were some days later than had been expected.

Melissa was just vomiting into a pot when her hostess came in. Lady Gifford had grown more stout since their last meeting, but her smile was kind and concerned as she saw that Melissa was truly unwell.

'You poor child,' she said. 'Leominster thought that you were pretending to be ill because you wished to avoid meeting him, but I told him that I was sure it was not so. He has lingered here on your behalf, Melissa, but I fear that he was forced to leave not an hour since. A messenger came from the King and he must ride with his men to meet him at Leicester.'

Melissa felt a rush of relief, but managed to control her satisfaction. 'I must ask for your pardon, Lady Gifford. I fear it was my fault that we were delayed, and even now I cannot rise from my bed.'

'Well, there is no hurry now,' her kind hostess said. 'Leominster will return after the battle is over and the King victorious, I daresay. Besides, as Gifford says, the betrothal may go ahead for someone may stand in as Leominster's proxy.'

'Ahh…' Melissa gave a cry of despair and was promptly sick again. The stench was vile and made Lady Gifford retreat towards the door. 'Forgive me. I am too ill to take part in any ceremony just yet.'

'Yes, I see that,' her hostess said. 'Do not worry about it for the moment, Melissa. I shall tell my husband that you must be allowed to rest.'

Melissa lay back as her hostess left. She was feeling dreadfully ill, but at least she had managed to delay her betrothal for the time being. She would find ways of delaying her marriage—and if in the end they forced her to it, she would take her own life.

'Help me,' she prayed. 'Please, help me…'

Melissa did not know whether her prayers were for God or the man she loved. Seeing Rob for a few minutes at Shrewsbury, had given her hope. She did not know why, because there was no reason that he should help her—and yet she would not give up just yet. Her salvation lay in delay and she would keep to her bed for as long as she could!

* * *

The Stanleys—a family of powerful English lords—had met and conferred with Henry Tudor, but they had refused to promise their help, though they would not oppose him. It was clear that they were still sitting on the fence, waiting to see which side was winning before throwing in their weight.

However, confidence was growing amongst the men on Henry Tudor's side. Reports were coming in that some of the lords promised to King Richard had failed to show, and that meant his force was much weaker than it might have been.

'I think it must be soon,' Owain said to Rob on the evening of the 21st of August. 'May God bless and keep you, sir.'

'Thank you, and my wishes are the same for you,' Rob said, and then frowned. 'There is something I think you ought to know—something your kinswoman Alanna Davies told me when I visited Morgan Hywell at Shrewsbury. Were you aware that Lord Whitbread might have killed his wife? He said that she died of childbed fever—but he beat her and she died of her wounds.'

'Alanna told me,' Owain said. 'She saw him leaving her chamber with blood on his hands and she was buried in the crypt at Meresham. It is the reason I have stayed close to Melissa until I was injured—because I have feared that he might do the same to her.'

'Have you considered that Lady Whitbread might still be alive?'

'Elspeth?' Owain stared at her. 'He murdered her that night—how can she be alive?'

'Alanna is no longer sure that her kinswoman is dead.' Rob explained what Alanna had told him and Owain drew his breath sharply, a look of something akin to despair in his eyes. 'She came to me and told me before I left Shrewsbury. She thought that you would want to know that, and believed I would see you before she does.'

'If God spares me, I shall find her!' Owain said, his eyes lit by a fervour Rob had not seen in him before. 'I shall bring her home and somehow the wrongs that have been done her shall be put right. And then I shall kill him!'

'We must hope that we shall both be spared,' Rob said. 'Be sure that your enemy is also mine, Owain. I intend that he shall not continue his evil ways for longer than I can help.'

'I pray that we meet in battle,' Owain said fiercely. 'I would glory in seeing his blood spilled on the field of battle.'

'Which, if our spies tell us truly, will be on Bosworth Field,' Rob said, and traced the line of the scar on his cheek with his finger. 'If Whitbread falls to me I shall not spare him....'

'You seem much recovered,' Lady Gifford said as she entered the bedchamber to see Melissa brushing her long hair. The sun was shining in through the small window, which she had opened to let in the warmth for the stout walls of the manor house made it feel cold even in summer.

'Yes, I am better,' Melissa said, for she could not face making herself sick again, and, besides, had no more of the water that had made her ill. She must make a recovery and hope to find a way to put off her betrothal by other means. 'I should like to walk in the garden I can see from my window—if that is permitted?'

'You are not a prisoner, my dear,' Lady Gifford said, though her smile was a little uncertain. 'At least, you have the freedom of the house and inner courtyard. You may not go outside the walls, of course, though where you would go is a mystery. I think your father and Gifford foolish to imagine that you would try to run away, for where could you go? It is several leagues to the nearest town, and if you sought help in the village they would bring you back to us.'

'Would you help me?' Melissa asked, because the lady had been kind enough. 'If I could reach an Abbey the nuns might take me in.'

'I do not think so, for the nearest has my husband as their

patron. They receive money from his good offices and would not give you sanctuary if he asked for you. I am sorry, Melissa, but I think you must accept your fate. You will find that few will accept you without a dowry, and your father would never release it.' She gave Melissa a sympathetic look. 'It will not be so very bad, my dear. I thought I should die when my father promised me to Gifford, but I have born him three sons, though two died in infancy. Now he leaves me to sleep in peace while he sports with his mistress.' Her mouth tightened and a bitter note crept into her voice. 'I have learned to find my own pleasures and I daresay you will find that, in time, you may reach a kind of peace, yourself. We must do as we are bid, Melissa, as you know, our male relatives see us as their property and we are powerless.'

Melissa turned away, fighting her tears. Lady Gifford had allowed a glimpse of her true nature to show through, and she knew she would receive no help from her. She did not wish to live in the way that the older woman had described, nor would she. If she were truly trapped in this place, then she would take her own life.

'You must dress and come down now,' Lady Gifford told her, a harder tone in her voice as she saw that Melissa was still stubborn. She gave her a straight look. 'Gifford will delay no longer. Your brother is to stand proxy for Leominster and you will be betrothed this day.'

Melissa felt as if the noose were closing about her throat. She wanted to run away, but knew that she had little hope of getting very far. She must wait a little longer, form a plan somehow. In the meantime, although binding, a betrothal was not marriage. It would count as nothing if she lay in her grave, though it would stand as a bar between her and Rob if they wished to marry…yet he despised her and it could mean little to him if she were the wife of another man.

She closed her eyes, and for a moment was swept back to the

day when Rob had told her that he wished to marry her. He had stood gazing down into her eyes, his mouth soft and generous, his eyes filled with laughter—and then he had kissed her. 'I shall love you all my life. No matter what happens…'

The sweetness of his kiss had made her feel like swooning with happiness and she had nursed her hopes of being with him forever—but then her father had come home and somehow he had known of their secret meetings.

'You will send him away,' Lord Whitbread had thundered, his hand gripping her arm so tightly that she had cried out in pain. 'If he dares to come here again, he will die—not quickly by the sword, but slowly and painfully. My torturer knows how to make men suffer….'

'Father, I beg you not to harm him,' Melissa had cried, tears running down her cheek. 'Why will you not let me marry Rob? He loves me and I love him….'

'He is the last man I would allow you to marry,' Lord Whitbread thundered. 'His father and I…' He shook his head. 'That is none of your affair. Listen to me well, Melissa. If you do not send him from you in a way that ensures he never returns, I shall make him suffer and you shall watch.'

So she had sent him away with cruel words and her brother had scarred him, had beaten him and humiliated him—and now he hated her. It was useless to hope that one day he would come for her, because she had killed his love. There was no one to help her. Only her wits could save her now.

Melissa was filled with dread as she went down to the great hall where her father's cousin was standing with Harold and others who would bear witness to the ceremony that day.

Her heart was beating wildly. She looked about her, feeling close to desperation as she walked to stand next to her half brother before the priest who would hear their vows. Harold had an evil grin on his face and she knew that he was taking pleasure from seeing her forced to do her father's bidding.

'So, sister,' he said in gloating fashion. 'I am to stand proxy for Leominster. Would that I were not forbid you by virtue of blood ties for I would soon teach you to mind me.'

'I would die before I wed you,' Melissa said, her face pale.

'May I begin?' the priest asked, and at a nod from the earl, began his intonation, which would bind Melissa to her promised husband. 'Lady, give me your hand for this ring will seal your promise.'

'No!' Melissa hid her hand behind her back. 'I shall not promise. I do not wish for this betrothal and I shall not marry that man....' She swayed and moaned, feigning faintness. 'I cannot. I am too ill....'

'Come, I have no time to waste,' the Earl of Gifford said, glaring at her. 'You will do as you are told, girl. I have dallied here too long already. I shall see you take your vows and then I must leave. I gave my word to the King....'

Even as he spoke a man wearing the livery of Leominster came rushing into the hall. He flung himself on his knees before the earl, clearly near to exhaustion, his chest heaving as he fought for breath.

'My lord! I bring news of a terrible battle four days ago. Alas, Richard has been defeated on Bosworth Field. Henry Tudor has the crown, taken from a thornbush where it lay after the King was slain. They say that all Richard's friends were killed as they fought to defend him, but that he fought on valiantly until he was slain.'

'God rest his soul!' the Earl of Gifford said, and looked slightly dazed, as if he were unable to believe what had happened. Indeed, his mind was reeling from the shock, for he was not sure what the news meant. 'This changes things,' he declared. 'We cannot now go through with this betrothal ceremony, Melissa, for your future husband may be dead—or taken as a traitor. We must wait and see what your father would have us do.'

Melissa felt a wave of relief sweep over her. She was still feeling overwrought and gave a little moan, half swooning into the arms of her ladies in her relief.

'Take the wench out of my sight,' Gifford said impatiently. 'I must ride to meet the new King for, unless I make my peace with him, there is no telling what may happen.'

'It was that I came to tell you,' the messenger said. 'My master bid me tell you to bring you the news. Henry has sent one of his most trusted officers north to subdue those who might take up arms against him, and he may come here.'

'You have delivered your message,' Gifford said. He was in a dilemma for he did not know what to do to protect himself and his lands. If he resisted the force Henry Tudor sent against him, he would be branded a traitor and his life might be forfeit—and yet perhaps all was not yet lost. There were others of Plantagenet blood that might be thrust upon the throne by right of force. Henry Tudor had taken it by the sword and he could lose it just as easily. A battle had been fought and the King was dead, but the struggle was not yet over. The upstart Tudor would discover that it was not that easy to subdue England's nobles. 'Go now...'

'But, my lord,' the messenger protested, 'the Marquis of Leominster begs you ride to him with all your men and help to protect his castle. He says that it would be best for all those loyal to the true successor to make their stand at Leominster, for it will stand a siege better than your house.'

Who was now the true heir to the throne? Gifford could not say with any certainty. If King Edward's sons were dead—or bastards as rumour had named them—where should his loyalty now lie? The sons of Richard's sister, Anne, perhaps or perhaps others with an equal claim—Elizabeth of York, for one.

With no clear claimant, Gifford decided that his loyalty lay with his own self and no other. He would remain within the fortified manor house that was his home and see what fortune brought.

Meanwhile, Melissa's ladies had taken her to her chamber, laying her solicitously on her bed. She recovered as a burnt feather was waved under her nose, sitting up just as Lady Gifford came in.

'Ah, you are better. It was simply a faint—and no wonder. Your brother, Harold, is in a fearful pelter to be gone, for he is wondering what has happened to his father.'

'Yes, I daresay he is anxious,' Melissa said, putting her feet to the floor. 'If anything should happen to my father he might be in difficulty—unless Father has secured the estate to him.'

'Surely he would not leave it to a bastard?' Lady Gifford said, and frowned. 'It should come to you or your children, Melissa. Oh, dear, Gifford is in such a mood and I cannot talk to him. You were not betrothed to Leominster, and yet I have a letter from him, telling me to make you ready for a journey. He wants you to go to him at his castle for he says that Henry will never breach its walls.'

'No, I cannot go,' Melissa said. 'We are not betrothed and it would not be fitting. My father would never agree.'

'No, I do not think he would,' the lady said, and sighed. She felt a surge of impatience as she looked at Melissa. If the wretched girl had done her duty they might have been rid of her long since! 'Had the ceremony gone ahead I could have sent you for you would have been as good as wed to him, but in the circumstances—' she shook her head '—I do not know what to do. We cannot send you home in these troubled times. Harold might have taken you had he waited but he would not...so I suppose you must stay with us for the moment. I do hope we shall not be under siege for long. It becomes most uncomfortable to say the least.'

'Yes, I daresay,' Melissa said. She had not experienced it, for her father was too powerful, but she could imagine that it was an unpleasant experience.

'I must go and check our stores,' Lady Gifford told her with a worried look. 'The last time Gifford quarrelled with one of his neighbours we were shut up in here for a month and the food was running short—any longer and we might have been eating rats.'

Melissa shuddered for she could not think of a worse fate. 'I think I would prefer to be hungry,' she said.

'Wait until you know what real hunger is,' Lady Gifford said. 'I must go, my dear. Please feel free to walk where you wish. You may come and help me if you feel strong enough.'

'I am perfectly well,' Melissa said. 'Pray, tell me what I may do to be of service?'

'Some of the men have gone hunting,' Lady Gifford said. 'When they return, we shall need to salt the meat so that it keeps longer. And there are fruits to be preserved for the winter. You may help with that, for we shall need all our resources if we are to resist a siege.'

'Then, I shall come down when I have changed into suitable attire,' Melissa said. 'Please do not let me keep you, my lady.'

As Lady Gifford went out, Melissa summoned Agnes to help her change out of her best silk gown into a kirtle of Wilton and a tunic of worsted, which were less costly than her best clothes and would do for the chore of salting down the fresh meat.

Her thoughts were busy as she changed, because she knew that she had been given a temporary respite. If her father still lived he would be determined on her marriage—if not to the Marquis of Leominster to someone else. Unless he had been killed on the field of battle or was the subject of an act of attainder, he would never give up his plans for her.

More importantly, what had happened to Rob? He might hate her, but she loved him still and she did not care what became of her as long as she might know that he was safe.

'I thank you for your support, Sir Robert of Melford,' Henry Tudor said. He had not yet been crowned the King of England, but he had assumed its majesty. It was now within his power to grant favours to those who had served him well, and none had done better by him than this man. Rob had fought valiantly in the field, and was respected by all. 'You shall have your rewards when I am truly King—but I would ask another service of you. There are lords in the north of England that I must either subdue or make peace with—namely Gifford and Leominster. They live no more than fifteen leagues apart. Subdue one and the other should fall— From the information my scurryers give me, I would say that Gifford will fall the easier. Control him first and he cannot come at your back when you have Leominster at your mercy.'

'And what would you have me do with them, sire?'

'Send Gifford to me unless he resists too long. Although I know him to be my enemy, he took no part in the battle. Therefore, I may imprison him in the Tower and pardon him in due course—if he will recant his loyalty to my enemies. Leominster will never give in. He will be tried and condemned to a just death—unless he dies in battle.'

'It shall be as you wish,' Rob said. 'I shall leave as soon as my men may be made ready to march.'

'Come to me when I am crowned,' Henry said. 'I would have loyal, brave men about me, Robert of Melford—and there are none braver I think.'

'Thank you, sire.'

Rob took his leave. As he walked back towards the camp where his men were resting, he was thoughtful. They had all worked hard these past days. Although the battle of Bosworth had lasted no more than two hours, because of Henry Tudor's brilliant stratagem—and perhaps Richard's depleted forces—there had been skirmishes. Rob's men had been sent to rout some of those who remained defiant and would not lay down their arms.

Rob had not expected that he would be released after one battle, however successful. Had King Richard not been caught in a difficult position it might have ended differently. After killing Henry's standard bearer and unhorsing the knight, Sir John Cheney, who was a veritable giant, Richard had been lost in the melee, his horse shot from under him by the archers, perhaps helpless in the mud of the churned fields. If he had escaped to fight again, he could well have been victorious for the Stanleys might then have thrown in their fortunes with him. Instead, Lord Stanley had found the crown hanging on the thornbush and brought it to Henry Tudor, declaring him the king.

It would take a serious rebellion to dislodge Henry once he had the throne secure, Rob knew—and it was to this end that some of the more troublesome nobles were to be subdued. Some would fight and might lose all they owned as well as their lives. Others might negotiate and thereby save their lives, even if their lands were forfeit, for often something was saved for their sons.

'Rob!' Owain came towards him. 'I have news that may interest you.'

'What news, pray?' Rob asked, his mind busy with plans for the task the King had given him. 'We must make ready to leave by dawn for we have more work to do before we can go home.'

'I have learned that Lord Whitbread is badly injured and like to die of his wounds,' Owain said. 'There is a dispute over his lands, for Harold of Meresham is a bastard. Some say that they will go to the lady Melissa's husband.'

'She is married then?' Rob felt the knife plunge into his heart. For hours at a time he had forgot her in the midst of battle, but she was always there at the back of his mind, waiting to plague him when he slept. She was proud and faithless, but the memory of their secret meetings, when she had given her kisses so sweetly, lingered still, and sometimes of late he had begun to wonder if he had misjudged her.

'I do not know,' Owain said. 'If they married her to Leominster before he rode to join King Richard it may be that he will inherit—but if she is not wed—' Owain frowned '—her father's cousin, Gifford, would then have guardianship of her and might use her for his own ends. With King Richard dead, I do not know who will protect her fortune.'

'She becomes Henry's ward,' Rob said, his mouth thinning to a grim line. 'I have work to do, Owain, for I am to lay siege to Gifford and then Leominster...' He frowned as something struck him. 'You said her father's cousin, Gifford—do you mean the Earl of Gifford?'

'Yes, sir,' Owain said, a hard expression in his eyes. 'It was to the earl's stronghold that they took her.'

Rob felt a foolish hope spring up anew in his breast, but he crushed it ruthlessly. There was nothing to hope for. She was proud and faithless, and he would be stupid to think otherwise.

'It may be that we shall find her there,' he said. 'Unless she is with her husband—and if so it will not be long before she is a widow.'

'If the King orders it so be it,' Owain said. 'I am with you, Rob, for if you go north I shall find my lady there somewhere...'

'Aye, your lady,' Rob said with a nod. 'We shall release her from her captors if she be a prisoner—but if she is a wife then she must face the consequences. Her husband has been attained a traitor and will be brought to face the King's justice.'

Owain looked at his face, seeing the hard welt of red that marred his masculine good looks. It was little wonder that he was bitter, but Owain knew him for a fair man and hoped that he would treat kindly with Melissa.

Melissa was tearing strips of white cloth for bandages. She had rolled several lengths and was wondering how much more would be needed when Lady Gifford came to her in the store-room, which was situated at the back of the great hall, near to the scullery and kitchens.

'Your uncle bade me tell you that he wishes us to gather in

the hall,' Lady Gifford said. 'He has received notice from the King's messenger that he is to surrender Gifford to His Majesty's commander and he intends to make his wishes clear to us, Melissa.'

'Will my uncle surrender?' Melissa asked, her heart beating wildly. She was not sure which would be the best, for if a stranger came to the fortress there was no way of telling what would happen to them all.

'I do not know,' Lady Gifford said. 'He told me to make ready for a siege, but now it seems that he is undecided. He may hope to make peace and bargain for his life and lands.'

'But you and your son?' Melissa asked, for the countess had a son of just seven years. 'What will happen to you—all of us— if he does not fight?'

'We must wait and see,' Lady Gifford said. 'If the King is merciful we shall be spared. I do not know this man he sends against us.'

'By what name is he called?' Melissa asked.

'He is called Sir Robert of Melford,' the countess replied. 'Apparently, he is well thought of by the King and is to be honoured for services given.'

'Robert of Melford comes here?' Melissa's heart was racing wildly now. A part of her longed to see Rob again, and yet she was afraid—afraid of the coldness she might see in his eyes. Even so, she would rather be his captive than another's, and deep inside her there was a small kernel of hope…hope that he might have learned to forgive her.

'You know of this man?'

Melissa looked into her eyes, her head held high. 'He is the man I would have married had I been free to choose,' she said. 'He loved me once, though no longer. My father tried to kill him and he has cause to hate me…' She choked back a little sob. If only she had disobeyed her father and somehow run away with Rob—but she had been given no chance. Lord Whitbread had kept her close until the moment Rob was seen riding up to the castle, and he had waited behind the tapestry to rush out and take her lover prisoner if she had done other than he ordered.

'We must hope that he is not a vengeful man,' Lady Gifford said, a little shiver running through her, for some men would use this opportunity to inflict a cruel punishment. 'But come, Melissa. Your uncle is waiting.'

'Should I not change my gown?' She looked down at herself for her tunic was stained and she would have preferred to look her best—especially if Robert of Melford was admitted to the castle.

Lady Gifford shook her head impatiently. 'No, come as you are. This is no time to be thinking of fripperies. We must not keep the earl waiting for whatever he decides to do may seal our fate one way or the other…and if this man is your enemy we may all suffer for it.' She gave Melissa a look of dislike, abandoning all pretence of being the kindly woman she liked others to think her. 'If we lose everything because of you…' Her eyes were dark with malice. 'Gifford belongs to my son. He is all that I have lived for—and one day he will be the master here. If your quarrels endanger that, you will be my enemy.'

'The man I knew would not take a petty revenge on women and children,' Melissa said. 'He may despise me, but he is not like my father—or your husband.'

'Let us hope for all our sakes that you are right!'

Melissa's heart was thumping as she followed Lady Gifford down the stairs. For days they had been preparing for a siege, but now it looked as if her uncle might have decided to open his gates and let the King's messenger in. If that man were truly Robert of Melford it meant that she would see him very soon. She had begun to believe that she might never see Rob again in this life and it was both thrilling and terrifying to know that he had come to subdue her uncle into submission.

What would he have to say to her?

Chapter Four

Rob halted his forces and looked at the fortified manor house that lay before them. It was strongly defended for it sat at the top of a rise and had stout walls surrounding the main buildings and courtyard, though there was no moat or drawbridge. Gifford had done away with the Keep of his ancestors and built himself a fine house, but it was more vulnerable than the castle that had once stood on this spot. The gate had been closed against him, but a battering ram would soon have that down and leave the courtyard open to him.

Rob still had nearly a hundred men that had been willing to follow him north on the new King's business, though many had returned to their homes after Bosworth. It was the custom after a successful battle and Rob did not blame them, for there were still harvests to be gathered and many of his force had been drawn from simple country folk. Those who remained were trained fighting men and sufficient in number to take a fortress such as this. However, Rob had seen no signs of men massing on the battlements over the gates or along the walls. It seemed that the earl was giving consideration to the King's demands.

Rob was surprised but pleased when he saw the white flag being hoisted above the gates. He had expected that Gifford would put up some kind of a fight, even though he knew his own force to be superior, for if his information were correct, Gifford had no more than sixty fighting men. Of course he might have mustered another hundred of the common folk to man the walls and throw stones at the attacking army, but it seemed that he had chosen otherwise.

As Rob watched, the gates opened and two riders came out to meet him carrying a white flag. He rode forward to speak with them alone, knowing that his archers were watching for treachery and had their arrows trained on the men coming to parley.

'I speak for the Earl of Gifford,' one of the men cried. 'Why do you come in force to our gates, Robert of Melford? We have no quarrel with you or yours. Depart and leave us in peace this day.'

'I am come on King Henry of England's business,' Rob replied. 'Your master has the King's commands. Lay down your arms and allow us into the fortress and there need be no blood shed, nor will your women be harmed or your buildings be torched.'

'Do you give your solemn word as a man of honour that the women, children and old folk will be safe—and do you grant safe custody to the earl and his family?'

'King Henry wishes to speak with the earl,' Rob replied. 'His wife and son will remain here as his bond. If he tries to escape on the journey to London, they will be taken to the Tower as the King's prisoners.'

'I shall return and give my master your terms,' the steward said, and, turning, rode away.

Rob rejoined his own ranks. He would prefer that Gifford surrendered for the sake of the women and children within the fortress, for otherwise many would suffer. He wondered if Melissa was still her uncle's prisoner and his heart beat faster at the thought of seeing her very soon. If she was here, it might mean that she had not yet been wed to Leominster.

What should he care for that? He knew from her own lips that she considered him to be unworthy of being her husband and the sound of her laughter that day had burned deep into his mind, taunting him whenever he softened his heart towards her. She had lied when she said that she loved him, and he had believed her. He must remember that she lied easily! He would behave as an honourable knight, and treat her well—but she would never blind him with her smiles and kisses again.

Melissa saw her uncle in close conversation with his steward. Hale had just returned from a parley under the flag of truce, and she wondered what they were saying. She had been upstairs to change out of her working gown into a tunic and kirtle of green and gold. On her head she wore a frette of gold-work trellis, her hair hanging loose about her shoulders. If they were to surrender the fortress to Robert of Melford, she would look her best when he first saw her.

She saw that her uncle had sent the steward off on another errand and, after some hesitation, approached him.

'What is happening, sir?' she asked. 'Are we to fight or surrender?'

'I do not have enough men to win the struggle,' the earl replied a little sourly. 'Some of my men rode with Leominster while I lingered here. If your intended husband sends reinforcements we might hold out—but I think he means to defend his own stronghold and will not aid us. Therefore, for the sake of my son, my wife—and you, Melissa—I have decided that I must surrender. Mayhap if I pledge allegiance to the King, he will spare my lands to me.'

'But can you in all honour pledge loyalty to a man you despise?' Melissa asked with a little frown. She had heard her father and half brother speaking of their dislike of Henry Tudor, whom they considered an upstart, and she wondered how the earl would swallow such humiliation.

'You know nothing of these things,' Gifford said, and glared at her. 'Go back to your sewing, niece, and leave this business to me.'

Melissa sensed that she had angered him without meaning

to, and was not surprised when he suddenly ordered her to return to her chamber.

'I have negotiated terms with this Robert of Melford,' he went on. 'It has been promised that the women and children will not suffer. But stay close in your room until you are sent for, niece.'

'Yes, uncle.' Melissa walked from the great hall, her shoulders stiff with pride. It seemed that even though the plans for her betrothal had failed, she was still at her uncle's bidding, still confined to her rooms as if she were a prisoner rather than a guest in his house.

She went upstairs to her chamber and took out her sewing as she had been bidden; she was feeling angry because her opinion had been dismissed as worthless. It was almost always so, she knew, for few women reached an influential position in life, unless they were queens or princesses, and sometimes not even then. Were any women valued and loved for themselves? Melissa asked herself a little bitterly. Or were they always considered merely a possession to be traded for power and wealth?

'Does something ail you, my lady?' Agnes asked, looking at her anxiously. She had heard the name of the King's commander and felt uneasy lest her mistress take this chance to punish her. 'May I do anything for you?' If Melissa ever guessed that it was she who had betrayed her secret meetings with her lover, she would surely beat her!

'You may take yourself from my sight until I send for you,' Melissa said. 'I have not forgotten or forgiven what you did to the Abbess, Agnes.'

'I beg you to forgive me,' Agnes said, throwing herself on her knees before Melissa. 'Your father was my master and I did only as he ordered me. I was to watch you whatever you did and make sure that if you visited the Abbess while he was absent, she did not give you anything.…'

'He did not order you to poison my aunt…or did he?' Melissa's gaze narrowed in suspicion. 'You swore to me it was an accident, but you lied, didn't you? You went to my aunt's chamber deliberately and you murdered her…' Melissa's blood ran cold as she looked at the girl in horror. 'He sent you to spy on me…it was you who told him of my meetings with Rob! Oh, how dare you ask for mercy when you have betrayed me so many times? Go from my sight or I shall have you whipped.'

Agnes burst into tears and ran through to the outer chamber.

How could the girl have betrayed her so cruelly? Melissa felt as if she were on fire, her mind working furiously as she thought about all the times her father had seemed to know what she was doing or thinking. She had trusted her ladies, often telling them her secrets—and Agnes had betrayed her to her father. She would send the girl away and ask Lady Gifford to supply her with another serving woman. She could hardly bear to look at Agnes now that she knew she was the cause of all her grief.

Laying down the embroidery panel she was working on, Melissa got up and went over to the narrow window to look out. The glass was grey and the view somewhat distorted, but she could see what was going on. A white flag had been hoisted over the castle walls. As she watched, the gates were being opened and men began to ride into the courtyard. Some of them were dismounting and there was some shouting going on, as if a few of the earl's men did not take kindly to the idea of surrender.

The courtyard was gradually filling with soldiers now, some of them in full armour, the sun shining on the slanted metal plates that were designed to deflect the missile from the deadly crossbow. Her heart raced as one of them took off his helmet and she could see his face well enough through the thick glass to know him. She recognised the powerful figure of the man she loved.

Rob was here! He was here and she would see him sooner or later, even though she had been ordered to stay in her chamber. Her anger at his manner towards her in the forest that day had long since gone. Would he give her a chance to explain that she had been betrayed and forced to do her father's bidding? Would it even matter to him now? She knew that she had killed his love the day she had sent him away, but perhaps he would help her to leave this place and seek sanctuary in a nunnery.

She looked down at the man in the courtyard below, accepting the surrender of Gifford Towers from the earl himself. She knew that her father's cousin must be angry and humiliated and she wondered that he had accepted his fate so easily. He had planned to fight at the start, but something had made him change his mind—what?

It was clear that the earl would not feel honour bound to keep any pledge he gave. Was he hoping that his captors would grow careless so that he might escape? Melissa was certain in her own mind that the earl did not intend to go cap in hand to the King and beg for mercy—which must mean only one thing. He hoped to win his freedom by other methods.

Should she warn Robert of Melford that Gifford was not to be trusted? Yet if she did that, he might be punished or sent to London in chains as a prisoner. And there was the question of his wife and son—and the entire household. Perhaps it would be better if she kept silent. After all, she had only her intuition to go on, and who would listen to the thoughts of a woman?

She turned away from the window and sat down, picking up her sewing. It was a pastime she normally enjoyed for it was a pleasure to see a picture take shape from her skill with the needle and the glowing colours of her embroidery silks were lovely. She knew that she might have to wait for hours before she was summoned, and she was comparing two strands of pink silk, which were slightly different in colour, when she heard voices and a noise in the outer chamber.

Something was going on! Melissa lifted her head, wondering about the commotion, but it did not occur to her that it was important for she did not expect to be summoned until well into the day, when refreshments were laid in the great hall. However, a moment later, the door was flung open and a man came in, still arguing with the women who were trying to bar him from her chamber.

'Rob...Sir Robert,' she said, for the anger in his eyes told her that she could look for no softness from him. Nothing had changed in all these weeks. He would always hate her. 'I had heard that you were coming. I am glad the earl offered no resistance for many lives have been saved.' Her eyes strayed to his face, for the red scar on his cheek was still as vivid and raw as it had been when she first saw it. Something made her ask, 'Does it still pain you?'

'Would it give you pleasure to know that it does?' Rob asked, and his hand went to his face, for he knew that she must be revolted by its ugliness. 'Your brother told me that I had insulted you—and this was my punishment. I bear it with pride, for it is a constant reminder of the perfidy of women.'

Melissa seemed frozen to the spot. She had risen to her feet when he came in, her embroidery falling to the ground. She ran the tip of her tongue over her lips, her mouth dry as she felt a spiral of fear run through her. He looked so angry, his tone so bitter. This was not the charming man she had fallen in love with so desperately, but a stranger. She was not to know that Rob was deliberately harsh, because he feared that he might weaken.

Her hand crept to her throat, for she was wearing the trinket he had once given her, and it hung from a ribbon at her throat. His eyes followed her movement and she saw him frown as he saw the jade heart.

'I told my father nothing of what happened between us,' she whispered, the colour draining from her face. 'We were betrayed by a woman who served me...' She could not continue for her throat felt tight with suppressed tears. 'I had no choice…' What was the use? He would not believe her. She raised her head proudly, meeting his eyes now as anger bolstered her courage. 'But believe what you will. It makes little difference now.'

Rob came towards her, his expression stern, unforgiving. 'I came to inform you that you are now my prisoner, lady,' he said in a voice hoarse with a mixture of emotions he did not care to acknowledge. 'By what name should I address you? Are you wed to the Marquis of Leominster?'

'No…he was called away and the betrothal by proxy did not take place,' Melissa whispered, her lips white. He hated her so! How could he not after what had happened to him? 'My uncle keeps me here until…' She faltered for she did not know how to go on.

'It is as well for you that you were not wed,' Rob said, still cold and distant. 'Had you been a wife you would soon have been a widow. Your intended husband took sides against Henry. He is known to be plotting even now to aid a rebellion and for that his life is forfeit.'

Melissa was trembling. Not because she cared what became of the marquis, but because Rob was so stern and she had never imagined that he could be like this. Even in the forest, when he had rescued her he had not seemed so cold. Indeed, as they rode together she had felt something between them, but now he looked at her as if they had never been lovers.

'What of my cousin, sir?' she asked. 'Will the King be merciful?'

'My orders are to send him under guard to London, where he will be imprisoned in the Tower until Henry has time to deal with him. He surrendered to me and took no actual part in the fighting. He may be spared if he swears loyalty to the King. That is not my business. My task was to take the fortress in Henry's name, which I have this day.'

'My cousin's wife and her son?' Melissa swallowed hard for she could see no softness in this knight. Where was the laughing, gallant man to whom she had given her heart? Had he gone forever? She thought that her brother's cruelty must have killed all that she had loved in him, and her heart ached for something lost.

'All the women and children will be treated fairly,' Rob said, his gaze intent. He showed no emotion and yet a little nerve flicked in his throat, as if he were fighting some strong emotion. 'I have not yet decided what shall be your fate, Melissa of Whitbread.' He frowned as she was silent, her face pale, eyes downcast. 'You do not ask for news of your father?'

Melissa raised her head, a spark of pride in her eyes now. 'I know that it was his intention to fight for King Richard. If he was not killed in battle he may be attained as a traitor, his lands forfeit…though his son took no part in the battle for he was here.'

'Do you plead for your half brother?'

'No…' Melissa took a deep breath. 'I have no reason to love him or my father—but I believe in honesty and fairness. I played no part in what happened to you that day, sir, but I beg you to forgive me—for it was done in my name.'

'Forgive you?' Rob's expression did not change, though she sensed his bitter anger. 'For the face that must frighten the children? For the pain I endured night after night—for the humiliation at Lord Whitbread's hands? For the lies you told me? How may a man forgive these things, lady? Tell me, and perhaps I shall.'

He had not forgotten how to mock her, but now she could no longer smile. He had teased her unmercifully as they walked and laughed together in the meadows, but his eyes had been warm and loving then and now they were like ice. The pain seared deep inside her, for she knew that it was impossible. No man could forgive what had been done to Rob—and she knew that all her hopes were at an end.

'For all or none, sir,' she said, a hint of pride in her lovely face as she met his angry gaze. 'If you can forgive one you can forgive all—but if not then you must hate me. Were there a way to turn back the clock and take away your pain, I would do it, but I think there is none.' Tears sparkled in her eyes but pride had come to her rescue. She would not beg nor would she weep. 'My future is in your hands, sir. I must do whatever you tell me.'

'Must you?' Rob came closer. So close that she could feel the cold anger emanating from him as an icy blast from the north winds. He reached out, his hands touching her hair. It fell in luxurious strands to her shoulders, tumbling down her back in soft waves. He let the red-gold strands trickle through his fingers, his voice thick with desire as he said, 'Your hair is even more beautiful than I remembered in my fevered dreams.'

'Rob…' Melissa's pulses raced as he reached out for her. He had taken off his breastplate of steel and he caught her to him, holding her pressed against the hardness of his chest, his leather jerkin soft and yielding to her hand. As she gazed up at him, his head came down and he took possession of her mouth—but his kiss was not like the others she had had of him. His lips were hard and angry as he took without giving, bruising, demanding and cruel. When he let her go, she put her trembling fingers to her lips, feeling as if she had been used, her eyes brimming with the shaming tears, which she still held back. 'Why…'

'So that you understand that you are my prisoner,' Rob told her. 'Mine to do with as I please. I have given surety for every lady in the fortress, save one. You will be given neither your freedom—nor a promise of safety. As yet, I have not decided what I shall do with you, but forget your ideas of marriage to the marquis, for that I shall never allow.'

Melissa felt her throat tighten. Did he imagine that she had wanted to be Leominster's bride? She had longed to tell him the truth, to explain that what she had done had been for his sake, but she could not plead with the man he had become. It would shame her to weep and beg and she would not give him the pleasure of seeing her humbled.

'I am yours to do with as you will, sir,' she said. He was angry and he hated her. Her heart felt as if it had been encased in ice. Even though his kiss had bruised and hurt her, she would still be his willingly if he asked it of her. She had loved him so much, but she would not risk further humiliation by showing him that she was still his for the taking. 'I acted as I did for good reason, sir—but I do not ask you to believe me. Nor shall I beg for your forgiveness. All that I ask in common mercy is that you will allow me to leave here. I should like to retire to a nunnery and become one of the sisters.'

'You ask too much,' he said. 'You and your family owe restitution to mine. My father died after a visit from your brother—and you gave me false promises and this—' he touched the scar '—do you not think that I am entitled to compensation for my injuries?'

'Yes, perhaps,' Melissa said. 'King Richard was the guardian of my fortune, but I know not what has become of it—take it, for it has brought me nothing but grief. I wish only to spend the rest of my life in sanctuary.'

'You think that gold will pay? It seems that you *are* your father's child, lady—but blood must be paid in blood.'

'Then kill me and have done with it!' she cried.

'Do not think that I have not thought of it…'

'Then do it now! I am willing to pay all my family's debts.'

Rob's eyes scorned her but he made no reply, turning to walk from the room without another word. Melissa stood where she was for a moment longer after he had gone, and then sank to her knees, covering her face with her hands.

Walking away from Melissa's chamber, Rob was churning with conflicting emotions. He had been harsh with her, because if he softened once she would worm her way into his heart again. For a few minutes as they first met, he had seemed to see the girl he loved and he had wanted to take her into his arms and kiss her, but then she had become cold and proud, and he was reminded of the day she drove him from her. And yet the memory of her brother's words was imprinted into his mind, words that had made him writhe in agony a thousand times.

She had been wearing the jade heart on a ribbon at her throat. Why had she kept that trinket? Why had she worn it—to soften his heart perhaps, to make him believe that she still cared for him? He would be a fool to believe in such sentiment! Harold's words were burned into his memory.

That was for my sister. She tells me you have insulted her.

She said that she had acted for good reason, implying that she was innocent. How could he believe her? His fingers strayed to the scar on his cheek. He knew that he must look ugly enough to curdle the milk, as the goodwives said to their children when they wished to frighten them with a monster. He had seen other women stare at the scar and turn away in disgust. Why should Melissa be any different? He was not particularly vain, but he knew that women had always loved him for his looks. That was now a thing of the past! He was scarred inwardly and outwardly, and the bitterness he had endured had made him harder.

He could not believe in love. How could any woman want his kisses now? Besides, she had never truly loved him—how could she when she had betrayed him to her father for the sake of wealth and rank? Why should he believe anything she said?

Yet the pride in her eyes as she told him to take his revenge on her—her scorn for the fortune she had inherited—and a look in her eyes that spoke of grief and sleepless nights, all these things told him that she was innocent. Was it possible that she had been the victim of her father's spite?

It was useless! He could not let down the shield he had erected to keep him safe in the dark hours. To believe her would be to love her, and that would make him vulnerable.

He fought the churning desire inside him. His men were even now making the fortress secure. He must decide what to do about the Earl of Gifford before moving on to attack Leominster's stronghold—and his thoughts concerning Melissa must be put aside for the moment.

Melissa was staring out of the window when the door of her chamber opened. She thought it was her serving woman and did not immediately turn her head, but then, hearing a man cough, she swung 'round, her heart thumping. For a moment she had thought Rob had returned, but she gave a cry of relief and pleasure when she saw it was Owain.

'My dear friend!' she cried, and ran to him, holding out her hands to greet him. He took them, raising one to his lips to kiss it lightly. 'I have longed for word from you, Owain. Forgive me for leaving you with the monks, but I dared not stay for fear of my father's anger.'

'How are you, my lady?' he asked, his eyes studying her face, seeing the shadows beneath her eyes and the grief she was trying to hide. Was he right to keep his secret from her? For years he had suppressed the longing to tell her something that might set her free. Perhaps one day, but the time had not yet come. He must first discover if the rumour that her mother lived had any truth in it. 'I have wanted to come to you, but I gave my promise to help put Henry Tudor on the throne of England—and this was my first opportunity.'

'So you fought with Robert of Melford for Henry Tudor?'

Owain nodded. He noticed signs of redness about her eyes and guessed that she had shed a few tears after Rob had visited her, though she had done her best to wash away the signs.

'Yes, my lady. He is a brave leader and men follow him willingly. We fought in the same battle, side by side with Henry Tudor. I admire him as a man and a leader—but I think he is very angry. He believes that you betrayed him to your father. And what was done to him was cruel. Harold had giv-en orders that he was to die, but I came upon them as they set about their wicked work and I killed them. I took him back to his family…but perhaps it would have been better if I had left him to die?'

'No! How can you say it?' Melissa cried. 'It is bad enough that he suffered as he did—but at least he lives…even if he hates me.'

'But you—do you love him?'

'I do not know…' Melissa raised her head. 'If I did, it would shame me to admit it, for he hates me.'

'Did you know what your father and brother planned that day?'

'Do you really need to ask?' Melissa's eyes filled with tears. 'Surely you know me better, Owain? I would have married him willingly, gladly, for I loved him—but my father told me that, unless I sent him away, he would kill him. Not easily with the sword, but a slow death by torture—and his family was to be destroyed, his home burned to the ground.'

'So that your father could take Melford's lands,' Owain said, nodding grimly. 'He has coveted them for many years—but the trouble began long ago. Your father wanted the woman Oswald Melford married but she told him that she would have none of him and took Melford instead. He was a mere country squire, his lands substantial but nothing to your father's riches, though he and his son have added to them over the years…'

'My father loved Rob's mother?' Melissa stared at him in as-tonishment. 'So that is why my father wanted to hear me hu-miliate Rob… He listened to me from behind the tapestry. I understand now why he was so angry. It was sweet revenge for what he had suffered.'

'Perhaps,' Owain said. 'I do not know if he loved her or if she merely wounded his pride, but I know that he never loved your mother, Melissa. He married her for the fortune she brought and he treated her badly, cruelly—and when your grandfather made you the King's ward he felt cheated.'

'Yes, I understand. I always wondered why he hated me.'

There was more, but Owain judged that she had learned enough for the time being. She needed to come to terms with things he had told her—the rest would keep.

'Rob believes that I betrayed him to my father, but it was not so. We were spied on by one of my women and she went to my father on his return. Had I been given the chance, I would have warned him not to come that day, but I was locked in my chamber until the last moment.'

'I believe you,' Owain said. 'I have always thought you innocent of any involvement in what Lord Whitbread did that night—but you cannot expect Rob to believe you so easily. Your…Harold of Meresham said that you were insulted by his attentions, and Rob believed him…though whether he does so in his heart I do not know. He was badly injured—not only the wound to his face, but another to his head. He was thrown over the back of a horse, his head down as if he were a beast killed in the hunt. Imagine the hurt to his pride as well as his face. It was a terrible humiliation for a young man—perhaps worse than the injuries he sustained.'

'Yes, I know that he suffered greatly that night,' Melissa said, a break in her voice. 'I would have taken my own life before I let my brother bring me here—but my father kept my woman Rhona as hostage and threatened that he would give her to Harold if I escaped him before I was wed. I had no choice but to come here, because I did not want her to suffer for my sake.'

'Lord Whitbread will take no more revenge,' Owain told her. 'He received a wound in battle that laid him low, and has since died of it. I have heard that Harold of Meresham claims his estate and means to petition the King.'

Melissa made the sign of the cross over her breast. 'I am sorry for Lord Whitbread's death,' she said, 'though he was never kind to me.'

'Harold claims what should by rights be yours, for he is a bastard. Do you not wish to make a counter claim?'

'I know that he has long been anxious to lay hands on my father's wealth,' Melissa said. 'He would have taken my own inheritance if he could, but my grandfather made provision, as you know. I do not grudge him my father's lands. After all, I have my own.'

Owain nodded. He would have expected no less of her. 'I believe Sir Robert has asked Henry Tudor to become the guardian of your grandfather's estates,' Owain said. 'But I do not know whether your father's wish will stand in law regarding the marriage…' He hesitated, overcome with the desire to tell Melissa the secret he had kept close so long. He must wait until he returned from his quest. If he found Elspeth everything would be different.

'Rob…Sir Robert says that I am his prisoner,' Melissa said. 'I think he intends to subdue Leominster for he is a traitor to the new king.'

'Yet if he treats for pardon and swears loyalty it may be that Henry will allow him to retain at least some of his lands—and marry.'

Melissa was startled. 'Surely I shall not be forced to marry him now that my father is dead?'

'I cannot be certain,' Owain said. 'I tell you only what is possible. Kings are no more to be trusted than ordinary men when it comes to such things. If it suits him, Henry may give you to any of his lords who have fought for him. Your lands are a rich reward for any knight. It is the custom of kings to reward those who serve them—and this one needs to keep the loyalty of his supporters, perhaps more than most. In England the custom of wealth and privilege is strong, and many nobles keep court and numbers of armed men that make them almost as powerful as the King himself.'

'Yes, I know. My father was one of them, I think.'

'He gave his loyalty to King Richard and for that his lands may be forfeit—but you played no part in the struggle and if Henry is fair he will return them to you or your husband.'

'Sometimes I wish that I had nothing.' Melissa sighed, looking so sad that Owain longed to put his arms about her and comfort her, but knew that she would be disturbed by such an act. 'But it makes me happy to see you, sir, for I have been much concerned.' She smiled at Owain suddenly. 'You know that you have always been dear to me.'

'I thank you for your kind words,' Owain said. 'There is something more I would tell you, but you must understand that it may come to nothing…'

'What is on your mind? I can see that it troubles you.'

'I am not sure that I should speak—perhaps it would be best to wait and see if I discover her…'

'Now you intrigue me,' Melissa said, and smiled. 'Pray, tell me what you mean.'

'I have been told something…concerning your mother.'

'I know that my father killed her. The Abbess gave me a letter describing my mother's murder before she died.'

'It is not that, though that is grief enough to bear,' Owain said. 'I have believed it these many years and sworn that he shall not lay his hand on you…but this may hurt you even more. Alanna says that she thinks Elspeth may yet live….'

'My mother still lives?' Melissa looked at him in bewilderment. 'How can she? I have visited her tomb every week for as long as I can recall…how can she live?'

'The story is thus…' Owain explained what Alanna had told Rob. 'I cannot say if there is a grain of truth in her suspicion, but it may be so.'

Melissa turned away and went to the window to look out. Her mind was whirling in confusion, her eyes burning with the tears his story had aroused. If her mother lived… How often she had prayed that they might meet, might talk and embrace!

'Why has she not come to me in all these years?' she asked as she turned. 'It surely cannot be true?'

'If she lives she must have run away,' Owain said, and his face twisted with grief. 'She was afraid of him. I would have helped her but I was not there at that time. I had returned to my home, for my family needed me—and, when I returned, it was to learn that she was dead. Alanna told me that he had beaten her and I would have taken revenge then, but there was a child—you. I vowed that I would protect you with my life.'

'Yet she might have sent me some word…a sign that she was alive.'

'I do not know whether the story is true or false,' Owain admitted. 'It might have been better had I not told you.…'

'No! I am glad that you did,' Melissa said, and her face lit up. 'Oh, if she lives…I must know it. I want to see her…to ask her all the things I have longed to know.'

'It is my intention to look for her,' Owain said. 'My reason for telling you was because I must leave you. I think you safe enough now that Robert of Melford has the castle secure. But I promise to come back to tell you what I have found.'

'Yes, thank you,' Melissa said. 'I wish that I might come with you. If I could I would ride away from this place now and never return.'

'But you are not free,' Owain said. 'Rob is a good man—but do not try his patience too far, my lady. There are others concerned in this and these are uncertain times.'

'Yes, I know,' Melissa said, and sighed. 'Lady Gifford fears for her son and his inheritance.…'

'Could you not tell him the truth, as you have told it to me?'

'No! He hates me and would accuse me of lying. I beg you, do not tell him for he will think that I have sent you to plead for me.'

'You know I would never betray you, my lady.'

'Yes, I know it.' She smiled at him for he had been her constant friend.

'And now I must tell you that Sir Robert bids you come to dine with him at table this night.'

'He sent you to ask me?' Melissa wondered that he had not mentioned it himself. She looked thoughtful. 'Tell me, where is Lady Gifford and her son?'

'Confined to her chamber for the moment, I think,' Owain said. 'She will remain there until after her husband has left on his journey to the Tower.'

'But that is unfair,' Melissa cried. 'She must wish to say goodbye to her husband, for she may never see him again.'

'Sir Robert is not minded for such leniency,' Owain said, and sighed for he had seen the look in his leader's eyes when he inquired if Melissa were still in the castle.

'Then I shall ask him to change his mind,' Melissa said. 'To prevent a wife saying goodbye to her husband is a wicked thing.'

She walked past Owain to the outer chamber before he realised what she intended. As soon as he understood what she meant to do, he followed, catching her arm.

'Have a care, my lady. He is very angry.'

'Then I can do no harm. He is already angry with me, let him be more so—but show kindness to others.'

'My lady…' Owain protested, but she would not listen. He followed her along a narrow gallery and down the stairs to the main chamber below. It was possible to see that Robert was standing there in conversation with the earl's steward, Sandro of Hale. Melissa hesitated as she reached the bottom stair but then went up to them, her head held proudly, her expression angry.

'Go, sir,' Rob said, dismissing Hale with a wave of his hand. 'Do all that you have promised and you need fear no harm to you or your people.' He frowned, his gaze narrowing as he looked at Melissa. 'What business have you here, lady? My orders were that you remain in your chambers until we dine this night.' It was dangerous for her to walk alone until he had things settled, for tempers were roused and in times like these men might do things that would shame them—and her.

'I came to plead with you to allow Lady Gifford to see her husband before he leaves for London,' Melissa said, but there was no hint of pleading in her voice. Her tone and manner was imperious and she was every inch the noble lady, for she had determined not to show weakness in his presence. 'She may never see him again and it is only fitting that she should take a proper farewell of her husband.'

'Indeed?' Rob glared at her, his mouth set in a thin line of disapproval. 'And who gave you permission to make this plea, lady? I think you forget your position here.'

'I may be your prisoner, sir,' Melissa said. 'But that does not make me your serf. I am still a lady to whom you owe at least courtesy—and I think you are too hasty in your commands.'

'And who told you what I command?' Rob asked, gaze narrowed, icy. 'I think you take too much upon yourself. Return to your chamber and stay there until I bid you leave it.'

Melissa turned, but even as she did so, she saw her aunt enter the great hall from a different direction. Lady Gifford went up to Robert of Melford, curtseying before him and smiling. She was dressed in a gown of blue silk, her head dressed with a chaplet of silver and looked very fine. She did not seem to be in any distress, and was clearly not confined to her chamber despite what Owain had believed. Melissa nodded to her and went past, climbing the stairs that led to the upper floor.

Owain met her as she reached the top. 'It seems that he has changed his mind,' he said, and frowned as he saw the lady of Gifford speaking with Rob. 'I should not have told you anything. Now he will be even more angry with you.'

'I care not for his anger,' Melissa said stiffly, for in truth she was feeling a little foolish. It seemed that Sir Robert was politely attending Lady Gifford, and as Melissa set foot on the landing immediately above, she heard her aunt laugh. 'I am content as long as she is not being treated harshly.'

Owain studied her proud profile as she passed him and went into her chamber. She had not made matters easier for herself— and yet he wondered what had made Sir Robert change his mind, for he had commanded that the earl's wife be confined to her room at the start.

Below in the hall, Lady Gifford was listening to the proposal made her by the man who had assumed command of her home.

'You are asking me if I would prefer to accompany my husband to London or remain here?' Rob nodded and she hesitated. 'What becomes of my son if my husband does not keep the terms of his bond?'

'If you go with him, you might find yourself imprisoned with the child somewhere. If you stay here, you are under my protection. For as long as you behave modestly and make no attempt to leave or to incite rebellion, you will be safe. These lands are now the property of the Crown, but Henry may decide to leave them in your care, lady. In time, your son may inherit, though that is for the King to decide. I do not know what is in his mind. If he gives the earl's estates to one of his knights...' Rob shrugged his shoulders.

'I think that I prefer to stay here,' Lady Gifford said. 'If we are under your protection we are safe for the moment. I have some modest lands that were left to me by my father. If it were permitted I might choose to retire there one day, sir.'

'All that is a matter for Henry,' Rob said. 'For the moment you may remain here. Once the earl has left for the Tower, you will be free to move as you wish within these walls and to run your household as before.' He hesitated, remembering Melissa's anger. 'Do you wish to take a private leave of your husband?'

'No, Sir Robert. All that I have wished to say to the earl has been said before you came. We understood how it would be...'

She hesitated once more. 'If I give my word that I shall not try to leave or to incite rebellion, please, may it be considered apart from the oath my husband may swear?'

Rob's gaze narrowed. 'Do you believe that he will break that oath?'

Lady Gifford was silent for a moment, and then, 'I do not know what he intends for he has not consulted me—but I do not wish my case to rely on his.'

Rob was thoughtful. She would not go so far as to betray her husband, and he could not demand it, but she had given him a hint of what might be expected.

'The earl has given me his solemn vow that he means to surrender his person to King Henry, and for that I have allowed that he ride like a man instead of being conveyed in chains like a felon. If he should break his oath to me, his life would be forfeit. Do you understand, lady?'

'Yes.' Lady Gifford raised her head, looking into his eyes. 'I care only for the life and future of my son. I would be content to retire to my late father's manor and live there in peace. A king is a king while he holds the throne, sir. I care not in what name he rules and shall never raise my hand against any that wear the crown of England.'

'Very well, lady. You may retire to your chambers until the earl has left these walls. Your word is given and I shall trust you for the sake of your son. But I warn you not to play me false for then I should not be so lenient.'

Rob watched as the lady walked away. He had sent for her before Melissa's outburst, but he was not sure if he would have spoken to the countess so fairly had she not accused him of being harsh. He knew that he had been cruel to Melissa at their first meeting, but the sight of her had roused such feelings that he had not been able to control his anger. Such a fierce desire had rushed through him that it had been all he could do to control it, and a kiss was the least he had wanted of her—but feeling her softness and the tasting the sweetness of her lips had thrown him into confusion.

Was she honest or a consummate liar? She had been angry in her turn when she thought he meant to treat Lady Gifford harshly. Her eyes had flashed green fire and she had looked magnificent. Her beauty stirred him, but, he realised now, it was her spirit and her courage that made her the woman she was— the woman he wanted above any other.

A wry smile touched his lips. He ran a finger down the length of the scar on his face, feeling the thick welt that of late had become inflamed once more. The bruises and slight cuts received in battle were healing—but the anger and grief at her betrayal still swirled inside him, eating at his pride.

He was not sure whether he wanted Melissa for herself or because he wished to take his revenge on her. She had humiliated him, even if she had been innocent of all that happened afterwards. If she loved him she would not have said the words that struck him to the heart.

He could live with what her brother had done, even with the knowledge that Harold had been the cause of his father's seizure—but he could not live with her betrayal.

Chapter Five

'Sir Robert has sent for you,' Agnes said as she came into Melissa's chamber later that afternoon. 'You are to dine with him in the hall this night.'

'I am not hungry,' Melissa said, a stubborn look on her lovely face. 'Send him my apologies but I do not feel well enough to come down this evening. And why are you here? I told you that I shall not have you serve me. In future, send one of the other women to serve me. You are a traitor and a murderer and I do not want to see your face again.'

'Forgive me, my lady. I did only as your father bid me. He would have punished me had I not obeyed him.'

'I do not wish to hear your excuses. Leave me and give my message to Sir Robert.'

Agnes shot her a scared look. 'But he will be so angry. You cannot refuse him, my lady. It was an order not a request.'

'I shall not come,' Melissa said. 'If you dare not tell him yourself, tell Owain. He will pass on my reply.'

Agnes shook her head and went away. Melissa got up and went over to the window, gazing out at the scene below. It was still light—the moon had not yet chased the sun from the sky—and she could see men walking about. It seemed that the livery of Melford was everywhere, and her uncle's men had either been disarmed, allowed to leave or perhaps imprisoned. It did not occur to her that many of them might have wished to throw in their lot with the King's commander and were even now sporting his colours of green and gold.

'Melissa—what nonsense is this?'

She heard her aunt's voice and turned to see Lady Gifford. She was a little surprised to see that her aunt had dressed in her best green gown with a sideless surcoat of cloth of gold. She was wearing her gold chaplet, her hair caught in a jewelled net.

'I thought you could not be ill for Agnes was afraid to speak. Why have you disobeyed Sir Robert's command?'

'I do not wish to dine with him.'

'Stop this foolishness and come down at once,' Lady Gifford said, and her eyes glinted with annoyance. 'You are a stupid girl and will make him angry—and we must remember that we are all at his mercy. Thus far he has treated us well, but he could make us suffer if he wished. You have no idea of what might happen if we give him cause for anger. If you knew what beasts men can be… I have seen women raped and men killed, my home burned to the ground when I was but a child. I became the King's ward and married a strong man, because I was determined that what happened to my mother would not happen to me—or my son.'

Melissa faced her proudly. 'Do you not think I have suffered enough? My father killed my mother when she was still recovering from my birth—and he hated me, losing no opportunity to humiliate me whenever he could. Until I was old enough to marry, he hit me and sent me to my chamber for the smallest of faults.'

'Then you should have learned,' Lady Gifford said, her mouth hard. 'A woman may persuade with gentle smiles and her body where she may not command. I have learned to keep a soft voice and bowed head, and because of that I won back my father's lands from a king's hands. But now my husband has been sent to London where he will no doubt be imprisoned in the Tower, and I am free of him at last. All I care for now is my son—and his inheritance.'

'I am not as you, madam,' Melissa said. 'I shall not smile when I am angry and I shall not beg for scraps of any man!'

'Then you will deserve all you get,' Lady Gifford snapped. 'But do as you are told and come down or the rest of us may suffer in your place!'

Melissa looked at her, a stubborn expression on her face. She did not wish to give in to her cousin's wife, and yet she knew that she spoke truly. A sigh escaped her, because it was not she alone that might suffer for her disobedience. She did not care what happened to her, but she could not risk harm to others.

'Very well, I shall come for your sake,' she said reluctantly. 'I suppose we must do as he says.'

'Yes, we must,' Lady Gifford said. 'For my part I hope to win freedom for my son and myself. I do not think that Gifford will abide by the promise he has given to surrender to the King—and I do not wish my son to be made a ward of the Crown and spend his life imprisoned somewhere. Robert of Melford is a fair and honest man. I know that the scar he bears is enough to send shivers down the spine, but if he speaks for us we may receive justice.'

'You think that the scar is ugly?' Melissa asked, because it had not occurred to her that others would see it that way. For herself she saw only the pain that he had suffered for her sake. 'I hardly see it.'

'It is not so noticeable when he turns his head,' Lady Gifford said. 'But I suspect it pains him at times. I would not dare to speak of it to his face.'

'Yes, I am certain of it. It was his reward for daring to ask for me in marriage.'

'Melissa! No wonder he looks so angry when he speaks of you.' Lady Gifford was horrified. 'You must not risk angering him further. Come down and smile at him, Melissa.'

'I cannot promise to smile for him,' Melissa said. 'But I shall come as you bid me. I would not bring harm to you or others.'

As she entered the great hall, where trestle tables had been set up for dining, she was aware that most eyes were turned on her. She looked straight ahead as she walked up to the high table, where she could see that Rob was sitting. He rose to his feet as she approached, his gaze narrowed as it dwelled on her.

She made a defiant curtsey to him. 'I am come, sir, as my aunt bids me.'

Rob nodded, and for a moment there was a flicker of a smile in his eyes. She had clearly come reluctantly. She had lost none of her pride, though it seemed that she had been kept almost a prisoner here. She had refused to be betrothed to Leominster and had kept to her bed for several days in defiance of her cousin's demands. He had learned this much from the steward Hale, who had seemed only too pleased to offer his allegiance and could not hide his relief that his former master was on his way to the Tower. It would seem that Owain was right and she had been reluctant to marry.

There was some dispute as to whether the betrothal had gone ahead or not. It did not matter. He had made up his mind. She would never be allowed to be Leominster's wife in truth.

'I see that you are come,' he replied, his smile fading as he gestured to the place at his left hand. Lady Gifford had taken her seat at his right, and Melissa had no choice but to do as he bid her. 'As I bid you, lady. Remember that it is *my* bidding that matters here.'

Melissa set her mouth stubbornly. She gave him a furious look but made no further comment. He could believe what he pleased. She did not care. He was not the kind, gentle, man that she had thought him, and she would not bow to his will easily. She had been a fool to give her heart to him, and she would cease to pine for what might have been.

Rob made the signal and the servants began to carry in the

platters of food. Spit-roasted capons, beef and a mess of belly pork and onions were accompanied by a dish of preserved plums and bacon. Bread trenchers were provided at the lower tables, though at the high board they were served on pewter plates. Small wooden bowls filled with scented water and napkins of English linen were placed to hand, for they ate with a knife and their fingers. A custard of eggs and bread sweetened with honey and dried fruits and a syllabub followed, together with a quince tart. All of it was washed down with quantities of ale or a rough red wine that Melissa found unpalatable unless sweetened with honey.

She ate very little, for the food seemed to stick in her throat. The men seemed in a merry mood and there was much laughter and some coarse jokes from farther down the hall, which might have made her blush had she been near enough to hear them.

Rob looked at her as she sat stiffly at his side. 'Is the food not to your taste, lady?'

'The food is very well, but I do not feel hungry,' Melissa said.

'Drink your wine.'

'I do not like wine, unless it has been sweetened—and this has not.'

'Why did you not say so?' Rob raised his hand, summoning one of the servants. 'Bring some sweetened wine for the lady Melissa.'

She glanced at him as the servant bowed and went off to fetch it. 'Thank you, but it was not necessary, a little watered ale would have done as well.'

'You are used to mead I doubt not,' Rob said. 'We drink it at home and it is much nicer than this....' He sipped the wine from his own cup and made a face. 'Your cousin had little taste in wine, lady. I think he did not pay much attention to the preference of ladies.'

'I hardly knew my father's cousin until I came here,' Melissa said, eyes flashing. 'But I have not found that men care for the opinion of ladies often in anything.'

'No?' Rob raised his brows. He turned to look at her. 'You must have been unlucky in the men you knew, lady. My mother was adored and given everything my father had it in his power to give her. Her wish was his command, and when she died his heart went with her to the grave.'

'Then she was fortunate, indeed,' Melissa said, and lowered her eyes.

'Yes, I believe she thought so,' Rob said, a little pensive, eyes seeming to look inward and not at her. 'My father never forgot her, even though she died long before he did....'

'He must have loved her very much?' Melissa studied his face, seeing that the harshness she had come to fear was absent, his eyes warmer than she had witnessed of late. Did he know that his father's wife was the cause of the quarrel between his father and hers? That it was the reason he bore the scars of her half brother's torture? 'I fear that my mother was not as fortunate.'

'No, I have heard that she was badly treated,' Rob said, and his expression softened, because he knew that it must have hurt her to learn of her mother's cruel death. 'It was a terrible thing and I am sorry for it.'

'You knew that she was murdered?'

'Your kinswoman, Alanna Davies, told me of it.'

'You have seen Alanna? Do you know where she resides?'

'Yes, but it would not help you to seek sanctuary there, lady,' Rob said, frowning again. 'Henry has taken over your guardianship, and will wish to see you when you leave here.'

'Am I to be his prisoner now?'

'Perhaps. For the moment your fate lies in my hands and I have not decided what it shall be....'

'Then I must wait upon your will, must I not?' She felt her cheeks growing warm for she knew that he was watching her.

Was he trying to read her thoughts? She prayed that he could not, for she did not wish to be an open book to him.

'Here is your wine. I hope it is more to your taste.' He turned his head and began to speak with Lady Gifford. Melissa looked at his face. She saw that his scar looked red and puckered, and realised that it was still tender for the colour was livid. It must have been so painful when it was done! Her heart ached for him, tears catching at her throat. He became aware of her scrutiny and turned to look at her once more. 'It is ugly and you are sickened by the sight. Is that why you do not eat?'

'Does it hurt very much?' Melissa asked and she wanted to reach out to touch it, but dared not. 'It looks as if it has been infected again. Have you no healing salves to ease it?'

'It does not hurt as it did,' Rob said. 'Megan will see to it when I am home again. It does not matter. Try your wine, lady.'

Melissa sipped it and nodded. 'That is much better, thank you.'

Rob looked at her for a moment. 'I have decided that you may move freely within the grounds, Melissa, though you may not leave them without my permission. We have secured the walls and there is no reason why you should not do much as you please.'

'I should like to help my aunt,' Melissa said. 'A house like this needs a great deal of management—and with so many extra mouths to feed we shall need more supplies of fresh meat.'

'You will make someone a good wife,' Rob said, and his mouth softened into a smile. 'Help Lady Gifford if it pleases you. I intend to stay here some days.'

'And what will you do with me when you move on?'

Rob's gaze narrowed. 'Are you anxious to journey home—or to the house of your betrothed?'

'I have nowhere to go, unless Alanna would take me in—or the nuns, as I asked you,' Melissa said. 'My half brother would not welcome me beneath his roof nor should I wish for it—and I have no betrothed.'

'Surely the contract your father signed makes you Leominster's property, whether or not the betrothal actually happened.'

'It is not for others to decide,' Melissa said. 'Am I not a ward of the King? You have just said it—and Owain told me that you had asked that Henry Tudor take charge of my estates. Why did you do that, sir?'

Rob was silent for a moment, then, 'I do not know, lady. Perhaps I thought to have them and you for myself.'

'Why should you wish for that?' she asked, looking into his face as she searched for the truth, and found nothing. 'If you believe that I betrayed you to my father, you must hate me?'

Rob smiled ruefully, 'Why indeed? It was a foolish whim, no more. Yet it protects you for the moment. Henry is too busy to give you or your estates much thought just yet. There is time enough to decide what should become of you.'

Melissa inclined her head. Her heart was aching, for it seemed that he was no different from any other man. He had protected her lands because he coveted them himself. If he decided he would wed her, it would be for advancement not for love of her—and she had thought him above such considerations. And yet what else should she expect? He might have killed her and taken them for himself. Perhaps she should be grateful that he had shown restraint—and yet she was hurt and angry. How could he shrug like that? As if those walks in a sunlit meadow had never been. Had he forgotten the days when they had lain together in the soft grass, touching and kissing and speaking of the day they were wed?

He had never gone beyond the bounds of chivalry, but sometimes she had wished that he had... Perhaps if she had truly belonged to him he would have refused to take his dismissal, he would have known that she would never say such terrible things to him unless she was forced. He ought to have known it! She felt a return of the anger that had sustained her earlier. He blamed her for his injuries—but he was not blameless. He must surely have known of the quarrel between his father and hers, but she had known nothing. If he had told her, she would never have encouraged him to come alone and unarmed to ask for her hand.

She raised her head proudly. 'May I go to my chamber now, sir? I am not hungry and my head aches.'

It was her heart that ached but she could not tell him that, for her pride would not allow it.

'Go then,' Rob said, seeing that her face was pale. He knew that she was distressed, and that it was his fault, but he did not know how to behave towards her. There was a part of him that longed to believe her innocent—that wanted to make her his own and never let her go—but a warning note in his head kept telling him that she was not to be trusted.

How could she look on a man so fearfully scarred with anything but disgust or loathing? Even if she had cared for him once—if her brother had lied to deceive him—she could surely not feel anything now? And that meant that her words of concern were false…and yet she had seemed to mean them. Her eyes had been moist with tears, her voice broken with emotion.

Damn her and all her kind! She was not to be trusted. She had nearly destroyed him once, he would be a fool to let her inside his defences again.

Rob lifted his wine and drank deeply from it. The taste was strong and not to his liking. He thrust it aside and drank from Melissa's cup, his lips touching where hers had been. He felt a sudden, sweeping pain and knew that he wanted her despite all, needed to hold her in his arms and taste the sweetness of her lips—and yet still his stubborn nature would not let him go after her.

He would not beg her to love him. He would have cherished her above all women, but now there was a barrier between them—a wall built of pain and pride and he did not have the courage to break it down. For if she guessed that he still wanted—still desired—her, despite all, she might laugh at him. At best she

would shudder when he touched her, drew her to him in bed—
and that would hurt far more than all that had gone before it.

He pushed the cup away and asked for ale. Perhaps if he drank
enough of it he could forget her and the hurt look in her eyes.

Rob knew that he had drunk too much as he went up the
stairs that night. He wanted Melissa. He had tried to remember his duty—that he had not yet finished the work he had
begun for Henry Tudor, but nothing seemed to matter except
this burning need inside him. He could think only of her lips,
her sweetness and the softness of her body as he'd held her
close to him when they rode through the forest on his horse the
day he saved her from those rogues. He remembered her when
they first met. He had seen her standing alone by the stream,
such a wistful look on her face that his heart had gone out to
her. He had dismounted from his horse, going to stand by her
side, as she gazed into the clear water.

'Why so sad, lady? Is there anything I can do to help you?'

She had turned to him then, meeting his eyes in wonder,
seeming surprised that he had spoken to her so softly, and then
she had smiled. Rob had fallen in love with her in that instant,
for it was like seeing the sun break through the clouds.

'I was thinking that I should like to walk into the stream for
it must be so cool and the day is hot.'

'Why don't you?' he had asked. 'I will turn my back while
you remove your hose, lady.'

'But I might fall and then…' She shook her head. 'It was just
a foolish whim.'

'You shall not fall, for I shall be there to hold your hand and
you will be safe.'

Melissa had looked at him with those wonderfully deep eyes
of hers for a moment, and then she had taken his hand. 'Yes, I
shall be safe if you are there to hold me,' she said. She had been
so trusting, so innocent and lovely…

Was all that false and what came after true? His thoughts were in turmoil, muddled by the wine and ale so that he could not tell what was true and what false.

He ran his forefinger over the hard welt of puckered skin on his cheek. The scar would grow less livid in time, but it would never fade entirely; it would always be there to remind him—and her.

Why should he not take what he wanted? He was the master here. He could make her do his bidding, take what he needed from her and then discard her. It was what most men would do in his situation.

His feet seemed to have a will of their own as he found himself walking in the direction of her chamber. Yet outside the door, he paused, the sensible side of his brain telling him to seek his own bed and sleep off the effects of the wine. His desire held him glued to the floor outside her door, and then he was lifting the latch, going through the outer chamber where her woman lay snoring.

He crept silently past her, lifting the latch of Melissa's door carefully and pushing it back to slip inside. A small candle had been left burning on the chest to one side of her bed. He frowned for such practice could be dangerous and if there were a fire she might be burned in her slumber, because she *was* sleeping. He put out the tiny flame between his fingers and moved nearer to the bed. There was just enough light coming through the window to see her as she lay there, one hand under her cheek.

For a moment he was tempted to lay down by her side, to take her into his arms and love her, but he smothered the urge. His head had cooled a little on seeing her, and he knew that it would be a base thing to take her unawares as she rested. He was about to turn away when she gave a start and opened her eyes.

'Who is it?' she asked. 'Agnes, is that you? What are you doing in my room?'

'It is not your woman,' Rob said. 'Do not be frightened. I have not come to harm you. I merely wished to see you.'

Melissa sat up in bed, drawing the covers up to her neck to cover herself. She was beginning to see better as her eyes became accustomed to the dark, and some of her fear ebbed as she realised that it was Rob.

'What are you doing here? Why have you come to my chamber in the dead of night?'

'I was on my way to my bed when I thought of you,' Rob said. 'Go back to sleep. I shall not disturb you further.'

Melissa gathered a silk coverlet about her, holding it tight as she got out of bed, for her night chemise was so fine that she would have felt naked in his presence without the cover. She stood looking at him warily, sensing that there was more to this than he would say.

'Did you think to ravish me as I lay sleeping?' she demanded. 'Where is your honour, sir? You have no right here. You must leave my chamber at once.' Perversely it was the last thing she truly wanted, but she could never tell him what was in her mind.

'Must I?' Rob had been about to leave, but her defiance inflamed him. He reached out, snatching the cover away from her, revealing the flimsy material that hid little of her body from his eyes. She was so beautiful, so desirable that he could not help himself as he moved towards her, reaching out to pull her hard against him. His head bent, he took possession of her lips, his tongue seeking and entering her mouth. She tasted of the honey she had drunk earlier and he slid his hand down the arch of her back, cupping her buttocks as he pressed her harder against him.

'No!' Melissa gave a cry of alarm as she felt the throb of his arousal. 'You must not do this, Rob. Please, I beg you—do not force me. Leave me now before it is too late…' Her head was whirling and she knew that if he persisted she could not resist him, for her body clamoured for his.

Rob's mind was confused, his senses inflamed. He knew that he wanted her more than anything he had ever wanted before in his life and he was tempted to throw her down upon the bed and make love to her. Yet even as his arms tightened about her, he glanced down and saw her pale, unhappy face, and something turned in his stomach. Realising that for the first time in his life he had been on the verge of taking an unwilling woman, he let her go, moving away from her. He breathed deeply, raggedly, staring at her hungrily as he fought to subdue his need.

'Go away, Rob,' she said softly. 'I beg you, leave me.'

'Yes,' he said, and shook his head. 'It was wrong to come here like this. Tomorrow I shall arrange for us to be wed. You shall be my wife before I bed you.'

'No, please…' Melissa stared after him as he left the room. She had wanted to marry him so desperately, would have died rather than marry another man—but now she was torn by doubts. Rob wanted her because she had lands and was the daughter of a lord. It was no different from her being given by her father to a man for the acquisition of lands and wealth.

She felt the tears well up in her eyes as she ran for her bed, and lay with her face buried in the pillows as she sobbed. She did not know why Rob had come to her chamber that night— or why he had changed his mind about seducing her—but she did know that she did not want to be married for the sake of her inheritance.

Rob awoke suddenly from the heavy sleep that had claimed him when he fell into his bed the previous night. He was aware of pain at his temples, and he blinked as he saw the sun streaming through the small windows of his chamber. He was a damned fool to have drunk so much ale the previous night. He had vague recollections of something he had done while in his cups, though he could not quite recall what had happened. He seemed to remember that he had gone to Melissa's chamber, where she lay sleeping and…

He groaned and splashed cold water into his face to freshen himself. He noticed that his scar had become more inflamed and that side of his face had swollen; it had begun to throb like the devil. He shrugged the pain aside, knowing that he had more important worries than an infected wound.

What had he done the previous night? His memory was hazy. He knew that he had wanted her, had kissed her—but what else had he done or said? Whatever it might have been, in the cold light of dawn he knew that there was only one cure for what ailed him. She must be his wife for he could not endure the gnawing ache the thought of her belonging to another man set up in him.

He would wed her, bed her and forget her! Was that not the age-old cure for the kind of lust that possessed him now? He nodded his satisfaction. Just because he ached to lie with her, it did not necessarily mean that he loved her. He would take her for the wealth and lands she would bring, the sons she would give him and the ease he would find in her soft flesh.

If Rob suspected that he was lying to himself, he was too proud to admit it. Even though the need for her nagged at him like the toothache, he still could not entirely forgive what had been done in her name. The bitterness had burned too deeply into his mind to be erased by a smile, even though her smile was something he craved as he craved the sweetness of her kiss and the perfume of her skin.

He finished his ablutions and dressed in a clean shirt, trunks and hose. He would wear a houppelande of green over a tunic of gold and a burlet of black velvet trimmed with gold and pearls in honour of the occasion. Today would be his wedding day.

Melissa awoke, shrugging off the dream that had caused her to toss restlessly on her bed. She had been so afraid but she could not recall why—though she seemed to remember that she was in a dark place. She had been cold and hungry and she had called someone's name as she lay on the chill of a stone floor, the life slowly draining from her. She had called but she had known that he would not come because he did not love her.

She threw back the bedcovers and got out of bed just as her serving woman came into the room carrying warm water in a pewter jug. The girl gave her an odd look but poured the water into a basin for her before laying out one of her best robes and kirtle.

'I have work to do, Morag,' she said with a frown. 'One of my old gowns will do for this morning.'

'But it is your wedding day,' Morag said. She gave Melissa a nervous glance, for she knew the lady's temper had suffered of late, and not knowing that Agnes had deserved her dismissal to the kitchens was afraid of the same fate. 'I was told to dress you in your finest clothes, my lady.'

'My wedding day?' Melissa wrinkled her brow. She knew that Rob had said he would marry her before he bedded her, but she had thought it merely an idle threat. 'I have no recollection of having been betrothed to anyone. Nor shall I consent to this wedding.'

'Please, my lady,' Morag said. 'Do not send me to tell him that you refuse for I dare not. He frightens me when I look at him…his terrible face…'

'Foolish woman!' Melissa was angry with her. 'It is merely a scar—a badge of honour for he had it in my cause.'

'Then, if the scar does not frighten you, why will you not wed him?'

'That is none of your affair,' Melissa snapped. 'I have my reasons but they are not for your ears. If you are afraid of Robert of Melford go to Hale and tell him I have refused to be wed.'

Morag shot her a scared glance but went off to do her bidding. Melissa washed and dried herself on a soft cloth, and then dressed in a reddish brown kirtle and a green wool tunic. She covered the top of her head in a cap of green silk, leaving the length of her hair free. Glancing at her reflection in a small hand mirror, she decided that she would do well enough for the work she intended that day, which was to help her aunt make an inventory of the linens and sort out those that needed mending.

She was about to leave her room when she heard the sound of a man's boots on the stone steps leading to her room and she went back inside quickly. She had her back turned and was looking out of the window when Rob burst into the chamber.

'Why have you dressed like that?' he demanded as she turned towards him and he saw that she was wearing one of her oldest robes. 'I sent word that you should prepare for our wedding.'

'I have no memory of consenting to marry you.' Melissa looked at him coldly, her green eyes flashing with temper.

'Have you not, lady?' Rob's gaze narrowed, but at the corners of his mouth a smile tugged, for to him she resembled an angry kitten. A feeling he had thought lost was brought to life within him, and he wanted to laugh out loud. 'How short your memory is, my sweet. For you once told me that you would marry no other.'

Melissa felt the fire spring up in her cheeks and her eyes dropped. 'You do ill to remind me, sir,' she whispered. 'I thought myself in love then, but now…'

'Now you wish to withdraw for you cannot stand the sight of my face?'

'No! That is not true,' Melissa cried. 'I am not such a shallow thing that I would flinch at the sight of a scar, besides, it is not so very dreadful.'

'Are you not?' Rob's gaze narrowed for he was not sure of her meaning. 'If the sight of me does not revolt you, why do you resist? Would you prefer to be the widow of Leominster?'

'No! You must know that I would rather have died than wed him,' Melissa said. 'I have decided that I do not wish to marry at all. Why should I be forced to be any man's wife? I shall petition the King to give me a dowry against my lands so that

I may retire to a nunnery.' Even as she spoke, Melissa knew that she did not want to spend her life with the nuns, but her pride would not let her give in just yet. He did not love her. If she married him he would discover that she still loved him and then she would be at his mercy. 'For pity's sake, let me go, sir.'

'No, I shall not,' Rob said, and his mouth settled into a grim line, the good humour he had felt vanishing. 'Why should I show mercy when none was shown to me?' He moved towards her, gripping her wrist firmly. 'If you will not be dressed as befits your station it is your choice, but you shall marry me, lady. The priest awaits us.'

'No!' Melissa tried to struggle free of him, but he had her fast and she could not escape him. She was forced to run to keep up with him as he propelled her from her chamber and down the stairs to the great hall below. 'I shall not give my promise. I refuse to wed you!'

'Refuse and I shall answer for you,' Rob said, giving her a hard look. 'You belong to me for you gave your promise freely, Melissa. In the old days that promise would have been binding in law, and in honour it is so even now. You are mine and I shall take what is mine, though you hate me for it.'

Melissa looked at him and saw his unyielding expression. She was angry, because despite her resistance she knew that in her heart this was exactly what she wanted. It was only her pride that stopped her throwing herself into his arms and telling him that she loved him and wanted nothing more than to be his wife.

She gave him a sparkling look but said no more, for in truth she did not know why she had fought so hard against him. It was merely pride after all—and what was the alternative? She knew only too well that if she were not wed to Rob she would be given to some other man of the King's choosing. He would show no more care for her wishes than her father had.

She gave up resisting as they entered the hall. Lady Gifford was there with the steward, the priest, Owain and Agnes. Lady

Gifford was dressed in velvet robes and frowned as she saw that Melissa was wearing an old gown.

'Why did you not choose your cloth of gold?' she asked as Melissa went to stand beside her. Melissa shook her head but made no answer. 'Well, I suppose it does not matter after all. Sir Robert is determined that the marriage should take place at once, and he must have his wish.'

Melissa shot a look of venom at her bridegroom but held her tongue. Once again, she was at the mercy of others. Lady Gifford would do nothing to anger the man who held her future in his hands, and there was no one else to aid her.

'I do not know whether this marriage be legal,' the priest said with a worried shake of his head as Rob told him to proceed. 'The betrothal ceremony was begun to the lord of Leominster's proxy—and there is a contract signed by the lady's father…'

'Do your work, priest,' Rob growled, 'and leave me to worry about the legality of the matter. If there be a matter of conscience I shall bear it, not you.'

'As you wish, sir.'

The priest was old, his beard grey, his eyes a faded blue. He did not see well these days and was unaware that the lady was not dressed for a wedding.

'Give me your hand, lady,' he said. 'You must put it into Sir Robert's and I shall tie it with this ribbon for the ceremony.

Melissa opened her mouth to protest, looked at Rob and shut it again, offering her hand. She felt a tremor run through her as it was bound with Rob's and the priest began to perform the ceremony that would make them man and wife.

'Do you, Melissa of Whitbread, take this man—Robert of Melford to be your lawful wedded husband, to love honour and obey him until death do you part?'

Melissa licked her lips, which were dry and then inclined her head.

'You must say I do, lady.'

She raised her head, looking directly at Rob, defiance in her face. 'I do…' she said in a loud clear voice.

'And you, Sir Robert of Melford—do you take the lady Melissa of Whitbread to be your lawful wedded wife until death do you part?'

'I do,' Rob said, and smiled as he looked at her. 'Until death and forever—for earthly death shall never part us.' He slid a heavy gold ring on to the third finger of her left hand.

Melissa felt a little jolt as she looked into his eyes. He looked at her as if…as if he meant those words. For a moment she felt that she might faint, for if the look in his eyes spoke truly he still loved her—or at least wanted her.

'You may kiss your bride, sir.'

Melissa gasped as Rob drew her to him, but instead of the passionate kiss she had expected, he merely brushed his lips over hers.

'I shall teach you what it means to be the bride of Robert of Melford later, lady,' he promised.

Melissa looked at him uncertainly as he drew back, her heart racing. He had a very different expression in his eyes now and it made her afraid. What did he mean? Did he intend to punish her for her defiance? She trembled inwardly for she was his wife now and must obey him.

'Where are you going?' she asked, as he turned away almost immediately.

'I have work to do, lady wife,' he said, and gave her a wry look. 'The fortress will not run itself. There is much to do if I am to leave it secure before I move on. Be patient, my love. I shall come to you later.'

Melissa stared after him as he strode away, feeling outraged. This was not how she had expected her marriage to be! There should have been feasting and merriment. It made her angry that he could just walk away from her, because he had work to do.

She wanted to rage at him, and wished that she had continued her defiance. How could he simply walk away, leaving her to wonder what was in his mind? It was unfair and arrogant and she hated him!

'Come, Melissa.' Lady Gifford was at her elbow. 'I shall show you what needs doing and then leave you for I must change. I never thought to be dressed more finely than the bride. Why did you not wear your best gown? I told Morag to prepare it for you.'

'You sent Morag to me…' Melissa was thoughtful. She had imagined it was Rob who had given the woman instructions to dress her as a bride.

'Of course I did, my dear,' Lady Gifford said with a smile. 'I know that Sir Robert is not the most handsome of men, because of that scar—but I believe he is not unkind. If you please him tonight, you will set the seal on your marriage. A woman should always try to please her husband, Melissa. If you wish to be happy do not be defiant or a scold—that way lies deep unhappiness, my dear.'

'Why must a woman please her husband?' Melissa asked, a flash of temper in her green eyes. 'Why should it not be the other way—a man may please his wife equally, may he not?'

'Yes, and perhaps he will—but you must be compliant and welcoming first,' Lady Gifford said. 'I tell you this for your own good, Melissa. A sullen wife wins no favours from her husband.'

'I thank you for your advice,' Melissa said. 'But if you please, I would make a start on sorting the linen chests.'

'Very well, go your own way,' the lady of Gifford said with a shake of her head. 'But if you alienate him, you may well come to rue it, Melissa. A man like that will take so much from a woman and no more, believe me.'

Melissa nodded but her expression was set. She was angry and humiliated by the way Rob had simply gone about his business, leaving her to do the same. She had just become his wife. Surely he could have spared a few moments to be alone with her!

* * *

Melissa called for the bathtub to be brought to her that afternoon. She had spent most of the day working and felt dusty and tired from her efforts, for she had sorted mountains of torn linen. Some had yellowed over time and needed to be washed, some were torn and fit only to be used as rags and some could be saved if a needle and thread was applied.

'We have done a good job this day,' Lady Gifford told her when they parted. 'It is always my intention to sort the linen each year, but it is seldom that I am able to do it as thoroughly. You have been a great help to me, Melissa. I think you will be an excellent chatelaine for your husband when he takes you home.'

'Perhaps…' Melissa had felt a little shiver trickle down her spine as Lady Gifford spoke. She was beginning to feel very nervous about the night ahead and wished that she might escape from her duty in this respect.

After the wooden tub was brought and filled with warm, scented water, Melissa sat in it, her knees brought up to her chest as the women soaped her back and then poured fresh water over her. It felt very good to be clean again for she was naked, having dispensed with the thin shift that was often worn for bathing.

When she was ready to get out, she asked for a cloth to be brought and then dismissed her ladies. Standing up, she wrapped herself about with the soft material, drying her skin and singing a melody that she had learned as a child.

Hearing someone come in, she spoke without turning her head. 'I think perhaps the blue silk gown and the white kirtle. And I shall wear the silver belt that is studded with crystal…'

'I think not,' a voice said, making her jump and turn to look at the man who stood there. 'I should like to see you dressed in green for I have brought you a gift.'

Melissa hugged the towel about her body, looking at him uncertainly. 'The blue is my best gown,' she said, her voice whispery and startled. 'I meant to wear it to honour you this night.'

'I thank you for the thought,' Rob said. 'But this will go better with green I believe.'

He handed her a small velvet pouch. She loosed the drawstrings and tipped the contents into her hand, gasping as she saw the heavy gold chain set with green stones. It was a very beautiful thing.

'I have never seen stones like these before,' she said. 'What are they called?'

'The French call them esmeraude, the Spanish esmeralda—but the man I purchased them from said they were emeralds and of a fine quality for they are not flawed.'

'Emeralds,' Melissa said, and nodded. 'I have heard of them for some say that they have magic properties and cure the falling sickness—but I did not know they were so beautiful.'

'I bought them to match your eyes,' Rob said, and his gaze lingered on the flesh that had been revealed as she let the cloth slip while she opened her gift. The swell of her breasts was open to his gaze and he moved towards her, his hand brushing against her flesh as he took the chain and held it to her throat. 'Yes, they will look well enough, Melissa. You will wear them and your green tunic this evening. There will be a feast tonight and I do not want you to shame me, as you did this morning.' He had donned his best for her and she had come dressed little better than a kitchen wench.

'If that is your command,' Melissa said stiffly. She had been pleased with his gift, but she did not like to be ordered what to wear. Or that he should imply she might shame him by wearing her old clothes.

Rob laughed. 'Scratch me with your claws if you wish, my sweet,' he murmured, 'but I shall teach you to please me whether you wish it or no.'

'Go away,' Melissa said. 'And send my women to me. I shall dress as I please, sir. I may be your wife, but I am not your serf!'

'Have I said that you were?' The smile faded from his eyes.

'Do as you wish, Melissa. I thought to please you, but if I have not I am sorry.'

He turned and walked from the room, still clutching the chain of gold and emeralds, but at the door he stopped and flung them down in disgust, as if he had had enough of her.

Melissa stood where she was for a moment as the door slammed behind him, then she darted forward to pick up his gift. She had not meant to slight what he had given her, for it was a magnificent present and she had never seen anything finer. It must have cost a great deal of money, and she had not thought Rob a particularly rich man. He possessed a sizeable estate but was not as wealthy as some of the powerful lords that owned vast acres. And that made his gift all the more precious for he had sacrificed other things to buy it for her.

She was ashamed of her sullen behaviour and determined to do better. Lady Gifford was right. She did not wish to turn Rob from her by being sulky and capricious. She would behave with dignity this evening in the hall and give him no reason to be ashamed of her.

She would wear her cloth of gold, which was her second best kirtle—and the green gown he admired. His gift would go very well with that, and she would fasten it about her waist.

She smiled as she fingered the chain of precious jewels. He had said that their colour matched her eyes, and that made her feel warm inside. If he truly loved her she would be happier than she had ever thought would be her fate.

'Love me, please,' she whispered. 'For I love you so…'

Rob watched as his bride approached the high table. She was wearing the gown he liked, with a squared neckline and a band of embroidered gold that crossed over beneath her breasts, emphasising the slenderness of her figure. The emeralds were fastened about her waist with a gold clasp. She looked regal, almost a queen as she came to take her place at his side. She was to sit at his right hand that night for as a bride she took pride of place over Lady Gifford.

His men got to their feet and cheered her as she walked through the middle of the hall, turning her head to neither side, her eyes looking straight ahead at him. Rob got to his feet. He took the hand she offered and raised it to his lips, pulling back the chair for her so that she might sit. He did not sit immediately, but lifted his wine cup in homage to her.

'I ask you all to toast my bride,' he said, and brought a roar of approval from the men. They all rose as one, her name on their lips.

'The lady Melissa of Melford!'

Melissa's stomach churned as they said her name, for until now it had not seemed real. She had spent her wedding day as she might have spent any other and it had hardly seemed that anything had changed, but now she realised that she was Rob's wife—his to order as he wished.

She had been defiant when he told her what he wished her to wear, but she knew that he had the right to do so. He had the right to order everything she did and to chastise her if she disobeyed him. But he would not. Surely he would not!

'Drink and eat, Melissa,' he told her as he resumed his seat. 'I think you will find the wine more to your taste this evening.'

She took a sip from the cup she had been given, discovering it was a white wine with a soft sweet flavour. It was delicious and cool, and she drank deeply before replacing the cup on the table.

'It is very good, sir,' she told him. 'I do not think I have tasted better—where did it come from?'

'I had it brought from France when I returned home earlier this year,' Rob told her. 'There were a few casks in my train, though most is now in the cellars of my home in Melford.'

'Your home…' Melissa faltered. She had no idea what kind of a house he lived in. Indeed, she knew hardly anything about the man she had married, except that his smile had once made her lose her heart to him. She wished that he would smile at her now, but his expression was serious. 'When shall we go to your home, sir?'

'Alas, I cannot tell,' Rob said, and frowned, for it was his greatest wish to take her there. 'I have more work to do for the King, Melissa. I must make this fortress secure and then…' He shook his head. 'But we should not speak of business this night. It is our wedding night.'

'You did not consider that this morning,' Melissa told him, a flash of temper in her eyes as she remembered how that had made her feel.

'Did that annoy you, my sweet?' Rob grinned at her. The pleasure he anticipated later had made him shrug off his anger at the way she had dismissed his gift. It seemed that she had changed her mind later, though he would have preferred to see the emeralds about her white throat. 'I had much to do and it could not wait.'

'The wedding might have waited until you had more time.'

'Swish your tail, my little kitten,' Rob said, much amused for it appeared that she had been offended by his neglect. 'Fear not, I shall make up for my offence this night.'

Melissa's cheeks flushed pink as she saw the look in his eyes. She turned her head away and spoke to Owain, who sat on her right hand. It was a little unusual for a man of his birth to be honoured thus, but she was pleased to see him there for she felt that he was the one person in her life who had always been constant to her.

'I am glad you are here, Owain,' she told him. 'There is no one else who means so much to me.'

'Thank you, my lady,' Owain said, and smiled for her words had pleased him. He had protested that it was not fitting when Rob told him he must sit beside Melissa, but now he was grateful to be so honoured by his friend. 'I am flattered by your words.'

'But I do mean them,' Melissa said. 'Lord Whitbread was

never kind to me. If I have known a father's love, it has come from you—and I thank you for it.'

'It was my pleasure to serve you.'

Owain's throat felt tight but he smiled and held his tongue.

'Will you dance, Melissa?'

Rob claimed her attention as he whispered against her ear. She looked at him in bewilderment, but even as she wondered a man got up from one of the benches and began to play his viol and sing.

'Michael is a minstrel,' Rob said. 'He asked if he might sing for us this evening and I said that I thought you would like it.'

'Yes, indeed I do,' Melissa replied. She smiled for the song was one of her favourites and told the story of a lady who left her rich husband to run away with the Gypsies. 'I have always loved this song.'

'It is a sweet enough tune,' Rob said, 'though I cannot approve the lady's choice.'

Melissa gave him her hand. 'Had I been forced to a marriage I could not like I might have done as she did.' Her eyes flashed at him, her head lifted proudly.

'Does that mean I shall have to lock you in the tower when we get home, Melissa?'

She had been speaking of the Marquis of Leominster, but she would let him think as he pleased. 'Perhaps,' she said, and gave him a challenging look. 'Do you have a tower at your home, husband?'

'Not like your father's Keep,' Rob said, and there was laughter in his eyes for he knew that she was tempting him. He led her onto the floor and they performed a stately dance of pointing toes and graceful curtsies from her, bows from him. Melissa was surprised at how well he danced until she recalled that he had lately been in France at Henry Tudor's court there. 'But there are tower rooms at the four corners of the main structure, though I think you will find them more comfortable than this house, lady wife.'

'Indeed?' she said, for she had thought the earl's home comfortable enough. 'I become curious, sir.'

'You shall see soon enough,' Rob said, and smiled. He bowed once more as the minstrel's song ended, leading her back to the table. When they sat down a fiddler began to play and some of the men got up to dance a jig, which was fast, furious and amusing. One of them did tumbling tricks and another juggled with clubs. 'We have no travelling players to amuse us—but some of my men thought they would supply the lack. I trust they do not displease you with their efforts?'

'No, of course not,' Melissa said, and clapped her hands as one of the men performed a mummer's dance for them. 'It is amusing to watch them, and I am grateful for their thought.'

'At home we often have entertainers,' Rob told her with a smile. 'My father gave them bed and board for a few nights and they came regularly. I think that I shall continue the practice for it passes the hours of darkness, do you not agree?'

'Yes,' Melissa said. 'Father would never admit them for fear that they carried disease or planned to rob him—but I watched the mummers on the village green sometimes and I have seen a miracle play in the marketplace.'

'Good,' he nodded. 'I see that we shall do well enough, wife. I think that you should go up now, Melissa. Let your women prepare you for bed and I shall come to you at ten bells.'

'Yes…' Melissa rose from the table, her head high as she walked from the hall. The men had been drinking steadily throughout the evening and she could hear some jests that made her cheeks burn, but she did not turn her head to look at them. They were entitled to make merry, but she hoped that Rob would not bring too many of them to her chamber for the bedding ceremony.

Alone in her room, she allowed Morag to help her disrobe and then dismissed her. She brushed her long hair for some time, feeling uneasy and then got up to pace about the room.

Melissa had no mother to advise her how to behave towards her husband—and Lady Gifford had told her that she must be meek and welcome her husband to her bed. Yet to behave thus was against her nature and she could not do it! Had Rob told her that he loved her, had he not threatened her, ordered her to wear what he chose, she might have been eager for his embrace. However, there was a stubborn imp on her shoulder that would not let her be the obedient wife her aunt had bid her be.

She went over to the window to stare out at the night sky. A sprinkling of stars lit the darkness, making her sigh for it was a night meant for romance. Yet she was a bride who did not know her husband's mind. She gave a little sob, covering her face with her hands for this was not what she wanted. She longed to be Rob's wife, but only if he truly loved her.

'Why do you weep?'

Melissa was startled for she had not heard him come in. She turned 'round to look at him. He had taken off the rich clothes he had worn for their feast and wore just a simple tunic, his feet bare. As he walked towards her she smelled a pleasant woody scent, mixed with the freshness of soap and she knew that he had bathed before coming to her.

'I was not weeping,' she said, lifting her head though she trembled inside.

'Do not lie to me, Melissa,' Rob said, and his voice was harsh. 'Do you fear me so much? I had thought that we did well enough together earlier this evening—but now you tremble.' His eyes narrowed. 'Is it because of this?' He touched the scar on his cheek. 'Do you feel revulsion at the thought of being kissed by a monster like me?'

'No!' Melissa cried, but she flinched away as he reached for her. 'No, do not touch me I beg you. This marriage was not of my asking. I do not know you....'

'You knew me well enough when you first promised to love me all your life,' Rob said, and his eyes sparked with anger. He reached for her shoulders, his fingers digging into her flesh, making her cry out. 'You are my wife, Melissa. And I shall take what is mine. You cannot deny me.'

'I know that I cannot,' Melissa said, and tears trickled down her cheeks, into her mouth. 'I know that I must obey you in all things and that I must smile and welcome you—but how can I when…'

'When my face gives you a disgust of me?' Rob let her go, his desire fading as he saw what he imagined was fear and revulsion. 'No, I should not have expected it. Well, I am not a monster, though you think it, lady, and I shall not force you to my will. You are mine and in time you must become my wife for both our sakes, but I shall leave you to sleep in peace this night.'

He turned and went out as silently as he had come, leaving Melissa to stare after him, the tears rolling down her cheeks. She sank to her knees, covering her face with her hands as she wept. It had all gone so terribly wrong. Rob thought that she feared him because his face disgusted her, but it was not so. She loved him so much that her heart was breaking, but her pride would not let her confess it, knowing as she did that he did not truly love her.

And yet he had given her a beautiful wedding gift that must have been bought before he came to this place. He had arranged a feast and sweet wine to please her and his men had entertained her. He must surely care for her, which meant that she had been foolish.

She had not intended to let him see her weeping but he had come upon her unawares. He had taken her tears to mean that she regretted her marriage to a man she disliked—but that was not so. She had wept because she wanted him to love her and she had thought that he did not.

If he did not love her, why had he not simply taken what he wanted of her? If she was no more than a piece of property he had taken by force, he might have used her as he would. It was what most men did after all. She was not so innocent that she did not know that many wives were desperately unhappy in their marriages. Yet Rob had not forced her. In his anger he had threatened that he would take what was his, but in truth he had done all he could to please her.

Melissa realised that Rob was suffering from hurt pride, just as she herself had been. He had been treated like a dog and disfigured by her brother—and he had been told that she wanted it done because he had insulted her. Was it any wonder that he had been angry? How could she expect that he would greet her with soft words and looks of love? She ought to have known that anger lent harshness to his tongue.

What could she do to repair the damage she had done? Should she go to him in the morning and beg his pardon? It would offend her pride to beg for his forgiveness, but if she must then she would do it. And yet… She took a turn about her bedchamber, her mind seeking an alternative to what seemed her only choice, and then she smiled.

She was not the meek wife that her aunt had told her she must be, but she did not believe that it was a meek wife that Rob wanted. If he loved her it was because she was bold and proud—and she would carry out her daring plan even if it was shocking.

She slipped on a velvet mantle over her night rail, and slipped out through the outer chamber. It was empty that night for she had sent her women to sleep elsewhere. She knew that Rob's chamber was at the far end of the gallery for she had seen it when she was checking the linen earlier. A few torches still flared in the iron sconces that held them to the stone walls, but Melissa could see easily enough by the light that came from an emerging moon and she fled along the gallery on bare feet. Outside the room she knew to be Rob's, she hesitated, her heart pounding.

Dare she go in without being invited? Would he still be awake or had he fallen asleep? It must be an hour or more since he had left her. She had spent some time in examining her thoughts and deciding what she wanted of her marriage, but now she knew. She knew what she must do, even if it meant humbling her pride.

Opening the door softly so as not to disturb him, Melissa let herself into Rob's chamber. He had not left a candle burning but the moonlight flooded into the room through an open window and she could see that he was lying in his bed. He had thrown down the gown he had been wearing when he came to her, and, as she approached the bed, she saw his naked shoulder for he had put off all but one thin cover, because the night was warm.

Melissa caught her breath, approaching as silently as she could lest he wake and challenge her before she could do what she intended. As she drew near, he groaned and cried out in his sleep. She froze to the spot for she thought that he would sit up and accuse her of something, but he merely sighed restlessly. She let her cloak slip to the ground, then lifted the thin coverlet and slid into the bed beside him, moving closer that she could feel the warmth of his body through her thin shift. She pressed her lips to his bare arm, hoping that he would wake and take her into his arms, but instead he moaned and threw out his arm as if in a dream.

Suddenly, she realised that he was burning up. It was not a dream but a fever! She jumped out of bed and lit a candle, taking it nearer so that she could see him more clearly. His face had swollen so much more since he had come to her, and she could see a yellow pus oozing from it.

It had taken harm and he was suffering from a virulent infection. Melissa knew that unless drastic steps were taken, he might die of such an infection, and she went to the door, shouting for help. A servant came running.

'My husband is ill,' she said. 'Is there a physician within the castle?'

'No, my lady—but Master Hale knows something of healing.'

'Then summon him at once, for it is urgent.'

Melissa went back to the bed to look at Rob. He was tossing and turning and he cried out a name—her name. She bent over him, touching the swollen flesh about the scar, discovering that when she pressed it more of the yellow pus came oozing out. She looked around and saw a bowl and ewer, and fetched them to the bed, standing the bowl on a small chest. She found a piece of cloth that Rob had used earlier to wash himself and began to bathe the infected wound, but as often as she wiped the pus away it came up again.

'That will not help, my lady.' The steward's voice made her turn to him with relief. 'The wound must be cut and cauterised or the infection will spread over his body. I told him earlier that it needed to be done, but he said it would heal.'

'Will it not hurt him to apply a hot iron?'

'He has known pain before, my lady. If nothing is done he may die.'

'Then you must do it,' Melissa said, blinking away the tears that threatened to spill over. 'Tell me what I must do, for I would help if I can.'

'Your task will come after,' the steward said. 'Return to your own chamber, Lady Melford, and I shall summon you when it is done.'

Melissa looked at him mutinously for she could not bear to leave Rob this way, but then she inclined her head. 'You will tell me when it is over?'

'Yes, my lady.' Hale smiled at her. 'Do not fear for him. He is a strong man and has suffered before.'

'Yes, I know.' She turned away but her heart was aching. Was it not enough that he had suffered once before for her sake—must he be tormented in this way? Yet she knew that the steward was honest and that she might trust him. Rob would die unless the infection was burned away, because he had neglected it and it had taken harm.

Melissa was spared the sight of Rob writhing in agony as his wound was opened and burned clean of the festering infection. When she returned in the first light of morning, Rob's cheek was covered with a wad of linen that hid the ugly sight from her.

'You may help to keep him cool and clean,' Hale said. 'But I shall treat his wound myself until I am satisfied it has healed sufficiently. Your task will be to make him stay in bed once he recovers his senses.'

'He will not like to be so confined,' Melissa said.

'I daresay not,' the steward replied. 'But had he taken more care at the start it might not have come to this…but he is not a man to worry about slight injuries.'

'You call it slight?'

Hale smiled oddly. 'Not my words, lady, but his. You must know your husband—he takes little account of physical pain.'

'No…' Melissa thanked him for his care of Rob and then went to take her seat beside the bed. There was nothing for her to do but watch over him, and keep him company when he woke.

Rob became aware of the stinging pain in his cheek as he returned to consciousness. It hurt like hell and yet the agony he had been enduring for some days had gone. He put a tentative hand to his cheek, discovering that it had a pad of linen fastened to it with bands of more linen, and it seemed to be less swollen than it had been that night…what night?

He struggled to remember, and then it came back to him. He had forced Melissa to marry him and discovered her weeping in her chamber. A smothered oath left his lips. He must have been out of his mind to force her to wed him, but the infection had been troubling him for a while before that and perhaps that was why he had done it. At least, he could think of no other reason for it was certain that she did not wish to be his wife. He moaned and opened his eyes to find her bending over him, a cooling cloth in her hand as she bathed his brow.

'What are you doing here?' he asked harshly.

'Where else should I be?' she asked, and smiled at him. 'You have been ill for nearly a week, Rob, and we have all taken a turn in caring for you—though you owe your recovery to Master Hale, for it was he who lanced the wound and applied the iron. It has almost healed and it looks so much better. Indeed, in a few months I daresay it will be almost gone.'

'Indeed?' he said, and frowned at her. 'Then I suppose I must be grateful for I believe it was badly infected.'

'Your cheek had swollen terribly and it was oozing pus. I tried wiping it away, but Hale told me that it would only become worse and that it must be lanced and cauterised. I feared that it would hurt you badly, but he said that you did not fear pain.'

'Of that sort, no,' Rob said, his eyes narrowed and suspicious. 'But why are you here? You did not need to tend me. There are plenty of servants to do that surely.'

'Yes, but I wished to help,' Melissa said. 'I was anxious for your recovery.'

'Had I died you would have been a widow and free to please yourself.'

'You think I would rejoice in your death? You wrong me,' Melissa said. 'But if it does not please you to have me here, I shall go.'

'Go then,' he said. 'I shall not detain you further—though I thank you for whatever you have done while I lay here.'

Melissa gave him a speaking look but said nothing. She had wept over him and sat by his side all through the fever, but it seemed that nothing she could do would please him. He could not forgive her.

Rob lay back against the pillows. He felt weak and ill, and his sickness was compounded by the knowledge that he had hurt her again. He had hurt her so many times, and it was not what he wanted. He wanted to make her smile and laugh as she had when he held her hand in the stream so that she should not fall. He wanted her to love him, but he did not know how to tell her. His bitterness had killed the sweetness that he had loved, and she was a proud woman—a woman he could not reach.

'You should not try to get up yet, sir,' Hale said as his master insisted on getting out of bed. 'You have been very ill—indeed, had your lady not called me that night, I think you would have died, perhaps by morning.'

'My wife called you— What night was that?'

'The night of your wedding, my lord. She was here in your chamber and she sent a servant to fetch me. As I have told you, I believe that her action saved your life.'

'And your own skill,' Rob said with a wry smile. 'I have not yet thanked you as I ought. You owed me no loyalty and yet you used your skills to help me—why?'

'Do you know what the earl would have done had he taken an enemy's fortress?' Hale asked. 'I have seen murder and rape and worse—and was sickened by it in my youth. You are not a man such as he and I should be proud to serve you. If you will have me?'

'I shall be glad of it, though I have a steward,' Rob said. 'But my wife has lands and we shall need a good steward there—if that would serve?'

'I would work in your kitchens if you asked it of me, sir.'

'I think we shall find better work for you,' Rob said. 'There will come a time when David is no longer able to fill his duties and for now—' he shrugged '—hand me my shirt, if you will. I must dress and go down or they will be thinking I am dead...'

'A day has not passed when you have not been asked for,' Hale said, but he handed him his shirt for he knew that Rob was not a man to be denied.

'So, you are better,' Melissa said when she saw him come down. She had been giving orders to one of the women who served her and went to greet him. 'Are you sure you should be up yet?'

'I am much better. I shall grow weak if I lie in bed longer, and I have things I must do,' Rob told her. His eyes went over her hungrily. She looked more beautiful than ever, and he knew that he must speak of what was in his mind. 'I must ask you to forgive me for what I said to you. It was harsh and unjustified, for Hale has told me that you found me, and that I might have died had I lain there all night. I have no clear memory of why you were in my room…'

'I came because we had quarrelled,' she said. 'It was our wedding night and you found me crying. You were angry and you left me…'

'And you came—for what reason?'

'Because I did not wish to quarrel with you. I know that you despise me…hate me…but I…'

'No, I do not hate you nor do I despise you,' Rob said. 'I cannot say that I love you, for the feelings I once had have…'

'I know that they must have died long ago,' Melissa said before he could finish. 'I do not ask that you love me, but I wish…'

'That I would release you? It is what I should have done, of course. I had no right to force you to marry me. I should have taken you to your kinswoman or…' He shook his head and smiled oddly, some of his old humour in his face. 'I cannot see you as a nun, Melissa. Nuns are meek women who give their lives to God and good works. I think you have too much spirit…'

'Yes, perhaps,' she agreed. 'I do not think it is truly what I want, though I would have accepted it rather than…be the wife of that man.'

'Did you hate it so much?' Rob asked, his eyes intent on her face. 'Why did you not ask me for help when we met near Shrewsbury that day?'

'There were two reasons,' Melissa told him, her voice calm and controlled. 'My father had kept Rhona with him, because he knew that I cared for her. He told me that if I did not go through with the marriage he would give her to Harold for his pleasure.'

'The devil he did! May his black heart rot in hell,' Rob said. 'And the other?'

'Harold would have killed you. He had ten men and you were alone. I would never do anything that might lead to your death.'

'Is that the truth?' Rob took her by the shoulders, holding her firmly but gently. 'If you were prepared to sacrifice yourself for Rhona—and to lose your chance to escape for my sake—why…'

She knew what he would ask. 'We were betrayed, Rob. Agnes told my father that we had been meeting. Foolishly, I told him that we wished to marry. I should have lied, pretended that we had met once by chance—and sent you word to stay away. I knew that my father did not love me, but I did not know that he hated you and your father.'

'You mean the quarrel over the land?'

'No—it was much more,' Melissa said. 'My father wanted to marry your mother but she refused him and married yours. I believe that was why he made me send you away. He could have barred you from the castle that day, for he was there, in the room, hidden behind the tapestry. But he made me hurt you. I knew that if I told you the truth he would punish us both and so I said all those terrible things…I wanted you to go because he had promised that nothing would happen to you if I sent you away, but he lied. He told me afterwards that he had given Harold permission to have his sport with you.'

'Why did you not tell me this before? In the forest—your father was not there that day.'

'You were so angry, so bitter. Would you have believed me?'

Rob looked at her, and then shook his head. 'No, I was too full of hatred even to listen.'

'But you do believe me now?' She looked into his face and saw that he was struggling to bring his feelings under control.

'I have not lied to you. But I can see that it is no use, you cannot forgive me.' She walked away from him.

Rob watched her go. He knew that he should follow and beg her to forgive him, and yet still the nagging doubts haunted him. He wanted to believe her...but he could not be sure that she was not lying even now. She was his wife and perhaps she thought that the only way she could find some ease in life was to deceive him...as he knew many women did when they were trapped in a marriage they hated.

He did not know what to do. He had forced her to become his wife, and yet he feared that they would never find happiness together if he held her to her vows. It might be possible to have the marriage annulled for it had not been consummated, and his illness would be testament to that...and yet it would cut the heart out of him to let her go.

He ought to do it! She had the right to choose.

Melissa tossed restlessly in her bed. Rob had offered her freedom. He would send her to her kinswoman Alanna Davies with an escort and then he would arrange an annulment of their marriage.

'It was wrong of me to force you to marry me,' he had told her at supper. 'I have no excuse for my behaviour towards you since I came here, Melissa. I have been bitter and angry and I blamed you for what happened when I knew full well that your father hated mine. Harold of Meresham is a bully and known for his barbarity. I should have known that you were blameless for what he did...as for the rest, I am trying to believe it was as you say. Forgive me if I do not say that I never thought you capable of such faithlessness, for I have and it will take some time to forget.'

'I forgive you and I understand,' Melissa had told him, retiring to her chamber, but now she was no longer so understanding. She had bared her soul to him, and still he held back—believed her faithless.

Getting out of bed, she wrapped her cloak around her and set off down the narrow passageway to Rob's chamber. As before his room was in darkness. But this time she had brought her own taper and she lit his so that the light flared, giving her a good view of him. He was sleeping and she saw that he had taken off the linen that had covered his wound. She bent over him to look at it more closely, pleased to see that it was healing well. He looked so peaceful and her anger melted. Smiling, she bent to kiss the scar. She would not wake him to quarrel with him now. It had been foolish to come here.

Rob was instantly awake as her lips touched his cheek. He gave a muffled shout of alarm, reacting instinctively. He jerked up, grabbing at her, pulling her down on top of him as he muttered something, his hands at her throat. She gave a little moan of fright, thinking that he meant to strangle her.

'Damn it!' he growled, and jumped out of bed. He stood looking down at her in bewilderment. He was completely naked, his body gleaming bronze in the yellow light, as if it had often been exposed to the sun. She could not take her eyes from him for he was beautifully formed, his muscles hard and strong, his stomach flat with a sprinkling of dark hair that arrowed to his manhood. 'What the hell are you doing, Melissa? I thought it was an assassin. I might have killed you!'

'You offered me my freedom,' she said. 'But I do not want it. When I thought you would die…' She shook her head. 'But you hate me still…'

'I do not hate you,' Rob said. 'Why did you come here on our wedding night? Was it to beg me to set you free?'

'No…'

'Tell me!'

'I came to you,' she whispered, sitting up against the pillows, her hair tumbling about her shoulders, a fiery golden mass against the soft cream of her skin in the candlelight. 'I did not mean to refuse you when you came to me earlier that night, Rob. I am a foolish girl and I was afraid…'

'Because of this, I know.' He touched the scar, and becoming aware of his nakedness reached for the gown he had discarded earlier.

'No!' Melissa rose from the bed, her hand moving towards him in supplication. 'Do not cover yourself, Rob. You are beautiful—all of you. It is not your face I fear. Please believe me. I hardly see the scar—it does not matter, except that I know it pains you.'

'Not so very much,' Rob said, his eyes narrowed as he looked at her. 'It is much better since it was lanced, for the poison has gone. If you did not feel revulsion because of this, what did you fear that night? Did you think that I would hurt you?'

'No…' Melissa had moved nearer to him. Greatly daring, her pulses racing, she reached up to touch his scar, tracing it delicately with her fingertips. 'I was afraid that you did not love me—and that you would laugh at me for loving you and break my heart.'

'Do not lie to me,' he said, though his tone was uncertain. He reached out for her, his hands cupping her head, one on either side, bringing her face close to his so that she felt the heat of his breath. 'Say only what you truly mean, Melissa, for I think I should kill you if I discovered that you lied.'

She smiled a little tremulously for she had begun to understand his threats came from his emotions. He did not always mean the harsh things he said to her. Perhaps it was only his hurt pride that made him say them.…

'I mean all I say,' she said, her throat hoarse with the fierce rush of desire that swelled in her as he kissed her. She melted into him, her body soft and pliant. 'Make me your wife in truth, Rob, for it is all that I wish to be, I promise you.'

He pulled her hard against him, his desire for her overcoming caution as he felt the sweetness of her surrender. She was dizzy with pleasure as she felt the surge of his need against her, the heat of his body penetrating her thin shift. And then he had lifted her in his arms, laying her down in the bed. For a moment he looked down at her, then, as she smiled at him, he came to join her, lying by her side, looking into her eyes.

'I shall not hurt you,' he whispered hoarsely. 'Even when I believed that you had spurned me for a rich marriage I could never forget you. I could never truly hate you, Melissa, though in my anger I tried.'

'I believed that you must,' she said, her lips soft and moist as she gave him a shy smile. 'I was angry for I thought you meant to use me as my father intended—and I was afraid that in time you would come to despise me for my weakness in loving you.'

'Despise you? No, not that…' He smiled as he touched her cheek and then bent his head to kiss her lips. 'I am not sure that I love you, Melissa, for I have forgotten how to love—but I know that I want you so much that my life would be useless to me without you. If that will content you, then we shall not seek an annulment—but speak now for if you do not it will be too late.'

'Rob—' she gazed at him uncertainly '—can you forgive me for what he did to you?'

'It was not your fault,' Rob said, his hand stroking the satin arch of her back. 'I blamed you in my bitterness, but I cannot put you out of my mind and must find a way to deal with it for both our sakes.'

Melissa nestled against him, comforted by the warmth and strength of his body. This was where she belonged, in his arms, held close to his heart. 'Then let us forget the past.'

Rob's arms tightened about her, his lips seeking hers in a kiss that left no need of words. As his tongue sought the warmth and sweetness of her mouth, she opened to him, giving herself up to the pleasures of his loving. His kisses made her melt with a fierce wanting deep inside her. His hands caressed and stroked her, his finger touching her in a place that had her gasping with sudden need, her body trembling with anticipation. Then he circled her nipples with his tongue, the slightly rough texture of his tongue making her breathe faster, her body arching to meet his as he entered her.

At first the pain was sharp but he hushed her cry with a kiss that soothed and reassured her, his body moving slowly, sensuously as she felt an answering need deep within herself. And when he withdrew, she reached for him, a cry of protest on her lips. But he thrust into her again, teasing her a little as he felt her instant response, her desire now as great as his own. Their bodies melded one into the other in a sweet coupling that swept them on a crest of love and passion to end in gasping pleasure as he gave a shout.

Pulling her with him, he rolled over to his back so that she lay half across his body, her face nestled against his chest, the tears trickling down her cheeks. His hand caressed her head, stroking the back of her neck.

'Do not cry, little one,' he said. 'It will not be painful another time. It is only the loss of your virginity that causes pain.'

'It hardly hurt at all,' Melissa lied, and she raised her head to look up at him. 'Besides, it is forgotten. My tears are of happiness, for I did not know that loving could bring such joy.'

'We have only just begun,' Rob promised her, his fingers running through the glory of her red-gold tresses. 'We shall learn to please each other even more as we go on, for we have all our lives before us.'

'Yes,' Melissa said, and snuggled against him. 'Nothing shall ever part us again.'

She lay nestled into his body like a trusting kitten. His power was like a mantle, wrapping her about, protecting her. Now that she was his, she believed that she had nothing more to fear. No one could take her from him now, because she was truly Rob's wife.

When he came to her again and again that night, seeming as

if his hunger would never be bated, she clung to him, giving herself up to his caresses with the abandon of a loving heart. She was his and it was all she wished to be.

'I love you, Rob,' she whispered as he slept beside her, the first rosy fingers of dawn seeking entrance at the window. 'I shall always love you no matter what.' And yet he had not said that he loved her. He wanted her, desired her…but did he love her?

Chapter Six

Rob was in the courtyard watching as his instructions were carried out. Before he could move on to take the castle of Leominster, he must secure Gifford. He could not afford to leave many of his men behind, and though many of Gifford's men-at-arms had come over to him, he could not completely trust them—or Lady Gifford. He would have to leave at least twenty of his own men here to help keep it for the King, for otherwise it might slip from his grasp. He was considering whether it might be as well to take those men that had come over to him when he left, for they would be more inclined to fight against Leominster than their lady of Gifford. She had sworn that she would never take up arms against a king of England, but an ambitious mother might do anything for her son's sake.

He decided that all was well and he would go in search of Melissa, and a little smile touched his mouth as he recalled their loving of the previous night. They had been wed for two weeks now and every night their pleasure in each other became more intense. Rob sometimes wondered at himself, for he had never expected to feel so much for a woman. Had he not been strict with himself, he could have dallied at her side all day and left his work—but he knew that he could not afford to neglect anything. At the back of his mind a shadow hovered.

He had dismissed warnings from the priest that perhaps his marriage was not entirely legal in the eyes of the church. It seemed that the ceremony for Melissa's betrothal had begun, though it had never finished—and of course there was the marriage contract. Leominster might be entitled to claim her as his promised wife.

Leominster's life was forfeit to King Henry, but while he remained at large there was a danger. Rob did not believe that the marquis would try to snatch her back, but kings were capricious creatures, and if Leominster were to treat for his lands, he might also be awarded his promised wife.

He would never give her up! Rob's expression was harsh. Melissa was his now, and he was determined to put his doubts behind him, though he had not quite been able to dismiss them.

He was about to go inside when he heard a shout and a moment later a rider came cantering into the courtyard. His frown deepened as he saw that it was one of the four men he had sent to escort Gifford to the Tower of London.

The man came up to Rob, bending his knee before him. 'Forgive me, lord, the news is not good.'

'I do not punish the bearer of ill news,' Rob said with a growl. 'Tell me the worst.'

'We watched the earl day and night, for you told us not to trust his word too much. There was always two of us on guard when we camped for the night, but last night when I rose to take my turn I discovered that the guards were dead. They had been taken from the rear, their throats cut. My companion was also wounded and I left him to make his way home as best he could while I rode to give you the news. I do not know why I was not murdered in my sleep, sir—except that I always rest sitting up with my sword across my body.'

'Perhaps you were meant to live to warn me,' Rob said, his mouth set in a grim line. 'I am at fault, Eric of Bolwood, for I should have sent him in chains as the King bid me. I granted him the dignity of an honourable surrender and therefore it is my blame.'

'Sir, I think the earl planned his escape, for we had camped some ten leagues beyond the boundary of the Marquis of Leominster's estate, and I think it was there that he would have gone for sanctuary.'

'Yes, I think you are right,' Rob said. 'He will have gone there with the news of what happened here.'

'Will they come against us, sir?'

'Perhaps. I have been preparing for such an eventuality. I had hoped to leave Gifford safe and then attack Leominster, but it is possible that he may come here…' Rob looked thoughtful. 'We shall make our plans for often surprise will win the day…'

'You were a fool to surrender to him without a fight,' William, Marquis of Leominster growled. 'I told you to come to me with your men and the women. We could have withstood a siege here for months had you heeded me. We might have traded for your manor when they wearied of the fight.'

'What if the King had sent more men to subdue us?' Gifford asked. 'Even here, we could not hold out forever against larger numbers. I thought it best to give my bond and then trick my guards and come here alone.'

The Marquis gave him a look of disgust. 'Now you have nothing and your bond is broken. Henry Tudor will have no mercy for you now, Gifford. If you do not end on the block, you will never be allowed to return to Gifford.'

'Unless we take it back from Melford,' Gifford said, his eyes narrowing. 'Henry has the throne, but who says he can hold it? It may be that if we show that we are not to be tamed others will follow. Richard may be dead, but his sister's son lives— and he may yet rule in the Tudor's place. In the meantime, we should teach Melford a lesson.'

'And how may we do that?' Leominster demanded, his

narrow-set eyes glinting with temper. 'Had you held out I might have come to your aid. As it is you have lost me my bride and the lands that are hers by right. And now you ask that I aid you in this struggle. Give me a reason—what benefit to me?'

'If you want the girl I know how we may get her back—and draw that upstart Melford from Gifford.'

'She belongs to me.' Leominster's gaze hardened. 'You say that the betrothal by proxy went ahead as planned. If that is so, she is mine by right and I shall take her from him. If he remains at Gifford yet, we may lay siege to it and…'

The earl shook his head. He had lied about the betrothal, but he needed the marquis's help. 'He is too clever for that, Leominster. He will have fortified it for a siege by now—but there is another way. We may take Melissa and draw the fox from his lair.' It would not suit him to have his manor laid waste by his ruthless neighbour. It would be much better if the fighting took place here at Leominster. 'You may withstand his attack far better than I could have had I refused to surrender.'

The Marquis gave him a withering look. He suspected the earl had taken the easy way out for his own reasons, but he had no such scruples. If it were possible to snatch Melissa from Gifford Towers without a fight so much the better. Once he had her within the walls of the castle, no man on earth could take her from him.

He looked at the earl thoughtfully. Gifford was more of a fool than he had believed. Yet if he knew a way to spirit Melissa away from the upstart Robert of Melford, he would have served his purpose. If the earl were disposed of, the Gifford lands might pass to him by right of force. Gifford had a young son, but children died easily and then with Melissa as his wife, he had as much right to his former friend's lands as anyone. His promised wife was a considerable heiress and he could come out of this with a great deal more power and wealth than he had expected.

'Tell me how this magic may be worked,' he said, for he could see no other way to gain his rights other by laying siege to the fortified manor house.

'There is a way in that no one but I knows of,' the earl said. 'It needs only one man to enter and snatch her from him...'

'If one man may pass then so may many.' Leominster growled. 'We could take a band of men in and come upon them by surprise.'

'You think that I shall reveal my secret to others?' Gifford tossed his head scornfully. 'No, that is not my intent, sir, for I should never lie easy in my bed again. The secret is passed down from father to son and shall never be told to others—but I will go in and bring her out to you, and then we shall return here. You will then promise to help me gain possession of Gifford once more when the upstart has been dealt with as I choose. I want him hanged, but not before he has been made to suffer.'

'Very well,' the marquis agreed. His narrowed gaze revealed nothing. Once he had the girl, he would dispose of this fool—but he would learn the secret of Gifford if he could. 'Bring her back to me and I shall help you gain what is rightfully yours.' A sword thrust in the dark once the deed was done, and the matter would be ended.

Melissa was singing as she worked at her sewing. She had finished mending the linen she had taken as her share of a dreary task and now she was planning a tapestry that she would take with her to her new home. It was to be a wall hanging for her husband's bedchamber at Melford, and she had decided that it should tell the story of the great struggle between the houses of York and Lancaster. Rob had told her that Henry's advisors wished him to marry Elizabeth of York, the lady with perhaps the most claim to the throne of England. If he did as they begged him, it might put an end to the wars that had lasted for so many years.

'Melissa…' She looked up as the door of her chamber opened and her husband came in. He was dressed in leather hose and a fine wool shirt that lay open to the waist, and her heart turned over at the sight of him. He was so handsome and she loved him. She never noticed the scar that marred one side of his face. 'Come down and walk with me, my lady. It is a warm day and you sit too long up here alone.'

Melissa got up and went to him, giving him her hand. 'I have been busy with the mending,' she told him with a smile. 'I did not wish to come down too soon for I thought that I might be in the way. I have seen how busy you are. Your men seem to train all day.'

'It is the only way to keep them fighting fit while we linger here,' Rob said. 'I wanted to talk to you, because I think we must leave soon.'

She looked at him anxiously. 'You are going to Leominster. I do not think the marquis will surrender as easily as my uncle did, Rob. I have heard that he is a harsh man and very proud.'

'Yes, I think that is true,' Rob agreed. 'We did not meet in battle, but I heard that he fought well and hard. It is because of his reputation that the King is determined to subdue him. Although the Crown has been won, it is not yet secure. Henry knows that some of the nobles will rebel against him. There are others with a claim to rule in his stead.'

'I think I understand,' Melissa said, 'and I know you must leave for it is your duty. But I shall pray for your safety.' Her eyes opened wide as she looked at him. 'What would you have me do?'

'That is my dilemma,' Rob said, and raised her hand to his lips to drop a kiss within the palm. 'I am not sure whether to send you back to Melford with an escort—or to leave you at Gifford until I can return for you.'

'May I not come with you?'

'A soldiers' camp is not the place for a lady,' Rob said, and smiled at her. 'I know you would accept the hardship without complaint, and I should like to have you near—but it would be too dangerous. I think you would do better to wait here until I come, though you may go to Melford if you wish.'

She knew that he could not truly spare the men to accompany her. Besides, Leominster was not so far away and he would send for her as soon as he was in a commanding position.

'I shall remain here until you send for me,' she said, and touched his cheek, her fingers moving over the scar, which was still livid though no longer throbbed with pain. 'But I shall pray that you come to me soon, my love.'

'I shall be no longer from your side than duty demands,' Rob told her, his voice hoarse with emotion. 'But I gave a promise and it must be kept, Melissa.'

'You would be less than yourself if you gave up your duty for my sake,' she said. 'When must you leave?'

'I think tomorrow at first light,' Rob said. 'We shall dine with the men in the hall this evening, and then I shall come to take my leave of you.' He longed to hold her in his arms and know the sweetness of her flesh, for it would have to last him some time, perhaps weeks or even months. He would not think that it might be the last time, for if he weakened he might stay here and never leave her at all.

Melissa dressed in her husband's favourite gown of green over a kirtle of cloth of gold. A net of gold sewn with pearls held her hair, and she wore the chain of emeralds about her waist. In bed the previous night, she had worn them and nothing else for Rob loved to see the jewels lie against her breasts. Her cheeks flushed a becoming rose as she remembered the way he had loved her, and she found that she was longing for that night when he came to her again. It would be for the last time until he returned—and who knew when that would be.

A little shiver ran through Melissa, a feeling of impending doom shadowing her as she dismissed her maid and prepared to go downstairs to the hall. Men oft died in battle, and Rob was not a man to hide at the rear while his soldiers were cut down in front of him. Her throat tightened with fear, for she did not know how she would feel if she never saw him again. She had given him her heart, but she was not sure of his and if he died she would never know if he had truly forgiven her.

Shaking off her anxiety, she left her chamber and made her way along the gallery. She was determined to show no distress, for this night was to be one of celebration. The men were in merry mood, though she knew that only watered ale was being served that night; it was a precaution against sore heads in the morning, for they would need to be ready to march soon after it was light.

A rousing cheer greeted Melissa as she entered the vast hall, for she was popular. Most of the men served Rob's family in one guise or another, though some were merely yeomen farmers and would return to the plough when he told them to go home. She smiled at them as she passed, her head held proudly, walking like a queen. Yet her pride had not prevented her from aiding the men in whatever way she could these past days, and many of them had benefitted from having their clothes washed in barrels by the women Melissa had sent to do their chores.

Rob stood to greet her as he always did, taking her hand and kissing it as he led her to her place at his side. He had provided more of the sweet wine she liked, and they toasted each other and their friends before the feasting began.

There were ribs of spit-roasted pig, pies of eel and trout, capons and pigeons in red wine, together with apples cooked in cider and boiled cabbage with bacon and cheese. Everyone ate heartily, entertained by the minstrel who had sung at Melissa's wedding feast.

Afterwards, she and Rob danced together, and some of the women from the manor joined in the merry jig that followed.

It was growing dark outside when Rob suggested that Melissa might like to go up to her chamber.

'I shall join you soon, my sweet,' he told her, and his eyes were dark with passion. She knew that he longed for her as she longed for him, and that, though he would not say it, their coming separation would be hard for him to bear.

'Do not be long, Rob,' she said. 'The night will soon be gone…'

She left him talking to the steward, saying good-night to her aunt as she passed, her heart racing at the thought of what was to follow. She must make this night special, so that Rob would remember it when he was lying on the hard ground with only a blanket to keep him warm.

Agnes was waiting in her chamber.

'Where is Morag?' Melissa asked. 'Why are you here?'

The girl looked at her nervously. 'She sent word that she was sick and could not come, my lady. I thought that you might allow me to serve you in her place.'

'I should have been told that she was ill.' Melissa frowned for she did not trust this woman. 'Well, I suppose, for this once—but I have decided that I shall not take you with me when we leave. I do not want you near me.'

'Do you wish to disrobe, my lady?' Agnes asked. Her eyes flicked away to the corner of the room, and Melissa sensed something was wrong. There was more to this than met the eye.

'What is it?' she asked. 'Speak now, Agnes.'

'Oh, my lady, forgive me…' Agnes said, a sob in her voice. 'I did not know how to warn you…'

'Warn me?' Melissa became suddenly aware that someone was behind her. She turned her head, but even as she did so, a heavy blanket was thrown over her, cutting off light and air so that she found it difficult to breathe. She tried to cry for help but the rough wool got into her mouth, choking her as she felt herself hoisted and thrown over a man's shoulder.

'Be quiet, girl,' a voice said. 'Behave and no harm will

come to you. I am taking you where you belong, to your rightful husband.'

Melissa struggled, kicking and pummelling at his back, but the blanket hampered her struggles and she was finding it more and more difficult to breathe. Her chest hurt and she was feeling faint, her resistance fading as she was carried away, through the secret passage that ran beneath the walls of the house itself.

It was some thirty minutes later that Rob at last entered Melissa's chamber. He had been delayed by one of his men, who had received bad news from home and asked to be released. Rob had given him leave, and then been delayed again by the steward as he was about to leave his own apartments. Impatient and eager, he had hastened to his love's chamber only to find it empty. He saw that the candles were still burning, but there was no sign of Melissa. She could not be in his chamber for he had left it only moments ago—so where was she? As his eyes travelled 'round the room, he caught sight of something gleaming near a tapestry that covered one wall of the room. Bending down to pick it up, he discovered that it was the chain of emeralds that he had given Melissa as a wedding gift. It had snapped at the fastener, something that must have taken some force for it was strongly made!

He looked at it in bewilderment. Once, he might have suspected her of breaking it deliberately in temper, but he knew her better now. She might be proud and defiant at times, but she would never do this to his wedding gift. Besides, she had been happy when she left him, her eyes promising a night of love and passion they would both remember.

Where was she? He felt the ice enter his blood as he wondered what had happened to her. Looking about the room, he frowned and then returned to the outer chamber. There was no sign of her woman, which was not in itself unusual, for Melissa often sent her to sleep elsewhere, he knew. And yet he had a terrible feeling that something was wrong.

Going to the top of the stairs, he shouted for Hale. A search must be made throughout the house and grounds for Melissa and there must be no delay.

The steward came running, his expression showing that he was already aware that something was wrong. 'Yes, sir? You wanted something?'

'My wife is not in her chamber,' Rob said, 'and her women are missing. I want them both found.'

'The woman called Agnes is belowstairs,' Hale said, his face grim. 'She was seen trying to sneak out with a bundle under her arm—she has taken some of your lady's jewels.'

'I shall speak to her at once,' Rob said. 'There is some treachery here, Hale. Double the guard and make sure that no one comes or goes.'

'Yes, sir.' The steward hesitated for a moment, then, 'There is a secret way into and out of the house, Sir Robert. Only the earl knows it for the secret is passed down from father to son....'

'It is as I might have expected,' Rob said, and swore furiously. 'He gave his bond too easily and broke it just as easily—he must have had something like this in mind from the beginning.'

'If it is my former master...' the steward hesitated, and then, 'I think he will have used her to bargain with the Marquis of Leominster. I daresay he hopes to draw you from here so that he may enter in secret and take Gifford back by stealth, thus saving it from being sacked as it might have been during the siege.'

'You are right,' Rob said, for he had already worked it out. The earl had known that if he resisted the siege he would likely be forced to surrender on harsh terms, and his property might have been destroyed in the fighting. It was not unknown for the home of a traitor to be burned to the ground. He had hoped to avoid such a fate, and to get his manor back by some other means. And now he had Melissa! 'Damn me for a fool! I should have had her guarded all the time.'

'You could not have known,' Hale said. 'I believe if you question the woman she will confirm what I have told you.'

'Yes, I daresay.' Rob's lips were white for, with Melissa in his enemy's hands, he was loath to move against Leominster.

He ran down the stairs to the great hall. Agnes was sitting on a bench, her head in her hands. When he spoke her name, she looked up at him, her face deathly pale.

'What have you to say for yourself, woman?'

Agnes trembled. 'I was afraid that I would be punished when you discovered that he had taken her. I took the jewels because I did not know where to go or what to do.…'

'You are a thief and perhaps worse,' Rob said, 'for if you knew he was here in the house why did you not warn us? And where is Morag?'

'She was sick and took to her bed. The earl said that he would kill me if I said a word to warn my lady,' Agnes said. 'He came so suddenly, and I did not know how he had got into the house. I did try to warn her but it was too late. He threw a blanket over her and was gone before I could do anything to aid her.'

'But you might have come to me at once,' Rob said, his eyes glinting with anger. 'Instead, you chose to sneak away with your mistress's property.'

Agnes fell to her knees before him. 'Forgive me. Allow me to seek the sanctuary of a nunnery and I shall bother you no more.'

'You deserve to be whipped if nothing more,' Rob growled. 'But I shall have you confined and kept here as a prisoner. It will go hard with you if my lady is harmed. Had you acted differently this night, we might have stopped her abductor from spiriting her away.'

He nodded to two of the men, who had been responsible for catching her as she tried to flee. They took hold of Agnes by her arms and took her off. Rob paced the floor, uncertain what to do next. It was almost impossible to discover the secret way. Besides, the earl would be long gone now. He must decide what to do next. Was Hale right in thinking that he would take her to Leominster? Was she to be used to gain the marquis's help in retaking the fortified manor house?

If Leominster had her...Rob might endanger her life by attacking the castle, and yet what choice did he have? It was his duty to the King, and his only real chance of getting her back might be by subduing Leominster.

Of Melissa's likely fate once she was in the hands of such a monster, Rob did not dare to think. Leominster thought to marry her to gain control of her lands, perhaps making himself so powerful that Henry was forced to treat with him. Melissa was his wife! She belonged to him, Robert of Melford. The marquis would be angry once he knew that he had been cheated of his prize. What would he do to her?

Rob was wracked with agony at the thought of what could happen to her. Leominster might consider that she was rightfully his—and that she had betrayed him by wedding Rob. He would punish her for that in some way. If he forced her to lie with him...the sickness swirled inside Rob's stomach for the thought was more than he could bear.

Leominster would die for it! He gathered all his strength of purpose, knowing that he must summon his men. Attack was the best form of defence. Leominster would have little time to take his pleasures if his castle were under siege. They would march tonight and attack as soon as it was light, perhaps taking the marquis unawares. Surely he would not have time to think of bedding her!

As he strode towards the door there was a commotion and some of Rob's men brought in a stranger. He was struggling and protesting that he wished to speak to Robert of Melford. Rob held up his hand.

'Let him speak,' he commanded, and the stranger was pushed forward and made to kneel. 'Well, tell me what you would say, sir.'

'I have news from King Henry,' the man said. 'He sends word that he will send you more men to help in the siege of Leominster. You are to begin it at once and Morgan of Hywell will join you with fifty men before three days are out.'

'Let him stand,' Rob said. 'Have you the King's seal to prove your words, sir?'

'Aye, I have, but they would not listen…' The stranger gulped. 'I found the body of a man outside your gates, sir, and I brought him in on my horse. They thought I had murdered him, but I swear it is not so.'

'It is the Earl of Gifford,' Owain said, coming into the hall at that moment. 'He has been knifed in the back and was dead when they took him down—but there was something in his hand.' Owain held out a scrap of cloth of gold. 'From her kirtle I think. Someone took her from him and killed him for his pains.'

'I would expect no more of a man such as Leominster,' Rob said, his mouth twisting with anger. 'I do not know why they fell out.…'

'Perhaps I may tell you,' Lady Gifford said, coming into the hall at that moment. Her head was held proudly, her face pale but determined. 'I know that Leominster always coveted my husband's lands for the forest abounds with game to the west and is a rich source of charcoal. To the east lies the sea. There are deposits of sea coal and good fishing, besides an opening to the ocean. Leominster has no forests of his own—and so he covets ours.'

Rob nodded, for a man might covet his neighbour's lands and many quarrelled and fought over them, taking what they could by force. It was a measure of the lawlessness that had come upon England these past years. 'By right they belong to your son, lady—though the King may have other ideas.'

'All I ask of you is to be allowed to retire to my dower lands,' Lady Gifford said. 'Let me bury my husband and leave, sir. I could not hold these lands against such as Leominster, even if the King granted them. My dower is but insignificant and may not arouse so much envy.'

Rob looked at her in silence for a moment. Perhaps he ought to send her to the Tower to await the King's judgement, but he would not see a woman so harshly treated. Besides, she had been kind to Melissa in her way. 'Go then, lady, for I leave here on the hour. I am sorry for your loss. Had your lord kept his word and given his allegiance to Henry, he might have lived—perhaps to return to his home one day.'

'I care not that he is dead,' she said, her head raised, eyes glittering. 'I live only for my son. He has been deprived of his birthright, but perhaps he may rise again to his rightful position one day. I shall not see you again, Robert of Melford—but if we meet it shall not be as friends!'

Rob watched as she walked away. Her last spurt of defiance had shown her true character. She had appeared meek and welcoming, but she had hidden her anger behind a smiling face. It was clear that the lady of Gifford resented what had happened here, for her son if not her husband or herself.

Rob had been determined to subdue Leominster for Henry's sake, but now he was impatient to begin his campaign. That monster had Melissa and he would not rest until he had set her free. He dare not think beyond that, for if she suffered at Leominster's hands…

The pictures whirled inside his head, and he groaned as he thought of her at the mercy of that evil creature. There were so many things that the marquis might do while he had her, and all of them sent shivers down Rob's spine. He burned with anger and frustration for, until he could break down Leominster's defences, there was no way he could reach her. The delay had been crucial for he could never hope to catch up with the marquis's men. She might even now be imprisoned within the castle walls.

'Do not fear for her,' Owain said, seeing the agony he was enduring. 'Melissa never bowed to her father's cruelty and she will not break now. Besides, the marquis will hardly have time to bother with her, for we shall be on them before they know it.'

'Yes.' Rob took a grip on his emotions. He had no time to dwell upon his own pain. He must take command of his men and do as the King had bidden him, for that way lay his only chance of salvation. 'But if he has harmed her, he shall know the agony of hell....'

Melissa's head was swirling as she felt herself lifted and carried from the back of the horse. She had no memory of how she had come to this place, for she had fainted, almost suffocated by the heavy blanket that had only now been removed from her head. It was dark and she could see little of her surroundings, even had she been inclined, though the clatter of horses's hooves over a drawbridge had told her that they must have arrived at Leominster's stronghold.

'What ails the girl?' someone asked close by. 'If you have harmed her, the marquis will have your head!'

'Nay, 'tis only a faint,' a man's rough voice growled. 'She was like it when we took her from Gifford, as you instructed.'

'What of the earl?' another voice asked. 'Did he give you any trouble? Did he show you the secret way?'

'He gave us the slip in the darkness, for we dare not follow too closely,' the first man said. 'He is dead as you ordered, my lord.'

'Damnation! It is a pity that he was too clever for you, but we will take it by force when we are ready. Very well, take her inside and see that she is locked in. I am too busy to bother with her just yet.'

Melissa heard it all through the haze that seemed to claim her senses once more. When they finally began to clear, she realised that she was lying on a bed with a feather mattress, and that the room was well lit with wax candles. As her sight returned and she could focus properly again, she saw that a woman was working at the other side of the room.

'Where am I?' she croaked, for her throat was sore. 'Who are you?'

The woman came forward and curtsied to her respectfully. 'So you have wakened, my lady. I am called Naomi and my lord says that I am to serve you.'

Melissa pushed herself up against the silken pillows. Her mind was beginning to clear, and she knew that her uncle had abducted her from Gifford, but something had happened after that… She had heard a shout and a muffled groan and then several voices. They had put her on a horse and someone had mounted behind her, holding her when she swooned. She thought that someone had said something about the earl getting what he deserved.

'Am I at the castle of Leominster?' Melissa asked.

'Yes, my lady. The marquis had you smuggled out of Gifford, where you had been held captive…'

'I was not a captive,' Melissa said, a note of anger in her voice. 'I demand to be taken back to my husband at once.'

'Your husband?' A look of horror came over Naomi's face. 'But you are the betrothed of the marquis…'

'I was married to Robert of Melford two weeks ago and I am his wife in every way,' Melissa said defiantly. 'Lord Leominster has nothing to gain by holding me here. Pray, tell him that I wish to leave at once.'

'Forgive me, my lady,' Naomi said, her face turning pale. 'If I dared to tell my master that he would have me beaten and thrown into the dungeons. Do not ask it of me. I would serve you well in any other way, bring you wine and food—but do not ask me to tell my lord that you have married another.'

'Very well, I shall tell him myself.' Melissa swung her legs over the edge of the bed, but as she tried to rise, her head swam and she lay back with a little moan. 'I cannot rise yet. Please, bring me water.'

'You are ill, my lady,' Naomi said. 'Stay there and I shall bring you water and a little wine. It has been a terrible ordeal for you.'

Melissa closed her eyes. She was feeling too dizzy to try to leave this bed for the moment; besides, she needed to think about her situation. How was she to escape from this place? She had found it impossible to avoid the eagle eye of the lady of Gifford, who had made sure that Melissa could not run away. But then Rob had come and he had married her, loved her in a way that had made her body sing with pleasure.

Surely he would come for her now. She was his wife, and he cared for her, even if he could not love her as he once had.

She knew that it had been his intention to lay siege to the castle, anyway. He would not fail her. Even if she found it impossible to get out, Rob would find his way to her. All she had to do was believe in him—and keep the marquis at bay.

For the moment she needed to sleep, but when she woke she would see what she could discover about her situation here. Was she to be a prisoner or would the marquis treat her as his betrothed wife? Not once he knew the truth!

He would be very angry when he learned that she was Rob's wife, but she could not be certain how he would react. She shivered, feeling suddenly cold all over. Everything she had heard of him led her to believe that she might suffer for his disappointment. She prayed that he would be too busy defending his castle to bother with her for a while. It might be better if she were to plead sickness for as long as she could.

She closed her eyes for her head was whirling again, and in truth she felt far from well. It was not long before she drifted into sleep, but soon she began to toss and turn restlessly on the pillows, crying out for Rob in her dream. She was in a dark cold place and she knew that she was dying. If her beloved husband did not come to her soon, she would die.

Rob sat on his horse looking at the stout walls of the castle. He had known it was well defended and he had made his plans accordingly. He would bring up his engines of war, the battering rams and ladders, protected by overhead shields that his men would use to scale the walls, but he knew that in the end he might have to starve Leominster's people out. He would not have cared for that, it was a practice often used when the fortress proved impregnable—but Melissa was a prisoner in there. If the others starved then she did, too. She might suffer far worse once Leominster knew that she was his wife.

He cursed that he had let her go alone to her chamber the previous night. Had he gone with her, she might have been safe in her chamber at Gifford, waiting for his return. Now he was not certain that he would see her alive again—and even if they both lived after this was finished, would she be the same? He knew the reputation of the man who had her now, and he was in agony for her sake. As Gifford's prisoner, she had been treated well enough, but now…

Leominster would not take kindly to the idea that the woman he had intended to make his wife had wed another, and if Melissa behaved in her usual proud, stubborn way…Rob did not dare to think of it for he was desperately afraid for her.

He turned to look at Owain. 'I need a volunteer to take my message to Leominster.'

'I shall go,' Owain said, meeting his gaze unflinchingly. 'If he hangs me, so be it—but if he lets me go I shall see what may be learned of her.'

'No, Owain, I cannot afford to let you go,' Rob told him with a grim smile. 'I believe you may do her more good by living than dying, my friend. I shall ask for volunteers from the men— but not you.'

Owain inclined his head, accepting that the man he had followed for Melissa's sake knew best, though he would willingly have given his life for her if need be.

'As you wish, sir.'

Rob summoned one of his most trusted officers and told

him that he needed a volunteer to take in the message to surrender, and, as he had expected, the man offered to go at once.

'You know the marquis's reputation, Rolf,' he said. 'He may take his spite out on you.'

'I go under a flag of truce, sir,' the soldier said. 'If he betrays it and I die this day, take my love to Bronwen and see that she does not starve.'

'You have my word on it,' Rob said, and clasped hands with him. He handed him the baton, which held the roll of parchment that Henry Tudor had signed, demanding the surrender of the castle. 'This is your authority. You come from the King of England, who is even now hastening to our aid with his troops.'

Rolf saluted him and turned his horse towards the walls of the castle, followed by the trumpeter who would blow his horn to attract the attention of those who manned the walls.

Rob and his men sat watching; they were out of range of the deadly crossbow or any missiles that might be fired at them by the great slings that had been erected on the battlements, and might be used for balls of flaming pitch once the fighting started.

The trumpeter did his work and men came to the edge of the battlements, looking down and calling out to know what was wanted. Rob's messenger held up his baton and called out in a loud voice that carried to both sides.

'I am come in the name of Henry Tudor, King of England by right of descent and conquest. He demands that you surrender to him as your lawful sovereign. If you now lay down your arms and swear an oath of fealty pardon may be granted and you may treat for your lands.'

A man had come to the battlements, looking down at the scene below. Rob could not see his face clearly enough to know him, but from his robes guessed that he was the Marquis of Leominster. This was the moment of decision, the one hope that everything might go well and he would soon be united with Melissa.

Something was happening…As Rob watched he saw the

marquis signal to someone and then a bowman appeared and took aim with his crossbow. His intention was clear and a cry of warning left Rob's lips as he saw the bolt fly. It pierced the helmet of the soldier who sat below on his horse, causing him to pitch forward and fall from his horse.

'Take my answer back to the upstart Henry Tudor,' Leominster cried out in a loud voice. 'I owe no allegiance to him. He takes the crown by force but while I live it shall never rest easily on his head.'

Rob's expression was grim. He saw that the some of his men had started forward. They had not waited for his order, their intention to recover the body of their officer.

'God damn him,' Rob said as they returned, carrying his lifeless form. 'We shall break down these walls if it takes a week or a year!'

His impatience knew no bounds. If Leominster would strike down a man who carried the white flag of parley and the authority of the King of England, what would he do to the woman who had been meant to be his wife but betrayed him with another? Melissa was Rob's true wife in every way. Leominster would be offended. He would not consider wedding her now, but would use her as he might any whore. He would do it from anger and from a desire for revenge against Rob.

A great sickness swirled inside Rob, for he knew of Leominster's reputation. He had ruined more than one woman and killed men as easily as another might swat a fly.

'Please, God, do not let her be harmed,' Rob prayed as he gave orders for his friend to be buried with all honour. 'Let me be in time, I beg you. Let me be in time...'

Chapter Seven

Melissa was awakened by noise in the courtyard outside her window. She pushed herself up against the pillows, realising that her headache had gone. She felt much better and wondered if the wine Naomi had given her the previous night had some healing property. As she considered whether she should get up to investigate what was happening outside, the door of her chamber opened and Naomi entered carrying a pewter jug.

'I have brought warm water so that you may bathe and dress, my lady,' she said. 'I hope that you are feeling better.'

'Yes, thank you. I believe I may owe that to you.'

Naomi smiled at her. 'I wished only to serve you, my lady. There was naught to harm, only to heal. My father was a physician and passed on some of his secrets to me.'

'You have used them well for I did feel truly ill last night,' Melissa said, and threw back the covers. The dizziness had passed and she was no longer feeling sick. 'What was the commotion I heard just now?'

Naomi glanced over her shoulder as if she feared to be overheard. 'I have not dared to look, my lady, but they say that Sir Robert of Melford has come with his army to demand the lord of Leominster's surrender in the name of the King.' Naomi held a gown of fine blue wool for her to put on. It was new and ob-

viously provided for her use by the marquis, a wedding gift
perhaps. She did not wish to wear it, but it seemed that there
was nothing else. Besides, the news had made what she wore
seem unimportant.

'Rob is here? Truly here?' Melissa's eyes lit with pleasure
for it was what she had longed for. Oh, if only he could be victorious and carry her off to his home, but she knew that it
would not be easy. 'What is the marquis's reply?' She sat down
on a stool, allowing the woman to dress her hair. Naomi
brushed it, twisting it into braids that were brought to the top
of her head and covered by an embroidered hood with lappets
of gold thread at either side of her face.

'He will not surrender,' Naomi said. 'He has the White Boar
as a part of his standard—and it is whispered that he was one of
old King Henry's bastards, though I do not know it for truth. He
supports the Earl of Lincoln's claim to the throne, as do others…'

Melissa nodded, for she knew that her father had chosen his
allies well. He would never have supported Henry Tudor and
she did not think the marquis would bend easily.

'If he will not surrender, what then?' she asked. 'How long
can the castle be defended?'

Once again, Naomi looked uneasily over her shoulder. 'I have
heard whispers that there is food for no more than a month at
most—but…' She went to the door and looked out, coming back
to her mistress. 'You will not tell anyone what I say, my lady?'

'If you give me a confidence I shall keep it,' Melissa promised intrigued by her woman's manner.

'I have heard that some of the men do not wish to fight,'
Naomi said. 'The marquis is not a popular master for he has
been harsh and ruthless with those who serve him. It is not certain, but I believe that some of them may rebel against him.
They whisper that it is useless for the King will not be denied
and then we shall all be traitors.'

Melissa's pulses raced. 'If only that were so,' she said, eyes glowing. 'If they could somehow force the surrender I know that my husband would be grateful…'

She broke off as the door was suddenly flung open and a man entered. He was tall and heavily built, though not fat. A great hulk of a man, his skin had a red mottled appearance and his beard was black as was his hair that hung almost to his shoulders. He was wearing a long gown of crimson velvet over a short black tunic and hose, his shoes of soft leather with buckles of silver, a flat cap of black velvet on his head. There was no doubt in Melissa's mind as she looked at him that this was the man she was supposed to have wed.

'Out, woman,' he said to Naomi, who gave her mistress a scared glance and then fled, clearly terrified.

Melissa had been sitting on a stool while Naomi brushed her hair. She rose to her feet, assuming the haughty air that Rob had found so amusing, but her eyes were cold, disdainful and did not hold the warmth that they had for her husband.

'By what right do you enter my room, sir?' she demanded.

'You are my promised wife,' Leominster said, his thick lips curling in a sneer as he looked at her. She was a little thin for his taste; he preferred women with more flesh than this proud beauty, but she would do well enough as the mother of his sons. He had spawned three already and killed as many wives, but women were easily come by. 'And this is my fortress. I go where I wish and none may deny me.'

'I am not your wife,' Melissa said. 'The ceremony was abandoned and Lord Whitbread is dead. The contract is void and I am now Henry Tudor's ward.'

'That upstart who claims the throne of England?' Leominster snarled. His eyes were slitted and angry, mouth hard. 'I swear I have as much right as he, though I would claim it for Lincoln not myself. I have no taste for kingship. I live as master of my own manors and here I am as powerful as any king.'

'I daresay you may rule your own people,' Melissa said, and

her expression was defiant, though her stomach was tying itself in knots. 'But you do not rule me, sir. I am not your wife and shall never be so. Indeed, I cannot for I am married to Robert of Melford—and all I own is his by right. While he lives, I can never be your wife.'

'You lie!' The marquis moved towards her like a snarling beast, grabbing hold of her by the top of her arms and shaking her. His fingers dug deep into the tender flesh and made her wince, but she gazed up into his enraged face, proud and still unrepentant. 'Tell me the truth, woman, or it shall be the worse for you!'

'I tell you nothing but the truth,' Melissa said. 'My fortune is in Henry Tudor's power to give or withhold—and my husband is Robert of Melford. We were wed more than two weeks since…' She gasped as he shook her, half lifting her from the ground in his fury and then throwing her back so that she fell to the ground and for a moment lay looking up at him. 'You can kill me if you wish, but it will not change the truth. I am the wife of another.'

'You would not be the first wife I had made forget her husband,' Leominster said with an ugly sneer. 'If I had the time I would teach you manners for you are a proud bitch. You are still of use to me. There is a chance that Henry will lose the crown as easily as he gained it, so I shall allow you to live for the moment. I would have taken you as my wife, but since you have given yourself to my enemy I shall have to think of some other use for you. Perhaps you may amuse my men…'

Melissa rose to her feet. Inwardly, she was feeling sick with fear for his reputation as a monster had not lied, but she would not allow him to see that he had frightened her.

'You may not have long to live, sir,' she said angrily. 'My husband is at the gates and he will come for me whether you defy him or not.'

'Aye, and so he may,' Leominster said, and the smile in his eyes made her stomach clench. 'But he will not find you. Had you been less proud, lady, I might have spared you—but you need to be humbled. I have no time to tame you for the moment, but I know of something that will quench the fire.'

He turned and departed from the room, leaving Melissa to stare after him. What did he mean? She felt cold all over and the dream that had haunted her came back as two soldiers entered the room. They hardly looked at her as they took hold of her arms.

'What are you doing? Take your hands from me! I demand that you release me at once. I am the daughter of Lord Whitbread and the wife of Sir Robert of Melford. You will be punished for what you do.'

'And dead if we disobey him,' one of the men said harshly. 'I beg your pardon, lady. What he plans for you is wicked and I do not like to do it, but I have no choice.'

Melissa struggled against them, fighting as they dragged her from the chamber. Naomi saw them and came running, her face pale.

'Geoffrey of Brampton,' she cried, 'what do you think you are doing to my lady? If you harm her you will answer to me.'

''Tis none of my doing, woman,' the man said. 'He has ordered us to shut her in the oubliette and we must obey him.'

Naomi gave a scream of despair. 'No, not there,' she cried. 'I beg you, Geoffrey, for the love you bear me—not there. She will die in that place. No one can survive it for long.'

'It is what he has ordered,' the other man said. 'If we disobey we shall hang from the battlements before the day is out.'

Naomi clutched at Melissa, trying to drag her away from the men, but the one who had just spoken hit her and she fell back, stumbling to her knees and screaming as they dragged Melissa away.

'Have pity for my lady. In God's name do not shut her in that terrible place.'

Melissa struggled as they took her down the stairs. She managed to break free for a moment and ran a few steps but she was caught and one of the men knocked her down. She hit her head against a stone balustrade, falling into the darkness as the man swept her up, carrying her over his shoulder like a sack of wheat.

'Naomi is right,' Geoffrey said. 'We should not be doing this, Jack.'

'I do my duty while he rules here,' Jack muttered. 'If your stomach is too weak for it, leave it to me. I have no mind to hang for her sake.'

Geoffrey nodded. He did not wish to hang, either, and might not have given the lady's fate another thought if he had not had hopes that Naomi would wed him.

'I'll come with you,' he said. 'But for goodness' sake at least give her a blanket, some food and water.'

'You do it if you want to,' Jack said. 'But she'll die anyway, unless he changes his mind. Once she is there it would take a clever man to find her without help.'

'Yes…' Geoffrey shuddered for the oubliette was below ground, hidden by a secret door and men had died there many times before. 'Poor lady. I pray God that something happens before it is too late.'

Rob greeted the messenger eagerly. He had sent out his scurryers to see if there was any sign of Henry's reinforcements, because it might be best to wait for them before making the first attack on the castle. Its walls were stout and defended on one side by sheer cliff that towered above the sea-foamed rocks below; it would not fall easily.

'What news?' he asked as the man dismounted. 'Have you seen anything of the King's men?'

'No, sir,' the man said, 'but at the fork I rode to the right and John rode left. He may have better luck.'

'Thank you,' Rob said. 'Rest and eat for we shall attack within the hour.'

He dare not wait too long for *her* sake! He strode away, giving orders to various officers as the preparations for the first assault began. Owain came up to him as he was speaking to the solider in charge of the battering ram.

'You do not wait for the King's men?'

Rob shook his head, his eyes narrowed, expression harsh. 'Every hour that we delay places her in more danger, Owain. If he has a battle on his hands he will not have time to think of her.'

Owain inclined his head, understanding Rob's impatience. 'There is news from the castle. One of the serving men slipped out through a side gate and came to us, asking for sanctuary. I cannot vouch for the veracity of his story, but the fellow says that there is a strong feeling against their lord amongst the men. Many of them are discontent with his service. They wished to surrender and are murmuring of rebellion.'

'What are you saying?' Rob asked.

'Perhaps it is not necessary to attack at once. It might be that a siege of some days would bring about a mutiny and surrender.'

'You think that I should wait?'

'It is your choice,' Owain said. 'I know you cannot bear to think of her at that monster's mercy—but suppose he took his revenge by killing her when you attack? If you give him a little rope he may yet hang himself.'

'What do you suggest I do?' Rob suppressed his impatience, knowing that his friend was speaking the truth.

'Send another messenger,' Owain said. 'Tell them that the King is on his way with more troops—and that if they resist they will be starved out and no mercy will be given. If they surrender, favourable terms will be offered to any that throw down their swords.'

'And who shall I send? The last messenger was killed.'

'Send me this time,' Owain said. 'I shall take more care than the last. He should have expected something of the sort for Leominster is known for his barbarity.'

'Go then and deliver the message,' Rob said. 'I shall wait—but if the answer is no, I shall attack at once.'

'Good.' Owain smiled. 'Should I be killed this day in battle or by treachery, tell my lady that I loved her.'

Rob nodded his head in assent, watching as his friend strode off to find his horse and a herald willing to accompany him. This time a party of four rode towards the castle and two of them were archers. Owain meant to give as good as he got, and he carried no flag of truce.

Rob watched as the herald blew his horn once more and men came to the battlements. He could hear much of what Owain cried for his words carried on the breeze.

'Lay down your arms and surrender now,' Owain cried. 'It will be so much the worse for those who refuse to surrender. The King comes with a huge army and this castle will be razed to the ground. Be warned, no mercy shall be given if there is resistance.'

Rob saw a man with a crossbow come to the edge of the battlements as before, but this time Owain's guard was too quick for him. The archer gave a shout as an arrow pierced his upper arm and fell back. Meanwhile, Owain raised his shield to protect himself lest another bowman attempt to fire, but nothing happened.

Rob could see that a man was at the battlements and seemed to be urging the men to fire again, but they were refusing to obey. He watched as Owain turned and rode back to him, a gleam of triumph in his eyes.

'I believe they have something to think about now, Rob.'

'It seems that your informant spoke truly,' Rob said. 'We shall wait here until Henry's men come up with us—but we shall draw up the cannon and fire a few rounds at the gate, just to show them we mean business.'

He went off to speak to the gunners and miners, whose job it was to bring up and prepare the guns for battle. To sit and wait and do nothing was more than he could bear. Melissa was within those walls somewhere—but was she still alive? What had that monster done to her?

Melissa was shivering. At first she was unable to see anything at all and she was terrified. Where was she? She had no recollection of being brought here other than the struggle with those soldiers as they dragged her from her chamber. She had been knocked down and had struck her head. She must have been out of her senses when they brought her here. The terror swept over her for she had never liked the dark and it was the stuff of nightmares to be locked in such a place.

It was cold and damp down here, and she could hear something…a rushing noise like wind or the sea. After a while, she realised that there was a crack of light coming from somewhere above her. As she began to get more used to the dim light she could see that the walls were hewn out of rock, but high above her was a natural crack. It was from there that the small amount of daylight was coming—but to what sort of a place had she been brought?

She began to find her way around the walls so that she stood under the crack, and looked up at it, but it was too small to squeeze through and obviously not the way out or in. Steadying her nerves, she pressed close to the rock face and inched her way 'round, feeling rather than seeing where she was going. Screaming and crying would not help her. She must discover where she was and whether she could find a way to escape. When her hands encountered something flat and protruding, she ran them over it, exploring the width, depth and height, before being certain that it was a step.

Oh, thank God! There was a way out, even if it was barred to her. She had thought that perhaps she had been lowered into a deep cavern and would be left to die. At least if there was an entrance someone might find her and rescue her. If Rob came in time…a sob of fear shook her as she sat on the bottom step and put her hands to her face. It was likely that the castle would not surrender and she might never leave this terrible place alive.

'Oh, God,' Melissa prayed. 'Let my death not be from starvation and cold.'

She knew that she would not be the first to be shut in an oubliette and left to die in that cruel fashion. Yet surely her death could not benefit the marquis. He would surely keep her alive if only to use her as a pawn in the game he played.

A renewal of hope came with the thought, and she stood up, determined to climb the steps to the top and discover what was there. She was halfway up when she heard a grating noise above her, and then there was light. A man's face appeared in the opening.

'Are you there, lady?'

'Yes,' Melissa cried. 'Have you come to let me out?'

'I dare not for he would have me hung,' Geoffrey of Brampton answered. 'I have brought food, water and a blanket. It is not much but all I could manage this time. I shall come again when I can. Take the basket as it comes down to you.'

Melissa could just about see the dark shape of an object coming towards her. She reached out for it, clutching it to her, her throat tight with emotion. At least someone knew where she was—and that someone was disposed to be kind to her.

'Thank you, sir,' she called. 'If you could get me out of this place I would see that you were rewarded.' She did not know whether he could still hear her or not, but she called again. 'Please bring me a candle next time for I do not like the dark…' The light was withdrawn and she could hear a grating being slid back into place

No reply came and she thought that he had not heard her. The blackness seemed complete again as she began the descent and, afraid to take a false step in the dark, she sat on the steps and lowered herself carefully one by one. Reaching the bottom, she sat on it and felt for the contents of her basket. On the top was folded a thin blanket. It would not keep her warm here, but it was better than nothing, and she wrapped it around her shoulders. Her searching fingers found a water bottle next and part of a loaf of bread, which when she tasted it was coarse and hard, but at least it was food. She sought for something more and to her joy found a candle and a tinder.

Almost weeping with relief, Melissa struck the tinder and lit the wick of the tallow candle. It was only a piece of one and would not last long, but it allowed her to see her surroundings. She was in a small cell of an uneven shape that looked as if it had occurred naturally rather than been built by human hand, and she believed she was actually inside the rock on which the castle was built—which meant that she must be near the sea. Perhaps that accounted for the cold and the damp in here. She shivered, glad of the thin blanket that had covered the food.

She decided that she would leave the basket at the top of the steps, for she could see her way clearly now that she had the candle, and there might be rats in a place like this. The thought sent shivers down her spine, but she conquered her fear. She carried the candle carefully to the top step and looked up at the grating above her. It must open into the dungeons of the castle, but there was no light and it was too far above her to reach. Someone must have either lowered her down into the oubliette or climbed down a ladder of some kind, which was then withdrawn.

She understood that there was no way of escaping. Anyone who was brought here died, unless the lord relented and allowed them to be brought out while still alive.

She thought that Geoffrey of Brampton had risked much for her sake by bringing her food and the blanket—so that might mean that the marquis had intended to leave her here to starve. It seemed that her survival lay in one man's hands, at least until Rob came for her.

'Oh, please come soon, my love,' she whispered as she

walked back down the steps to the bottom. 'Come soon for I do not know how I shall bear it if no one comes to help me.' He would come for her, he must! She was his wife and he would take her back for pride's sake if nothing else. She must not lose faith in him for if she did she might as well die.

She sat down and ate half of the bread, taking several sips of water, though she left some for later. She rather thought that the daylight had faded, which meant that she had only her small candle to light the darkness. If she used all of it at once, she might be in darkness for hours. She steeled her nerves and blew it out, keeping the basket close to her as she sat on the bottom step, the blanket around her, huddling her knees to her chest.

She would try to ration the light so that she could see when she needed to, and perhaps she might even sleep if she rested her head against the wall. She closed her eyes, willing herself to think only of good things.

Rob cared for her in his own way. He would come for her— and they would be together again. If Geoffrey of Brampton continued to bring her a little food she could survive. She would survive until Rob came for her!

Rob lay on the hard ground, his head on a folded blanket, another over him. His trusty sword was at his side beneath the blanket, because in times like these it was best always to be ready. He had slept only for a short time and fitfully, for his mind would not let him rest. He sensed that Melissa was suffering, though he knew not how or why, but he felt it as a physical pain inside.

'Damn his soul to hell!'

Rob threw off the blanket and got to his feet. There was no sense in trying to sleep for he knew that he would not. He had delayed his attack, because he knew that Owain was right. It would take more than the men he had with him to subdue this castle, and he did not wish to lose lives unnecessarily. It was always best to weaken the opposition, who would receive no supplies of any kind, and would in time starve unless they surrendered.

The castle had its back to the sea and the cliff face was too steep to climb. Leominster could expect no help from the sea. He was surrounded on three sides by open land to the right, a village to the left and the main approach from the front. Rob would make his attack on two sides when the King's reinforcements came up, and he did not think it could be long delayed now.

For two days they had waited, now and then firing the long guns, which directed heavy iron balls at the gates. So far they stood against the heavy battering they had received, though seemed to be considerably weakened. Rob knew that a deter- mined charge with the battering ram could break them, but first they would have to bring up a bridge to cross the steep ditch that was the first line of defence, and which contained black, stinking water.

He walked as far as the cliff edge, gazing out across the sea. It was beginning to get light, the start of their third day outside the walls of the castle. He could wait no longer! If Henry's men did not arrive today, he would throw everything he had against the enemy. If he did not, it might be too late.

'Melissa,' he whispered, his voice hoarse with the grinding ache of his agony. 'I never told you that I loved you. I do not know if you are truly innocent, but God help me, I am nothing without you, my love. If you are dead this life holds nothing more for me.'

'Where are you going—and what have you in that basket?' Geoffrey of Brampton froze as he was challenged. He had waited for nightfall before attempting to visit the dungeons again. It would have been only his second visit for he had been on constant duty at the battlements and dared not leave his post.

'It is only some food,' Geoffrey said. He knew the soldier

who had challenged him. 'Bread and water merely. I have been ordered to take it to a prisoner.'

'Let me look,' the soldier said, and snatched the basket from him. He removed the velvet cloak that Naomi had pressured Geoffrey into bringing, looking at it suspiciously. 'What's this?' He took out a chunk of cheese. 'You know the orders. All food like this is only for the officers. I should report you for stealing from the kitchens.'

'Please don't,' Geoffrey said. 'Take it for yourself. I was given it by someone, but bread alone will do for the prisoner.'

'Is it the woman?'

'Yes…though if he knew my neck would be stretched before morning.'

'Go on then,' the guard said. He broke the cheese in half, replacing half in the basket and covering it with the cloak. 'Poor soul. She will perish in the end, but it is a kind thought. I have not seen you.'

Geoffrey thanked him and went down the narrow, curving stair that led to the dungeons and the torture chamber deep beneath the castle itself. He shivered for he had heard screams coming from here often enough and prayed that he would not feel the torturer's hot irons. There were still some prisoners awaiting their punishment, and he could hear their moans, and cries for help as he passed through with his torch, but he dared not stop to aid them. His mission was to take food and water to the lady and leave as swiftly as possible. He had not wanted to risk visiting the oubliette a second time, but Naomi had promised that she would be his wife if he helped her lady, and he wanted her. Mayhap he was a fool, but he would risk it.

He turned into the dark tunnel that led even farther down into the bowels of the earth, carrying his torch aloft for there was a trap for the unwary. To the right at the end of this tunnel was a crossways, and to turn the wrong way in the dark would lead to certain death for there was a steep drop down the face of the cliff at the end of that tunnel.

At the end of the left tunnel was a wall of rock and at the base was the grating, which was the only way into the oubliette. It was opened by means of a sliding mechanism and the steps below were reached by using an iron ladder that was secured to the rock face. Some prisoners were merely tossed into the cell and died of their injuries, but Geoffrey and Jack had carried the lady down between them. It was too dangerous for one man to attempt it alone. He slid the grating back and knelt down to peer into the darkness, holding his torch.

'Are you there, lady?' he called.

'Yes, I am here,' Melissa's voice replied. 'I feared that you would not come again, sir. Please help me. I do not know how long I can survive this torture.'

'Naomi has sent your cloak,' Geoffrey called to her. 'There is a small piece of cheese and a loaf of bread and two candles. Take the basket and I will come again when I can.'

'Will you not help me to escape?' Melissa asked, a sob in her voice for she had spent one whole night in darkness. 'For pity's sake, help me, sir. I beg you not to leave me here alone again.'

'Forgive me, I dare not,' Geoffrey said, and slid the grating across. 'Keep faith, lady. Your lord is at the gates and there is talk of mutiny inside the castle. In a few days we may be forced to surrender. I shall come again.'

He turned away, his conscience nagging at him. If she were brave enough to help herself, he might have brought her up. It would not have been easy to hide her, but with Naomi's help he might have managed it. He thought that he would talk to Naomi. Perhaps together they could work out how to get the lady out of her prison. He knew that at least half of the men were resentful of their situation. Some spoke openly of a mutiny, though others were too afraid of the consequences if they failed.

Yes, he would return and speak to Naomi, he decided as he neared the end of the tunnel leading to the torture chamber. If she agreed that it was worth the risk they would get help and then he would go down and help the lady climb to freedom.

It was as he stepped out into the open space that housed both dungeons on one side and the torture chamber on the other that they jumped on him. Four armed men, catching him by the arms as he struggled and fought them.

'What are you doing?' he demanded, for he knew them all and thought of them as his friends. 'Let me go. I do no harm. Will of Amlea, would you betray a friend?'

'It was your own fault. You have been taking food to the lady,' one of them said. 'The marquis has given orders that you be taken and kept under guard until he has time to decide what your fate should be.'

'He is a monster and would leave the poor lady to starve,' Geoffrey said. 'We should fight against his tyranny and open the gates to the King's emissary. It will go hard with all of us if we do not.'

'Be quiet, fool,' Will Amlea said. 'If the wrong ears hear you we shall all be dead. If we had not come ourselves, you might have found yourself a prisoner here. At least you will sleep in the guardroom instead of the dungeons this night.'

'You know I am right,' Geoffrey said, looking at their faces. 'I have served the marquis faithfully, though sometimes what he forced us to do turned my stomach—but this is more than any decent man can take. To leave a woman of gentle birth in a place like that is evil....'

'You speak truly but it is dangerous to listen,' one of the men said. 'We can do nothing for her until he is forced to surrender.'

'And who is brave enough to stand up to him?' Will asked. He looked at his friends. 'I will stand if you will come with me.'

They murmured together for a moment, and then one nodded his head. 'I will stand with you—but we are not enough.

We must ask others to join us. If twenty agree, then we can take him and open the gates.'

'Forget your duty. You could not find me,' Geoffrey said. 'I shall talk to Naomi. She knows several of the servants who are ready to rebel. If we gather enough, we may take him while he sleeps.'

'Aye, we're with you,' the men agreed. 'If you can bring in others, we shall join you.'

Melissa rested on the bottom step, her head against the wall. She had put her cloak around her shoulders and was sitting on the folded blanket, because the chill of the stone had seeped into her and she was shivering. During the first night, she had explored her prison with her candle, discovering the bones of more than one poor wretch who had died in this terrible place.

She had screamed with fright when she realised what she was looking at, but then she realised that she had nothing to fear from the dead. They had suffered even as she was suffering now, and she felt that their spirits were close, comforting her.

'We had no friends to help us,' they seemed to say. 'You are luckier.'

Could she really hear their voices and feel their spirits or was she losing all sense of reality? Melissa knew that she could not bear the darkness much longer, and she was using her candles recklessly. Her head ached and her feet felt as if they were frozen. It was so very cold and she was hungry. She had eaten all the food from her basket and the coarse bread lay uneasily on her stomach, making her feel queasy.

She felt the tears begin to trickle down her cheeks, but she dashed them away impatiently. Feeling sorry for herself would not help. She must be patient and not give way to despair. Her only hope was that Geoffrey of Brampton would return—and that next time he would help her to leave this place. If he did not come soon, she thought that she might indeed lose her mind.

'Rob, my darling,' she wept. 'Please, please come for me. I need you so. I need you so.'

During the hours of darkness the only thought that had sustained her was that her husband would not rest until he found her. She knew that he cared for her, desired her as his wife, and for a moment she smiled as she remembered the sweetness of his loving, the touch of his hands.

'I love you, Robert of Melford,' she said, lifting her tear-stained face. 'You will come for me. I know that you will come for me…' It seemed to her then that she heard something…like the pounding of the sea or the roll of thunder.

Pray God, it was the guns of Rob's army!

Rob told the men to take their positions for battle. They had a bridge that would hold the battering ram as it was brought against the gates, and the first move was to bring that up to the castle under covering shields that would protect the engineers from the arrows and iron bolts of the defenders. Rob's engines of war had been pounding the walls for an hour and now it was time to go forward, for though the wall was not yet breached it had begun to show signs of cracks that might bring it down soon enough.

He mounted his horse for he intended to be one of the first into the castle when it was finally breached. At that moment, he saw a man riding hard towards him, and hesitated waiting for his scurryer to come up with him.

'What news?' he demanded. 'Have you seen Henry's army?'

'Yes, sir. He comes now and will be with you within thirty minutes at most.'

Rob gave a great shout of joy for he knew that once the reinforcements reached them they would win the day. Leominster could not fight the overwhelming odds that would now be ranged against him. He held up his arm giving the signal for the great machines of war to move forward, his knights and foot soldiers lining up to make the charge that would distract the archers while the bridge was secured and the battering ram brought into play.

It was as they rode towards the castle that they saw the white flag hoisted above the battlements. Rob stared at it in disbelief for he had not expected the surrender until the walls had been breached and Henry's men came up to reinforce them. However, even as the bridge and battering ram was brought up to the moat, the drawbridge came down with a rattle and fell into position, almost as though the ropes that held it had been hacked through with a sword rather than let down as normal.

Now some of the men and women were coming out, a crowd of them about forty strong, cheering and carrying sheets or shirts, anything white that they had been able to lay their hands on. It was mostly village folk who had been caught inside while at their work, and now came running, eager to surrender and pledge their loyalty to the new king.

They cried out to Rob that they had never wished to resist, begging for clemency. He waved them on, letting them pour down the hill towards their homes. Calling to some of his knights, he rode towards the bridge, still wary for there had been no official surrender from Leominster himself and this might be a trap. However, as he rode across the bridge, he saw that one of the officers had drawn the soldiers up into a neat formation. None of them were wearing arms. Their leader came to meet Rob, his sword laid across his hands as a sign that he was willing to surrender it.

'The castle is yours, Robert of Melford,' he said. 'The Marquis of Leominster has been confined in the guardroom and we have taken charge of his men-at arms. Those who would not agree to the surrender are locked in with him, though now that it is over I believe most will be willing to swear an oath of fealty.'

'And you are?'

'My name is Will of Amlea,' the soldier said. 'I am a free-man and gave my service to Leominster as my overlord—but he has become a monster and I shall serve him no more. I will serve you if you wish it, Robert of Melford.'

'Thank you. You may keep your sword and speak to me of this again later,' Rob said. He looked about him, raising his voice so that all might hear. 'There will be no bloodshed un-less a sword is raised in treachery against us. The King follows close on our heels and he will deal with your master. This castle and the manor of Leominster is hereby declared the property of King Henry VII of England. Let no man attempt to succour the traitor, Leominster, on pain of death.'

Dismounting, he looked at the man who had offered the sur-render, for it was clear that the others had deferred to him. 'Take me to Leominster himself,' he said. 'I wish to speak to him.'

'Yes, sir,' the man said. 'Please follow me. You need not fear that this is a trap. Many of us wished to surrender from the start, but we were not brave enough to defy him. But what he did to the lady was so evil that it turned our stomachs...'

'He has harmed Melissa?' Rob's hand went to his sword. 'Is she dead?'

'I do not know, sir,' Will of Amlea replied. 'She has been im-prisoned in the oubliette and few return from there. Only one or two of the men here know the whereabouts of that dread place.'

'But someone must have put her there!' Rob glared at him, a red mist forming before his eyes. 'What kind of a monster would do that to a gentle, sweet woman? Tell me, where is she?'

'I do not know exactly,' Will said, and looked uncomfortable. 'Two men took her there, that is true. One of them died last night as we seized the marquis and made him a prisoner—and the other is badly wounded. I am not sure who else knows the way, though I can guide you to the tunnel that leads to her prison.'

'Then, take me,' Rob said. 'Leominster can wait.'

'But there is a trap,' Will told him. 'It may be best if you speak with the marquis first, sir. One way is false and leads to certain death.'

'Then, I shall see Leominster first,' Rob said. He was chaffing with impatience for every minute that Melissa spent in such a terrible place might be her last. He knew how she must be suffering for it was the punishment given only to those who were intended to die; forgotten and abandoned, it was a cruel, evil torture for death often came too slowly in these hidden places.

Following Will of Amlea to the guardroom, Rob's mind was enduring a mental torture the equal of anything that Melissa had felt in her cell. Was she still alive? Or had she been thrown down into a hole to die like a rat? The pictures crowded in on him, searing him like hot irons as he felt the pain she must be enduring.

Several men were locked into the guardroom. He could hear their shouts as he approached and his heart hardened. These were the men that had stood with the marquis until the last. He would not grant them their freedom. They could wait until the King came and be judged as the traitors they were.

'Forgive us, sir,' several voices cried out. 'We feared our master and would beg to be allowed to surrender to you and the King.'

'Keep your excuses until the King comes,' Rob said, his expression one of anger and bitterness. 'Where is Leominster? Bring him out!'

There was some jostling and shouting, and then a man was pushed forward to the front of those crammed into a small space. Some of them jeered at him, and Rob knew that they must have suffered from his injustice times enough to hate him.

'Release me at once,' the marquis demanded of Rob. He was angry and humiliated, his thick lips curled in a snarl as he gripped the bars of his cell. 'I shall know how to deal with the turncoats who put me here.'

'You will answer to the King,' Rob said. 'I neither know nor care what becomes of you.'

'Then you will never see your wife again,' Leominster said

with a cruel leer. 'She may yet live. I am not sure how long it takes a woman to die of starvation, but it will be slow and painful.'

'Damn you!' Rob grabbed him by the throat through the bars, his hands tightening sufficiently to make Leominster gasp and choke before he was released. 'I'll see you put to the irons if you force me. You will see hell before she does! Tell me where she is or I'll kill you myself.'

Leominster put his hand to his throat, his eyes narrowed and cold. 'You will pay for that when Henry grants me leniency. As for that bitch you wed when she was promised to me—she may die for all I care. I'll not tell you where she is though you put me to the rack.'

'Damn you to hell!'

Rob drew his sword, but he felt a touch at his elbow and turned to look at Owain. 'You gave your promise, Rob. Besides, a woman who claims she served Melissa wishes to speak with you. She says that she may know where you can find Melissa.'

'No woman knows the secret,' Leominster sneered. 'But run to your death, Melford. I shall lay no flowers on your grave.'

Rob turned his gaze on him. 'If she is dead you will not see the morning,' he said, and turned away, following Owain outside.

The woman waiting there came forward, making a curtsey. 'I pray you find my lady before she dies,' Naomi said. 'My man took her food and water, but he is lying wounded and cannot aid you. Last night when they brought him to me, he said that you must not turn right at the crossways for it is certain death in the darkness....'

'Will of Amlea spoke of a trap,' Rob said, and nodded his head. He looked about him seeking and finding the man he needed. 'Come, Owain, the men can deal with this and Henry will be here soon. We must find her before it is too late. You—Will of Amlea—lead me to her.'

Will inclined his head but looked doubtful. 'He told you nothing. I can lead you to the tunnel but it may be dangerous.'

'Take me there and I ask no more,' Rob said. 'But it must be soon.'

'Come with me, sir. She is imprisoned in the bowels of the earth. Below the castle there is a tunnel and at the end of it a natural chamber that may be entered only from above. There is no light in the tunnel and one way lies the sea and a sheer drop. I have never been beyond the torture chamber and the dungeons. But I can show you the entrance.'

'Then lead me there and I shall find her,' Rob said. He glanced at Owain. 'You are with me?'

'Always, my friend,' Owain replied. 'I guard your back as I have in battle for though we have had fair words from most here, I trust few.'

They followed Will into the main body of the castle, passing through the great hall to a room at the rear. Will pulled aside a tapestry, revealing a door. It opened when he pulled a lever in the wall, and he stood back for Rob to enter.

'You go ahead of us with this torch,' Rob said, taking one from the iron bracket on the wall. 'Lead the way down, sir.'

'Yes, sir, to the tunnel,' Will agreed. 'But from there I have no knowledge which way is safe.'

'Leave that to me. I will lead then and you will follow, Owain in between us.'

Will bowed his head. Robert of Melford was no fool. In this instance he had no need to fear treachery for Will of Amlea was a man of his word. He would not go back on it or hinder their progress, though he would not wish to blunder on in the dark without a hint of where they were going.

They walked down the narrow stone stairway that led to the dungeons and the torture chamber. Seeing that there were prisoners and that a bunch of keys hung on the wall, Rob took them down and gave them to Owain, bidding him to set the poor devils free.

'The King comes and you are pardoned in his name,' he

called out. 'Go from here and do no wrong to any man and you will not be harmed.'

'God bless you, sir,' one of them cried. 'If you seek the lady you must hurry for it is four days since she was brought here and she may not live much longer in that cursed place.'

Rob needed no urging. Will was standing at the entrance to a tunnel. He went ahead of him, holding another torch to light their way. It was dark and narrow and the smell was foetid, the walls damp to the touch. He could see that they were coming to a crossways and he turned to the left without hesitation, stopping to glance back as he sensed that the man behind had hesitated.

'Are you sure this is the right way?' Will asked, looking uneasy. 'Be careful as you go for there could be a sheer drop before you know you are upon it.'

'This is the way, for Naomi told me that her man had imparted the information to her while he was still conscious. I trust her— she had no need to tell me unless she wished to help my lady.'

'It was Geoffrey of Brampton who brought food here,' Will said. 'If it were not for him we might never have risen against the marquis—but it was either see him hang or do as he begged us.'

'If he lives he shall be rewarded and his woman with him,' Rob said. He stopped as he saw that the tunnel ended in a solid wall. 'Damn it! Have we taken a wrong turn? Should it have been the other way after all?'

'It must be here,' Will said, and brought his torch forward. They both saw the grating at the same moment. 'Down there! See, there is a lever on the wall, sir—and an iron ladder. Fix your torch in this bracket and see if you can move it….'

Rob did as he suggested, pulling on the lever. The grating began to slide across, but stuck halfway, the metal rusty and ancient. He bent down and pulled at it with his bare hands, shifting it little by little until it was wide-open.

'Hold your torch so that I see down,' Rob instructed. 'Melissa—are you there?' He waited but there was only silence.

'Melissa! Answer me if you can. It is Rob. I am here at last, my love.'

This time he thought he heard a slight moan. It was obvious that though he might be able to jump to the first step, he could not get back without some form of help. Glancing about him, he saw that an iron ladder was bracketed to the wall, and realised that it was the only way down and out. Dare he go down and leave Will here alone? He hesitated but then he heard voices and he saw that Owain had come, two of the released prisoners following.

'I have to put this ladder through the opening and climb down there,' he said. 'I need someone to hold the ladder and I may need help to get her up.'

'I'll come with you,' Owain said, but Rob shook his head. He looked at one of the prisoners. 'You there—by what name are you called?'

'John of Leominster,' the man replied. 'I am cousin to the marquis but he feared I coveted his lands and he imprisoned me two months since, because he knew that I supported Henry Tudor. I will willingly help you with the lady, sir.'

'I shall go down first and see if she is there,' Rob said. 'When I am on the bottom rung, hand me down a torch so that I may see where she is—if she is here.' As if in answer to his words, there was a moaning sound. Rob put the ladder in place while Will and Owain held it steady at the top, making sure that it could not fall while he was on it.

He took the torch while he could still reach, and then turned to look about him. Seeing a huddled figure lying at the bottom of the steps, he gave a cry and went quickly down to her, turning her so that he could look at her face. She was clearly ill, and her skin felt damp and cold to his touch. Feeling the icy chill of the cell, he shivered.

'It is a wonder that she survives in this place,' he said. 'But she still lives. Come down and help me carry her up the ladder, John. She is not heavy but it will be easier with the two of us. I do not wish to risk injuring her.'

'I am still strong enough to help her,' John of Leominster said. 'I had friends who brought food for me, though had my cousin had his way I should have been dead. The only reason he did not put me here is that he feared my friends might take up arms against him if they learned that he had had me murdered.'

Rob lifted Melissa in his arms. 'Wait near the top of the ladder,' he instructed. 'I shall hand her up to you and the others may help you to lift her out of this cursed place.' There was a note of anger in his voice for what he had seen had enraged him further. 'I swear that that devil shall pay for this! Only a monster would have done this to a gentle lady.'

'You have my support,' John of Leominster said. 'My cousin knew that I would have joined Henry Tudor had he not imprisoned me, and taken half the village with me I daresay. Some of his men would have joined me, too, for he is hated and feared by most.'

'They rebelled against him or we might still be at the gates,' Rob said. 'Take care now, John. Do not let her head bang against the iron grating as you draw her through. I would not have her suffer more than she already has.'

'Trust me, I have her securely.'

'We have her now.' Owain's voice came down to him. 'She is safe, Rob. Come up yourselves. We shall form a sling to carry her through the tunnel, using her cloak and this blanket. She is breathing still, though very pale. Pray God, that she will recover once we have her in her chamber.'

Rob came up after the others. Owain and some of the other men had gone ahead, carrying their precious burden through the tunnel. He looked down at the oubliette and shuddered.

'There are the bones of others less fortunate lying there,' he said to Will. 'You should form a working party to bring them up so that they may be decently buried by the priest—and then this tunnel is to be blocked up. No one must ever come here again.'

'You are right,' Will replied, and shuddered. 'I shall have it seen to immediately. Once the remains are removed, the tunnel will be bricked in so that no one can ever be shut up down here in the future.'

'Yes, that is the best,' Rob agreed. 'To use gunpowder might cause damage to the structure of the castle and bring it down upon our heads. Brick it up and mark it with the sign of the devil so that no one is ever tempted to open it.'

They followed the others through the tunnel to the chamber that had housed the torture chamber and dungeons. Rob took Melissa into his arms again now that their path was clear. He looked down at her pale face, fearing the worst for she had not murmured since he brought her out of the cell, but her eyelids flickered and he knew that she was still alive.

'Lead the way,' he said. 'I must get my lady to a physician for she needs attention or she will surely die....'

Chapter Eight

'I fear she is very ill, sir,' the physician said to Rob after he had examined her. 'She has taken a virulent fever and is like to die. I am not sure that I can save her. Perhaps hot coals to her forehead or the leeches…' the man broke off as he saw Rob's expression. 'To cool the bad humours in her blood, my lord. It is a recognised cure…'

'Damn you,' Rob muttered angrily. 'You are nothing but a fool, sir. Get out of my sight for I shall not answer for my actions if I see your face again.' He went to sit by Melissa's side as the man left hurriedly, bending over her to stroke the damp hair from her forehead. She had been so cold when they first brought her here, but now she was burning up with fever. 'You must not die, my love,' he said hoarsely. 'Do not condemn me to a life alone, Melissa, for I shall never love another.' There was no sign that she had even heard him and he got to his feet as the door opened behind him and Naomi came in.

'How is she, sir?'

'No better. That fool of a physician said she was like to die. I sent him away. My father said they were all knaves and he was right. I wish that Megan were here! I know that she would help her.'

'I believe that I can help her if you will trust me, sir,' Naomi said. 'You have no reason to believe me for it was my Geoffrey that helped take your lady to that dread place. He knew that it was wrong, but like others he feared to disobey his lord.'

'I believe he took her food, water and a blanket—your doing I suspect?'

'I could not bear to think of her there,' Naomi said. 'If you will forgive him for the wickedness he has done, I shall do all that I can to save her.' She looked at Melissa as she threw out her hand and moaned.

'Has he recovered from his wound?'

'He will have pain for some time yet,' Naomi said. 'But I put the hot irons to his wound and it will heal, and I have given him something to cure his fever. Now I would help my lady— if you will permit it.'

Rob hesitated for a moment. He wished that Megan were here for he knew that he could trust her, but Naomi seemed honest and he had no choice.

'I shall leave you to tend her then,' he said reluctantly. 'But I shall return soon and sit with her. I cannot be by her side all the time for there is work I must do—but I shall come as often as I can.'

'I shall tend her and my young sister Rosalie will help me, sir. I swear on all that I hold dear that I will never harm her.'

Rob inclined his head. 'I shall trust you because I must,' he said.

'I understand your doubts, sir, but you may take my life if I fail you.' Naomi stood proudly before him, her gaze unflinching.

Rob smiled wryly. 'I am a fool, forgive me. I shall leave her in your hands.'

Naomi smiled and took her bowl and pitcher to the trestle table that stood opposite the bed, setting them down while she prepared the mixture that she hoped would ease her lady's fever.

Melissa was tossing and turning in her fever as Naomi approached the bed. She suddenly opened her eyes and sat up, staring in front of her.

'He comes…' she cried, and gave a cry of terror. 'The winged monster comes for me…'

'Nay, sweet lady,' Naomi soothed her. Melissa had fallen back against the pillows, her brow bathed in sweat. Naomi wiped it away with a cool cloth, smoothing the perspiration from her neck and shoulders and her arms. Then she lifted her a little with one arm, holding a pewter cup to her lips, the liquid dark and thick as it trickled into her mouth. 'Drink, my lady. 'Tis bitter but it will help you.'

'Thirsty…' Melissa moaned, and swallowed as the cup was tipped against her lips so that a good measure of the cure went down her throat. She pulled a face at the bitter taste, but after a few moments it seemed to calm her.

'That is good,' Naomi said, and smiled as she lay Melissa back against the pillows. 'Rest for a little now, lady, and then Rosalie and I will bathe you and make you comfortable.'

She smiled as the door opened and a young girl came in carrying a jug of warm water. She set it down on the trestle and stand, coming to the bed to look down at Melissa with pity in her eyes.

'Is she very ill, Naomi?'

'Yes, I fear she is, sister.'

'Can you cure her?'

'You know that I can, as long as I am not questioned. I have never dared to use all my arts in this place for I feared to be taken and hanged as a witch, but it is different now. I think Robert of Melford trusts me—and as long as he does not interfere I shall save her. But everything must be done in the right way, the leaves and berries gathered at a certain hour. The healing arts are not just in the cures themselves, but in the words that must be said as they are prepared and administered. It is to God that my prayers are given, but some believe that the words I use invoke the devil.'

Naomi's art had been taught to her by her father, who had

studied medicine in the great universities of Florence, Milan and France and had been a skilled physician, welcomed at the courts of foreign princes. Yet she knew that his methods were frowned on by the new school of thought that believed the use of religion in medicine to be blasphemous.

'You know that I shall not betray you,' Rosalie said, looking anxiously at her sister. 'I do not have your skills, Naomi, but I believe in you. I have seen you cure others that the doctors said would die.'

Naomi smiled at her. 'Then between us we shall nurse my lady back to health again, but you must swear never to reveal my secrets to another soul.'

Rob sat by Melissa's bed. For three days and nights the fever had raged and it seemed as if nothing would abate it. He knew that Naomi was using all her arts to help Melissa, but he was afraid that it would not be enough. He leaned forward, stroking her cheek, the tears trickling silently down his cheeks.

'If you die I do not know what I shall do,' he whispered. 'It is not seemly for a man to weep and beg, Melissa—but I love you too much, my darling. I shall have no wish to live if you leave me.'

Melissa's eyelids fluttered. She moaned and moved her hand on the bedcovers, as if searching for something. Rob took her hand and held it, then carried it to his lips, kissing it, his expression tortured as he felt the frustration surge in him.

'I beg you not to die,' he said, his voice breaking on a sob. 'My darling, do not leave me. Please do not die…'

'Rob…' It was a mere whisper, barely audible but he heard it and leaned closer.

'Melissa…' he said hoarsely. 'I am here. I am with you, my dearest love.'

'Water…' she said. 'Thirsty…'

Rob got up and went over to the jug standing on a coffer in the corner. He poured some water into a cup and brought it back to her, standing by her and slipping an arm beneath her as he lifted her, making it easier for her to drink. She took a few sips and lay back. Seeing that she was lying awkwardly, Rob lifted her while he rearranged her pillows. As he did so, a small pouch was dislodged and fell to the floor. He bent to pick it up, noticing that it had a pungent smell. He settled Melissa and walked away to look at the pouch more closely in the light of the candle. As he did so, the door opened and Naomi came in. She saw at once that he had found the charm she had placed beneath Melissa's pillows.

'It aids her sleep,' Naomi told him. 'She was dreaming of the monster that came on wings to carry her down to Hades. Since I placed the charm beneath her pillow she no longer cries out in fear.'

Rob's eyes narrowed as he looked at her. Naomi was a pretty woman, a little plump for his taste, but comely. 'Are you a witch?' he asked, and smiled as he saw the fear leap into her eyes. 'No, do not fear me, Naomi. Megan is a wise woman and some would name her a witch, but she has helped us many times. I know that there are many things that we do not understand, and if you have the magic arts you use them for good not evil.'

'I have been called a witch,' Naomi said. She faced him proudly, though her heart was hammering for she knew that if he condemned her she would die by the rope. 'I use my arts to help but only those who give their permission, for I know what my fate would be should I be suspected of witchcraft. I should be hung and then burned—perhaps before I was truly dead.'

'It is a wicked practice,' Rob said, 'for many an innocent woman has been sent to a cruel fate for doing nothing but trying to help others. You may rest easy, lady. I shall not betray you—unless you harm my wife. I should show no mercy then…'

She broke off as they heard a cry from the bed.

'He comes…the monster comes…' Melissa moaned and

sat up, her eyes wide and staring but not seeing them. 'He comes for me…'

Naomi took the pouch from Rob and went to the bed, placing it under Melissa's pillow. She stroked her forehead, crooning something that Rob could not understand for it was in a tongue he had never heard before. As he watched, the fear left Melissa's face and she fell back to her pillows again, seeming to rest more easily.

'I believe the fever is waning,' Naomi said as she turned to him once more. 'If I am right she will be better by morning.'

'I shall thank God for it,' he said. 'And you, Naomi, for I think that without your care she would have died.'

'Leave her to me now, sir,' Naomi said. 'There are things I must do for her—and I believe you have much to occupy you here.'

'Yes, you are right,' Rob agreed. 'Before the King moved on, he bid me secure the castle. He has taken it and all the manor lands for himself, but he appoints John of Leominster, the marquis's cousin, now steward here, to run it in his absence. I am to return to London as soon as Melissa is well, for he wishes to speak to both of us again.'

Rob inclined his head to her and turned to leave. He knew that the Marquis of Leominster had been sent to the Tower in chains to await his fate, which, despite his pleas, would probably be death by the axe. Rob could not find it in his heart to feel pity for the man after his cruelty to Melissa. Indeed, only the King's arrival had stayed his hand, for after Rob had seen how ill she had been treated, he had wanted to kill Leominster with his bare hands.

Henry had taken charge once he arrived. Some men had been hanged, others allowed to swear fealty to him as King. Some of the men of Gifford and of Leominster had asked to follow Rob; others were to return to their homes, which would now be passed to new owners. For though the King had seized both Leominster and Gifford, he might give them as a gift to one of the nobles that had served him well. The favours cost him little personally and would help to secure the loyalty of those he gathered about him, and he would need that in the coming months. England would need a steady hand at the helm if the civil wars that had raged these past years, tearing the country apart, were to end.

Rob had been promised new honours when he next saw the King, for Henry would be crowned soon enough. Rob was summoned to bring Melissa and attend the coronation, and only then would he be allowed to return home with his wife.

Henry had frowned when Rob told him that he had married Melissa, for in truth he had had no right, except that of conquest. However, once her story was made known to him, Henry had wished him well. Perhaps because he too had taken what he wanted by force.

'You have served me faithfully, Robert of Melford,' he said. 'Bring your wife to me in London and we shall see…'

Rob had watched Henry ride away. He would keep his promise to attend the coronation. He prayed that Melissa would have recovered and be well enough to accompany him by then.

Melissa opened her eyes and gave a little moan as she felt the pain at the back of her head. Her head was aching terribly and she felt so very thirsty; it was strange but the light seemed to hurt her eyes at first and it was several minutes before she could accustom herself to it.

'My lady, you are awake at last,' Naomi said, and bent over her, laying a hand on her forehead. She smiled because it was cool and dry. 'It seems that the fever has left you. Your husband will be pleased when he comes to see you.'

Melissa frowned for her thoughts were confused and she could not think clearly. 'My husband? I do not remember…' She sighed. 'My head aches so much.…'

'It is because of what happened to you,' Naomi said. She fetched a cup of wine mixed with herbs, holding it to Melissa's lips. 'Sip a little of this, my lady. It will ease your headache and in time you will remember—though perhaps it might be best if you did not remember all of what has happened.'

'Have I been ill?' Melissa pushed herself up against the pillows. The effort was almost too much for her and she closed her eyes, feeling weary. 'What happened to me?'

'You have had a fever,' Naomi told her. 'Your husband brought you to me and I have nursed you. He comes every day and every night to spend time with you, but he has much to do for he is charged with securing the castle before he leaves.'

'The castle…' Melissa wrinkled her brow for there was a strange blackness in her mind and she did not know where she was. 'Am I married to the Marquis of Leominster?'

'No, lady,' Naomi said. 'He was the monster who hurt you so. Your husband is Robert of Melford—do you not recall that you married him before you were snatched from Gifford and brought here?'

'Rob…' A little smile touched her mouth for she remembered that she loved him, but she had no memory of having wed him. 'Am I truly his wife? I remember that we rode together on his horse through the forest and he held my hand as I walked in the stream…' She looked at Naomi in wonder. 'I remember that we pledged ourselves one to the other…but my father made me send him away. I cannot remember our wedding…' She looked at Naomi. 'I seem to remember that my father sent me to be married to the Marquis of Leominster…'

'You were married to Robert of Melford at Gifford,' Naomi said. 'When they brought you here, you begged me to help you escape but I dared not. And then…' Naomi faltered for she did not know whether she ought to tell Melissa that she had been imprisoned in the oubliette. If her mind was shutting out the terrible memory, it might be that she would not be able to bear the truth. 'It was the Marquis of Leominster who had you snatched from your kinsman's home and brought here—and it was he who made you ill.'

'I see…' Melissa frowned. She was beginning to remember snatches of things but there were dark patches in her mind and she was frightened to examine them. 'You are sure that I am married to Robert of Melford?'

'Yes, my lady. Quite sure.'

'Then I am content,' Melissa said, and closed her eyes. She seemed to fall into a deep sleep almost at once.

Naomi looked at her in concern. She had not expected this and it made her anxious. It was true that she had hoped her lady would forget the terrible experience of being shut in the oubliette, but she had not thought that she would forget her marriage. Robert of Melford might be angry with her for he might blame her for his wife's loss of memory.

Rob stood looking down at Melissa as she slept. She had been sleeping for a long time, but Naomi had said that it was good. She needed to sleep because of all that she had suffered. As he watched, the urge to kiss her came to him, and he bent down, brushing his lips over hers. She stirred and murmured something, and then she opened her eyes and smiled at him.

'Rob…' she said sleepily. 'You are my husband…'

'Yes, my darling,' he said. 'We were married at Gifford—do you not remember?'

'I am not sure,' she said. 'I remember that day in the forest…and that day in the meadows when we promised to love each other.' She saw the scar and frowned. 'Your poor face…what happened to you?'

'Do you not remember?' he asked. Melissa shook her head, seeming puzzled and anxious. 'It does not matter. It was inflicted on me by an enemy, but he is dead now. All that matters to me is that you should be well again.'

'I am very tired,' she said. 'I have been ill but I do not know why. I suppose I had a fever…please, may I be alone now?'

'You have had a fever, my love,' Rob said. 'Sleep now and

you will feel better soon. When you are well again we are bidden to the King's coronation.'

Melissa nodded. His words seemed to come from a long way off and she was drifting again, drifting into sleep. There was something at the back of her mind that frightened her. She did not want to think about it! She pushed it away, because she knew that if it came to her she would die.

'Yes, go to sleep now, my dearest,' Rob said. 'I shall see you in the morning.'

As he went outside, he met Naomi. She was carrying a clean nightrobe for her mistress and a small flask of dark coloured liquid.

'She does not remember what happened to her in that terrible place,' he said. 'Was that your doing?'

'No, I swear that I have done nothing to erase it from her mind,' Naomi said, a flicker of fear in her face for she could see that he was troubled. 'She is shutting out the pain she cannot face, for she remembers some things and not others— though whether she wishes it so or not I cannot say.'

'She did not recall this,' Rob said, touching the scar on his cheek. 'Does that mean she wants to forget it exists?'

'I do not know these things,' Naomi said. 'My knowledge is of the body not the mind. Forgive me. I cannot tell you what is in her thoughts.'

Rob nodded and walked on. He was not sure whether he believed her or not, and wondered if he had been entirely wise to let Naomi tend Melissa. Naomi had saved Melissa's life—but she seemed subdued, unlike the woman he adored. He prayed that it was not her experience in that cursed place that had changed her, for it would grieve him if her spirit had been broken.

Damn them to hell! He cursed Gifford for stealing her away and Leominster for incarcerating her in that oubliette. Yet there was nothing he could do but wait and hope that his love would return to him. He must be patient and not push his claims for she might shrink from him. He loved and wanted her, but she seemed fragile and tired and he was afraid of causing her more pain.

Perhaps it would be best if he did not visit her too often. She would be better in the company of her women until she was feeling truly well again.

Melissa woke again to see that the sun was filtering through the small window high up in her chamber. It was hazy, seeming to be filled with dust motes that danced and fell, disappearing as they reached the shadows. She sighed and stretched for the shadows were in her mind, hovering like dark-winged monsters waiting to pounce on her if she let herself remember.

She was no longer feeling so very ill. Three days had passed since she first recovered her senses, and she was remembering more all the time. She had not remembered what had happened to Rob's face when she first saw the scar, but since then she had begun to piece things together. There were still gaps in her memory, but she had remembered that it was her half brother who had scarred and nearly killed Rob, though it was her father who had given the order—and he was dead, killed in the battle at Bosworth Field.

She felt nothing for her father. He had never loved her. She could not recall having been truly loved in her life, though the Abbess had been good to her. Something had happened at the Abbey, but Melissa could not remember exactly what. She knew that her aunt had died, but there was more…it was lost with the other frightening things that she had somehow shut out of her mind.

Did Rob truly love her? When he smiled, she thought he did, but she was certain of nothing. She seemed to be trapped in a kind of limbo that made her feel uneasy and nervous. She did not think that she had always been this way. Something had happened…something so terrible that it had brought down a curtain in her mind, leaving her afraid of what lay behind the shadows. She wished that she could remember exactly what had hurt her so much, because then perhaps she could learn not to be afraid, but no one would tell her. Naomi said that she had been very ill and it was best to forget, but she could not help wondering what had made her so ill. Naomi claimed that the Marquis of Leominster was to blame for her illness, but she did not recall ever meeting him.

What were they hiding from her? She would have asked Rob but he seemed to be distant from her. He treated her kindly enough, asking how she felt and if she needed anything—but he did not kiss her or tell her that he loved her. Had they quarrelled? Is that what she was frightened to remember?

Sighing, Melissa pushed back the bedcovers and put her feet to the floor. She wished that she could remember their wedding and what had happened since. Had she been happy until she was snatched away from Gifford? She knew that her feelings for Rob were still tender—but how did he feel about her? If he loved her, why was he keeping his distance from her? It was too difficult, for thinking made her head begin to ache again, and she was afraid of what she might discover if the curtain in her mind came down.

Rob saw Melissa coming down the stone steps that led from the tower that housed her bedchamber. He caught his breath for she looked so beautiful, and yet there was a fragility about her that had never been there before and it caught at his heart, making him almost fear to touch her. He was aware of a sweeping grief, because he could not forget that day in the woods when he had first seen her. She had been so proud, so full of life and confidence. It hurt him to see the hint of fear in her eyes, to know that it was justified after she had been so cruelly treated. She must have lost her trust in men in general—and perhaps in him.

'Are you feeling well enough to come down, my love?' he

asked, going to meet her as she reached the bottom step. 'Naomi said that you had a headache earlier so I did not disturb you.'

'Yes, I did have another headache,' Melissa said, and sighed. He looked so handsome if one did not notice the scar. In her mind he was always as he had been in the forest the day he had rescued her. 'But it has gone now. I am much better, thank you.'

She was so polite, so gentle and there was hesitancy in her when she looked at him. Rob missed the fierce spirit that had been hers, his heart breaking as he saw the questions in her eyes. What was she thinking? Did she wonder if it was he who had hurt her? He had been harsh to her and it would be no wonder if in her confused state, she imagined that he was responsible for what she had suffered. He had considered whether it would be best to tell her the truth, though Naomi thought not. For the moment he had let her have her way. Had she not nursed Melissa so devotedly, his beloved wife would undoubtedly have died.

'Do you think that you could be ready to travel by the end of the week?' Rob asked. 'I am bidden to Henry's coronation. I do not wish to leave you here, Melissa—and the King would speak with you—but if you are not well enough I shall make your excuses.'

'I think that I shall be well enough to come with you,' she replied, a slight frown creasing her brow. 'When shall we go home, Rob? I do not like this place. It frightens me. I do not know why, but when I wake in the dark something…' She shook her head. 'I should be glad to leave here with you.'

'Then we shall leave in three days,' he said. Perhaps it was the shadow of her ordeal here that hung over her. She might begin to recover when they were well away from it. He smiled at her, thinking that she was even lovelier than she had been at the start—but he did miss that sparkle in her eyes. He prayed that it was not gone forever. 'It is pleasant out, Melissa. Would you care to walk with me for a little?'

'Yes, I think I should,' she agreed, and laid her hand on the arm he offered. 'I do not think we have had much time to walk together since we were married.'

'We have had little enough time to know one another,' he replied. 'We shall begin to repair that lack, my lady. Tell me what you liked to do when you were a child—and I shall tell you of my own childhood.'

'Yes, I should enjoy that,' Melissa said. She smiled but her eyes held a sad, faraway look as if she was not really with him. 'I believe that I had a nurse when I was small. She told me stories of my mother…' She frowned as she looked at Rob. 'Is my mother dead? I cannot remember.'

'You were told that she died soon after you were born,' Rob said. 'But your kinswoman, Alanna Davies, told me that she might still be alive—and I believe Owain told you.'

'Yes, I think I remember something…the lily…someone gave Alanna a lily,' Melissa said. 'Owain promised that he would try to find her if she still lives.'

'He stayed with me until he knew that you were safe— but he left us then to travel to the Isle of Ely. He will do all he can to discover if anyone has seen her.'

'That is kind of him,' Melissa said. 'But he has always been kind to me. My father and half brother were not so…' Her eyes came to rest on his face. 'Shall you care for me, sir?'

'Do you not know that I love you?' he asked, and he felt a sharp pain strike him to the heart as he saw the uncertainty in her face. 'I know that I was harsh to you. It took me a long time to forget my bitterness, but when I thought you would die…' He frowned because he was still haunted by his dread of losing her. 'Do you remember nothing of the nights we spent together?'

'Please do not be angry with me,' she said, and her hand trembled a little on his arm. 'I do not remember our wedding, though I know that it happened. I remember riding through a forest on your horse—and that we pledged our love in the meadows, but so much is shrouded by a kind of mist. It hovers but I cannot quite recall it.'

'How could I be angry with you when you have been so ill?' Rob asked softly. 'I want only to make you happy again.'

'I believe I am happy,' she said. 'In my way. I know that I am not as before, but I cannot help myself. Forgive me if I disappoint you, husband.'

'You do not disappoint me,' he said, and took her hand, kissing her fingertips. 'I love you and I want you to be truly well again, Melissa. You know that I would do anything for you, my dearest.'

They were outside now, walking in the courtyard garden behind the castle. Beyond the wall, the sound of waves crashing against the rocks could be heard. Melissa frowned as she heard it for it triggered some memory—something that she did not wish to recall. She shivered suddenly, and felt as if she were suffocating. What lay hidden in her mind that frightened her so?

Rob had promised that he would do anything for her. She wanted to ask him what had made her ill, to tear away the curtain in her mind but she was afraid of what might be revealed.

'Could you send word to my kinswoman Alanna?' she asked. 'I would like to see her—and Rhona. I think there was a woman who served me by that name.'

'Yes, that is so,' he replied. 'I shall send word for them to meet us in London—but is there nothing else you would have of me, Melissa?'

'Nothing for the moment.' She smiled at him. 'The air is pleasant. I am enjoying our walk, sir. I hope that we shall walk together like this when we are at home.'

'Yes, perhaps we shall,' Rob agreed. He longed to sweep her into his arms and kiss her, to love her as he had on the night that she came to him, but he knew that she was not ready for his kisses. 'Perhaps I should tell you about my home, Melissa? I think that you will find it more comfortable than this cursed place.'

'Oh, yes.' A little shiver ran through her. There was something about the castle that frightened her. 'I am sure that I shall. Please, do tell me, Rob. I want to hear all about your home and your family....'

He nodded, smiling as he saw that the colour was returning to her cheeks. It was the shadow of the castle and what had happened here that hung over her. She would be better once they had left it behind. He for one would never wish to return. If he had been free to choose, he would have carried her off to his home at once, but the King had commanded him to be present at his coronation and he could not disobey him.

Melissa looked at Naomi as she prepared to leave that morning. She had been feeling a little better since her talk with Rob three days earlier and was looking forward to riding her palfrey. It would be nice to be out in the open air and away from the castle.

'Are you sure that you do not wish to come with us?' she asked the woman who had cared for her so kindly during her illness. 'I am certain that my husband would find a place for you and your man at his manor.'

'I thank you for the offer, lady, and I shall miss you, but we have decided that we do not wish to move southwards,' Naomi told her. 'Sir Robert has already rewarded me for my service. Geoffrey says that he shall give his allegiance to no master again. He wants to set up his own alehouse and I shall go with him as his wife.'

'Then I shall not press you,' Melissa said. 'But I do thank you for your kindness to me—and this is my gift to you.' She slid a gold ring from her little finger. 'It will serve as a reminder of my friendship if ever you should need me.'

'Thank you, my lady,' Naomi said. 'I think you will be well now. You no longer need my potions to help you sleep. I wish you a long life and happiness with your husband, for he is a good man and will take care of you.'

Melissa thanked her and went downstairs. One of the other

women who had helped to serve her was to accompany them as far as London and then return north to her home, for Melissa hoped that when they arrived, Rhona might be waiting with Alanna Davies.

Rob led her horse forward as she walked out into the courtyard, shivering a little in the cold breeze that had sprung up. He gave her his hand, helping her to mount the sidesaddle, and smiled up at her.

'Are you certain you can manage? You do not wish me to take you up pillion with me?'

'I think I can ride well enough,' she said. 'You must not worry about me, Rob. I am much recovered now. My headaches have almost gone.'

'I am glad to hear it,' he said. It was true that she seemed a little better each day. He had great hopes that once the castle was left behind, she would begin to recover her spirits. He had not yet attempted to make love to her for he did not wish to distress her, and he was not sure that she would welcome him to her bed. He must be patient until she was herself again. 'We shall ride as far as the village of Oxton today, where I have friends and we may stay in comfort for the night at their home. I do not wish to tire you too much, Melissa. We shall travel in easy stages for we have plenty of time. Henry will not be crowned until the end of the month.'

Melissa nodded and smiled. Already she was beginning to feel better as they rode away from the shadow of the great castle. Something had happened to her there. Perhaps she would remember it one day, but until then it hovered at the back of her mind, a dark menace that made her afraid to sleep alone.

She hoped that Rob would come to her chamber when they reached his friends' home. He had hardly visited her in her chamber since the first time that she awoke and saw him there. Melissa did not know why. If he loved her as he claimed, why did he not wish to make love to her? Did he still blame her in his heart for what her half brother had done to him? He spoke of love, but was he only being kind because she had been ill?

She put her troubling doubts from her mind as she rode, Rob just a little in front of her, his men to the front, side and rear. They had still more than seventy men-at-arms and at least another thirty retainers so were a large party, causing the village folk to stare at them as they passed. Some of the women came out to wave and one ran up to Melissa's horse, offering her a bunch of daises picked from her garden.

'God bless you, lady,' she cried out. 'It was you that brought Robert of Melford here and he has been our salvation. The monster that treated you so ill took my son and I never heard of him again. I think he died in some wretched hole beneath the castle. God be praised that you were saved. But you owe your life to your husband, for it was he that saved you.'

'Enough, old woman,' Rob said, and threw her a silver coin. 'Off about your business. My lady wants none of your tales.'

Melissa was shivering. She did not know why, but the old woman's story had sent chills down her spine. She wished that she might have spoken to her for a moment longer, to ask her what she meant, but Rob was clearly impatient to be on his way and she would not cause him more delay. He had lingered long enough for her sake, and they must reach their destination in time for the coronation.

Yet she could not resist looking back at the old woman. What had happened to her son and why had he been left to die in a hole in the ground? It was true that things like that happened to those who angered great lords—especially one with a reputation like the Marquis of Leominster.

A picture of a man's face flashed into Melissa's mind. She could see his fleshy lips and the anger in his eyes as he grabbed hold of her arm, threatening her. A little sob of fear rose to her lips but she crushed it, deliberately bringing down the curtain in her mind. She did not want to remember what came next. She was sure that the man she had pictured was the marquis. She had made him angry and he had punished her, but she did not want to remember what had happened after that…it was a dark shadow at the back of her mind and she meant to banish it.

Rob turned to glance at her, frowning as he saw her expression. 'Take no notice of the old crone,' he said, sounding angry. 'She is probably mad and does not know what she says.'

Was he trying to protect her? Melissa wondered why he did not want her to remember what had happened to her. She was afraid of lifting the curtain in her mind, but she might not have been if Rob had been there to explain what had happened before he came.

Perhaps when they reached Melford he would have more time for her. She wanted to ask him what had really happened to her, because she might be able to face the horror that menaced her if he was there to hold her when the darkness fell.

They stopped that night at a modest manor house in the village of Oxton. It was but a small place on the borders of Sherwood Forest, but there was a fine Norman church and a stream running past the churchyard as far as the Dover Beck half a mile or so to the south.

It seemed they were expected and a plump, smiling woman came out to greet them, welcoming them to her home. Her husband, a tall, thin man with a serious air followed her out and gave orders for the accommodation for the men, most of whom would be sleeping in the barns and stables.

'I am Lady Anne Shearer,' the woman told Melissa, giving her a warm embrace. 'Come in, my dear, for I have heard that you have been ill and must surely be tired of your journey. It is chilly for the month wears on and we shall soon have winter upon us I daresay. Come to the fire. There's mulled wine to warm you and food waiting on the boards.'

Melissa smiled at her, allowing her to usher inside to the

large chamber that was their living room. The house had not been built above a score of years and was a modern, comfortable manor house rather than a draughty fortress. She felt immediately at home, holding her hands to the fire and smiling as the woman fussed over her.

'You are too kind, Lady Anne,' she said. 'I am much better now I promise you.'

'But you still look a little fragile,' the kind woman said. 'Take a seat on the settle by the fire and put this cushion at your back, my dear. I hate to travel, though my husband says that we must go south for Henry Tudor's coronation. I am not sure that I would wish to, for I tell you plainly that I am a Plantagenet at heart, but I suppose he may trace his ancestry back to John of Gaunt.'

'And you are a rattlepate, Anne,' her husband scolded with a smile. 'It will not do to speak that way now. Henry is king whether it pleases you or no—and you may think yourself fortunate our guests are friends or you might find yourself in the Tower.'

'No, I do not think so,' Rob said with a smile for his hostess. He had noticed her kindness to Melissa and would not have her scolded. 'Henry knows that not everyone will welcome him or his line—but if he marries Elizabeth of York his claim will be all the stronger.'

'If he does,' Sir Henry Shearer said with a wry look. 'I have heard he is a mite reluctant, but we must hope that sensible counsel will prevail. You go to the coronation I believe?'

'Yes, indeed, for I was bidden by the King,' Rob said. 'I would not offend him for the world, though it is my hope that I may be allowed to return home before too long has passed.'

'There will be rebellions,' Sir Henry said. 'Take my word for it. I know that Lovell and the Staffords are dissenting. I think they will try to press the Earl of Lincoln's claims.'

'I trust you will not be led astray,' Rob said. 'Believe me, Henry Tudor is not a man to be easily dislodged. He has taken the crown and he will hold it no matter what he has to do…'

'You do not want to listen to politics,' Lady Anne said, drawing Melissa away. 'Now that you are warm, I shall show you to your chamber. Let us go upstairs and then we shall eat.'

Melissa was drawn away, listening to her hostess's chatter with half an ear. It was the first time that she had met any friends of Rob's other than the men who fought by his side. She was interested in hearing how long they had known him and whether they were relatives, but Lady Anne was gabbling about inconsequential things and Melissa did not wish to interrupt her.

'Now this is yours and Rob's chamber,' Lady Anne told her as she showed her into a medium-sized room that was well furnished. It had rush matting on the wooden boards, a large bed, chests on stands and a huge armoire in the corner. 'I daresay you may have been used to having your own rooms, my dear, but I am afraid we have only the one guest room. The house is not large enough for a family of eight—we have six children, you see, and their nurses. However, you have not been wed long and I daresay you will not mind.'

'No,' Melissa said, and smiled as she glanced at the large bed. 'No, I do not mind at all.' At least she would not be alone when the darkness came this night. Rob would be there to protect her from the monsters in her mind....

Chapter Nine

It had been one of the most pleasant evenings of her life, Melissa thought as she went up to the bedchamber she was to share with Rob that night. Lady Anne and Sir Henry were considerate, generous hosts and they had a delightful family. Their eldest son was thirteen and quite the gentleman. He had been allowed to dine with them and had sat by Melissa, entertaining her with stories of his adventures at the school he had attended until that summer.

Melissa had also met the other five children of the marriage, three daughters and two more sons, one no more than six months old. She had enjoyed her brief visit to the nursery, and was enchanted with the loving relationship that existed between Lady Anne, her husband and children.

'I did not know that it was possible to live as happily as you do,' she told her hostess as they walked up the stairs together that night. 'Thank you for sharing your home with me. It was a pleasure to meet your beautiful children.'

'We do have a fine family,' Lady Anne said, and glowed with pleasure at the compliment. 'But do not imagine that they are always as good mannered, my dear. They were on their best behaviour for your sake—especially my darling James. I was very proud of him this evening. He intends to seek a position at court when he is sixteen, and his manners are so pretty that I think he may succeed.'

'Yes, I am sure he will,' Melissa agreed.

She wished her hostess good-night and went into the bedchamber. A fire had been lit in the large, ingle-nook fireplace, which made the room warm and comfortable. Instead of jumping into bed at once after she had undressed as she had often done in her father's draughty house, she sat by the fire in her night rail. She had thrown a thin wrap about her shoulders and was sitting gazing into the fire when the door opened and Rob entered.

She turned her head and smiled at him. 'It is such a luxury to have the fire, Rob,' she said. 'There was nothing to keep me warm at the castle and my father did not believe in fires on any but the coldest of days.'

'This is how a home should be, Melissa,' Rob said. 'Henry was my friend when I was at school. Our fathers sent us away to learn to be gentlemen when we were very young. The school was at the house of the Earl of Scarborough, and though I missed my home I made many friends there.'

'I like your friends,' she told him, a little nervous as she stood up and went to him. 'I am glad you brought me here, Rob.'

'Then it was the right decision,' he said, and reached out for her. He kissed her forehead and then released her. 'Go to bed and sleep if you can,' he said. 'I have things to do and shall be late. I shall not disturb you.'

Melissa watched him leave, and then sat down on the edge of the bed. Why had he not stayed with her? He was kind and considerate, but he had left her to sleep alone yet again. Was it possible that he had married her simply for the lands she brought him?

Her heart did not want to believe it but her mind would not settle and it was a long time before she slept.

Downstairs, sitting before the fire, Rob was restless. He had longed to take Melissa in his arms and kiss her until she melted into him, as she had at Gifford. He wanted to have her wake beside him in the morning, to touch her and feel the softness of her flesh against his, to love her in every way.

He was almost sure that she would have come to him if he had pressed her, but he was afraid that if he asked too much too soon he might lose her or crush her spirit forever. She had suffered too much from the brutality of her father and half brother, and her ordeal in that terrible place had almost killed her. He must curb his impatience, win her to him slowly and teach her to trust him. It was little wonder if she did not trust him for there was a time when he had been harsh with her. He bitterly regretted it now, and wished that he might take back all the bitter words, but there was no way that he could erase that time from her mind.

All he could do was to hope that one day she would remember everything, and that when she did she would be prepared to forgive him.

In the morning, Melissa decided that she was a fool to doubt her husband. Why would he speak to her so kindly if he did not care for her? He was always so busy, and it might only be that he had not wanted to disturb her when it was done. She must be patient and wait for him to speak of whatever was on his mind, for sometimes when he looked at her she fancied she saw doubts in his eyes.

They had decided to stay another day with Lady Anne and Sir Henry, and Melissa spent the morning in her hostess's still-room helping her to bottle plums and pears.

In the afternoon she and Lady Anne sat at their sewing together while the gentlemen were out seeing to estate matters. The evening was spent happily in talking and laughing.

'I shall miss you,' Lady Anne told her as they went up the stairs later that night. 'I hope that you will come and visit us again one day, Melissa.'

'I should like that very much,' Melissa said. 'And I hope that you and your family will come to us when we are settled. We must keep in touch and always be friends. You have such lovely children…' There was a slightly wistful look in her eyes, though she was not aware of it.

'I shall write to you when my husband has occasion to send a letter to yours,' Lady Anne promised and smiled at her. 'But it will not be long before you have your own family to care for, my dear.'

Melissa's smile dimmed, for there would be no children if Rob did not come to her bed. 'Yes, perhaps. I hope it will be so for I should like to have several children.'

'You were an only child?'

'I have a half brother, but he never liked me.'

Was it because of what Harold had done that Rob still stayed away from her bed? Melissa's memory was still hazy in places, but some things had become clearer. She remembered that Rob had been angry for a long time. If they had quarrelled after they were married, it might explain why he was still so distant with her.

What would she do if he never forgave her? The thought of empty years ahead without love to warm her was somehow worse now that she had seen what life could be like in a happy home.

She could only pray that one day Rob would love her again.

Before she went to sleep she prayed that her husband would forgive her and she also prayed that Owain would be successful in finding her mother. It seemed unlikely that she lived, for surely she would have made some effort to see her only child?

It was a mystery and Melissa could only hope that one day she would know the truth.

Owain had not stopped or spared himself on his journey. He had been impatient to set out on this quest since Rob told him that there was a chance that the woman he had never ceased to love might still be alive.

He had believed Elspeth dead, and that her husband had

been responsible. When it happened he had been away visiting his home. Owain was a freeman, his small property consisting of a few fields and a cottage managed for him by his brother Edgar of Harleston. In his youth he had been ambitious and had entered the lord of Meresham's service with high hopes of preferment. However, he had soon enough discovered that his master was a ruthless man, and his wife a beautiful and gentle woman who was cruelly treated.

Owain had transferred his allegiance to her, though the only way he could stay by her side was to wear Lord Whitbread's colours. When he had discovered that Elspeth had died of a fever after giving birth to a daughter, Owain had remained in his service, because he had known that it was the only way he could keep an eye on Elspeth's child. He had had to watch Melissa being ill treated, able only to comfort and care for her from a distance. He had been there when she needed him, but he knew that she did not need him now for she had Rob to care for her. Therefore he was free to follow up this tale of a woman who might be Melissa's mother.

Now he was approaching the Isle of Ely, and he could see the great towers of the magnificent cathedral that had been begun by Saint Ethelreda. It was here that Alanna and her kinsman Morgan of Hywell had come to pray for the miracle that would cure Morgan's son. Apparently, a search had been made for Elspeth once before, but this time it would be thorough. Owain would not rest until he had explored all the avenues that were open to him.

If she still lived, he would find her. He frowned for he wondered why she had never tried to contact him or her daughter. He knew her as a loving, sweet lady, and could not believe that she would simply forget either Melissa or him.

If she had not tried to see them, it was for a good reason. And that meant that she might not wish to be found. But Owain was determined both for his own sake and hers, to say nothing of Melissa who wanted the story to be true so desperately.

Perhaps Elspeth was afraid of her husband. If that were the case Owain would be able to reassure her that she need no longer fear him—if and when he found her.

The noise and bustle in the streets of London surprised Melissa. It was a cool day in early October when they at last reached the city for they had made their journey in easy stages, staying with friends or at the various inns on their way. Rob had sent word ahead and a house had been secured for them. Situated close by the river, it was a large building with an undercroft and a timbered frame that protruded above the lime-washed stone walls below.

Passing through a busy market square, where the vendors were selling everything from the heads of pigs, fish and offal, to leather goods and iron pans, Melissa was forced to hold a scented kerchief to her nose. The stench was unpleasant in the narrow medieval streets, where an open ditch ran through and contained all kinds of filth thrown into it by an uncaring populace, but when they reached the newer houses built farther out it was much better. Here the streets were wider and there were still fields and gardens, which would be filled with perfume in the summer.

She was feeling weary as Rob helped her to dismount, for they had travelled many leagues these past days. However, as she went inside the house a woman came to meet them. She stared at her curiously for she seemed somehow familiar.

'Are you my kinswoman, Alanna Davies?'

'Melissa, my dear child,' Alanna cried, embracing her. 'I have thought of you so often and wished that we might meet. Owain has spoken of you to me, but while your father lived it was impossible to meet. This is a happy day.'

'Yes, indeed,' Melissa said, for she had taken to the kindly woman immediately. I too have wanted to meet, for there are things you may be able to tell me of my mother....'

'Yes, for we were close when young. I went with her when she married and I witnessed her suffering. I was so happy when I learned that you had been wed to Sir Robert, because he is a good man and I hurried to do his bidding and meet you here.'

'Alanna,' Melissa said, kissing her warmly. 'It is so good to see you at last. I would have asked you to come to me after the Abbess told me that you were with my mother shortly before she died—but my father would not have allowed it.'

Alanna made the sign of the cross over her breast. 'Lord Whitbread is dead. I cannot say that I am sorry, for he was not a good man, but I hope that he is at peace.'

'Yes, though perhaps he does not deserve it,' Melissa said, and frowned. 'My mother has been often in my thoughts of late. If she is still alive there must be a reason why she did not seek me out, for I do not think she would have forgotten that she had a daughter.'

'Yes, you are right,' Alanna said, and looked puzzled. 'I too have wondered and I cannot imagine what would keep her from you, my dear. But we shall speak of this another day. Come in, for you must be weary.'

'Yes, I am a little,' Melissa agreed. She turned to look at Rob as he entered the hall. 'Alanna is here.'

'I am glad,' Rob said, and came to take her hand. He smiled at Alanna. 'You are welcome, mistress. I hope that you will stay with us for as long as you wish.'

'She could come home with us, couldn't she?' Melissa asked, looking at Rob with a hint of pleading in her eyes.

'Of course, my love,' he said easily. 'Mistress Davies is welcome to make her home with us if she so chooses. She would be company for you when I am from home.'

'That is generous indeed,' Alanna said. 'May I think about it for a few days while you reside in London? Morgan of Hywell has been good to me, but I think he may take a bride soon and then I might prefer to live elsewhere.'

'Then come back to Melford with us,' Melissa urged.

'I shall tell you in a few days,' Alanna said. 'Now I shall take you upstairs. You will be pleased to know that Rhona is here and eager to be reunited with you. She told me that she was glad to leave the castle for she has been treated ill and forced to work in the kitchens since you left.'

'My poor Rhona. I was distressed when my father would not let me take her with me, but it is all so much better now,' Melissa said. 'I am so pleased you are here. It was good of you to come, Alanna.'

'It was your husband who sent me the money to travel,' Alanna said. 'No doubt he wanted to please you, for I understand that you have suffered much since I last saw you—as has he, the poor man. That scar must have been painful when it was first inflicted.'

'I think it still pains him at times,' Melissa said, 'though Naomi gave him something for it and I believe that it is beginning to heal at last.'

'It does not disturb you?'

'No, for he is my husband and I love him.'

'You are truly fortunate to have found such a man,' Alanna said. 'I loved a man once but he did not notice me...' She sighed and then her expression changed, becoming uncertain. 'I must tell you that your half brother is in London. I have heard that he came to petition the King for the lands that were your father's. He claims them as his right as Lord Whitbread's natural son, but I do not know if his plea will succeed. You are the true heir to the Whitbread lands, Melissa.'

'I do not care for my father's lands,' Melissa said. 'I do not think that Rob wants them, either. What is ours by right is the estate left to me by my grandfather. If the King will grant us those lands, then Harold is welcome to Meresham.'

'It is not that simple,' Alanna told her. 'Harold might indeed have a right to them for I believe it was your father's intention to leave most of his wealth to him—but your father has been attained as a traitor and the lands are to become the property of the Crown.'

'I see…' Melissa frowned for she was not sure what would be the outcome. 'I know that Harold feared my father would leave his manors to my sons, but he must know that it is different now.'

'Be careful of him,' Alanna warned. 'I think he might do something violent if the King thwarts him. Especially if he believes that you are to benefit instead.'

'But I do not want Meresham nor any of my father's lands,' Melissa said. 'And Rob has told me that he does not intend to claim them in my name—only those lands that were my grandfather's and mine by right.'

'You have told me and I believe you,' Alanna said, still looking anxious. 'But your half brother probably believes otherwise. Now that you are come to London he may well imagine that you mean to claim what he thinks of as his.'

'Rob will tell him that it is not so if they meet,' Melissa said. 'I hope that I need never see him again.'

The subject was dropped for they had reached the bedchamber, where Rhona was waiting to greet her mistress. The woman broke down in tears for she had believed that she would never see Melissa again and was overwhelmed when embraced.

'Oh, my lady,' she sobbed. 'I thought you might be dead for I knew that you were to wed that evil man….'

'I think he tried to kill me,' Melissa said, 'for he hoped to claim my lands one day—but he is the King's prisoner and I am here.'

'The Marquis of Leominster was hanged,' Rhona said, and made the sign of the cross over her breast. 'I saw the crowd yesterday at the gates of the Tower, where his body has been displayed for all to see. They say that he went proudly to his death, cursing the name of Tudor with his last breath.'

Melissa turned pale, feeling a little weak at the knees. 'I

pray that God may give him rest, though I cannot pretend to feel sorrow at his death or the manner of it. He was a wicked, cruel man.'

'They say his lands are forfeit to the Crown,' Rhona said as she took her mistress's cloak from her. 'Had you been his wife, you might have found yourself a prisoner of the Tower.'

Melissa shivered, for she knew that she could not survive being incarcerated in a prison again. 'Please, do not let us speak of these things. I am married to Sir Robert of Melford and I wish to forget everything else that happened to me.'

'Forgive me, my lady,' Rhona said. 'Some of your things were sent here ahead of you and I have prepared them. Would you like to wear your blue tunic or the green?'

'I think I shall wear the blue this evening,' Melissa said. 'But I need some new gowns. We must send for the silk merchant and have him bring some samples of his wares.'

'There are many silk merchants here in London,' Rhona said. 'We could visit some of them and you would have a wider choice of cloth.'

'Yes, perhaps,' Melissa agreed. 'I must have a new gown for the King's coronation after all…'

'I would come with you if I could,' Rob told Melissa a day or so later when she spoke of her desire to have a new gown made for the coronation. 'However, I have been bidden to attend on Henry this morning. You must take both Alanna and Rhona with you, my love—and I shall send two of my men to accompany. Your brother will hardly dare to accost you for if he harmed you, he would certainly incur the King's anger.'

'I do not fear Harold,' Melissa said. 'I should not have gone so easily with him the last time had I not feared what my father might do to Rhona. Harold does not have the same power to frighten me. I know that he hates me for he fears that I shall claim my father's manors, but he can do nothing to harm me now.'

'I know that he has petitioned the King, but thus far Henry has refused him an audience. I believe he is waiting to hear what I have to say on the matter.'

'You will not claim my father's manors?'

'I have no use for them. My own lands are sufficient in themselves, though your lands would be something to pass on to our children, Melissa. I shall ask Henry for justice for you but nothing more.'

'It is as I thought,' Melissa said, and smiled. 'My brother need not fear me—so why should he seek to harm me?'

'He has no cause,' Rob agreed, but frowned. 'Yet do not trust him, my dearest. He has a vicious nature and might seek to harm you for his own satisfaction.'

'Then I shall stay well clear of him,' Melissa said. She moved towards him, gazing up at him. 'It is some days since we were apart for more than a few hours. I shall miss you, Rob.'

'I shall be back this evening and we shall dine together,' Rob told her. 'Enjoy yourself and make sure you buy some material for your kinswoman and Rhona, as well. They should both have new gowns for the coronation, too, even if they only stand in the street and watch the procession.'

'How generous you are,' Melissa said. 'It was in my mind but I did not like to ask for I have no money of my own as yet.'

'You will have,' Rob promised her. 'I am certain that Henry means to grant you all that is yours by right.'

'Tell him that I send my good wishes and my duty.'

'Yes, of course,' Rob said. 'I must go for I may not keep him waiting.'

Melissa was feeling pleased with herself as she left the merchant's house. She had visited several in the thriving community, which housed cloth merchants of all kinds, selling good English wool, velvet, exquisite linens, damask and fine Italian silks. Since the Chinese monopoly had been broken, the home of beautiful silks in the western world was Italy, where some of the finest materials were produced, and transported to many countries, including England. It was from a selection of these figured silks that she had bought lengths of cloth for herself and her women.

'We have been very extravagant,' Alanna said as they left the last shop they visited. She was carrying some small parcels that contained laces and braid, but the bolts of cloth would be delivered to the house later that day. 'I hope that Sir Robert will not be displeased.'

'No, I am sure he will not,' Melissa said, 'for he said that I was to buy all that we need. We ought to look for a shoemaker for we shall need new shoes, but perhaps that will keep for another day.'

'Oh, yes,' Alanna agreed. 'I think they are situated a little distance from here.' She glanced across the road at the Cheapside Cross, which marked one of twelve places where Queen Eleanor's coffin had once rested, erected to her memory by King Henry III. Alanna frowned as she saw that a man was staring at them. 'Is that who I think it is, Melissa?'

Melissa followed the direction of her gaze, a chill running through her as she saw the man. It was her half brother, Harold, and from the way he was staring at her, he had lost none of his feeling of resentment towards her.

'Yes, I believe it is,' she agreed. 'He seems to be alone. Do you think that we should speak to him?'

'No, I do not,' Alanna said. 'Sir Robert said that you were to stay well clear of him, and I think it would be best if you did as he bid you in this instance, Melissa.'

'Yes, perhaps you are right,' Melissa said. Had she been left to herself, she might have wished her half brother well and told him that she did not mean to claim the estates that he believed his by right, but in the circumstances she decided that her kinswoman was being sensible. It would be best to stay away from him. She merely nodded her head in passing, walking to where her litter was waiting, for she was to be carried to the river and would be rowed out to the landing stage at the bottom of the garden that Rob had hired for their use. From there she and her ladies would walk up to the house through the gardens.

From across the street, Harold of Meresham watched her leave. She had several servants and armed men with her, and he knew that in his present circumstances he could do nothing to ensure her sudden demise. His mouth screwed up with bitterness, for he had just come from the King's court at the Palace of Westminster, where he had been told once more that an audience was denied him. He had been commanded to return to his home and wait until the King's judgement on the matter was sent to him.

Smarting from his humiliation at the court, where he had been made aware that he was a bastard and of very little consequence, his eyes followed Melissa until she entered her litter and was carried away.

How he hated her! If Lord Whitbread had married his mother he would be the rightful heir, and even when a man had been attained for acts of treachery his estate usually passed to his legitimate son. Harold had taken no part in the battle at Bosworth and he regretted it. He would have liked to be there and to have seen it end otherwise. It had in his opinion been a shameful affair, which had lasted no more than two hours, and perhaps finished as it had only because Richard had been killed. Had it ended as he believed it ought with Richard triumphant, Harold might even now be lording it at Meresham. However, his father had commanded him to Gifford and he had obeyed, as always.

He turned and walked away. That proud bitch would have everything and it was not fair. She should have been the wife of a traitor and condemned with him to imprisonment or death instead of being received as the wife of one of Henry's favourites.

As he waited in the draughty passages and courtyards of the

King's court, he had heard whispers about Robert of Melford. It was said that he was to be created an earl for the favours he had rendered the King. The prospect of his half sister becoming a countess, feted at the court at which he had been treated little better than a leper, rankled in his breast.

Had she been alone this day he would not have hesitated to do her some harm. If he could think of a way to murder her without being caught and hung, he would do it. She must surely be alone sometimes. Perhaps not here in London, but perhaps when she went home to her husband's house at Melford.

An unpleasant smile lingered about his mouth. He would bide his time, and when the chance arose, perhaps in a few months when she was no longer so closely guarded…then he would take great pleasure in breaking that slender neck with his bare hands.

Rob left the King's presence and went outside into the chill of a grey autumn day, feeling slightly stunned. He had not expected to be elevated to the rank of an earl. Nor had he been expected to be given the lands and manors of Gifford.

'I ask for nothing more than my wife's own lands to be restored to her,' Rob had said when it had been explained to him that he was being rewarded for coming to Henry's aid with a strong force and for putting down the rebellious lords Gifford and Leominster.

'You have served me well, Lord Melford,' Henry told him. 'I have other plans for Leominster's manors, and those of your wife's late father—but Gifford's are yours by right of conquest. You are the kind of man I would have on my side in the coming months. I know that there are dissenters—Lovell and the Staffords may try to put Lincoln in my place. You are free to go home after the coronation, but keep your men at the ready for I may have need of you again.' He smiled a little grimly. 'Your wife's lands are hers by right of inheritance, and I do not interfere with the law, even though she became my ward when I took the Crown. You deserve wealth and honours, Robert of Melford—and they are yours.'

Rob could say nothing but express his gratitude and promise that he would answer Henry's summons if need be. He had hoped to earn honours and perhaps win wealth when he offered his affinity to Henry Tudor in France, but he had been given so much more.

'In the matter of the legality of your marriage,' Henry went on as Rob was silent. 'It is true that Leominster might have had some claim on her—but he was a traitor and has met his death as he deserved. You have my permission for the marriage, and if I were you, I would have it blessed in church once more so that when your son is born, no man can point the finger and say he is not legitimate.'

Rob thanked him again. He knew that one of the first things Henry had done on returning to London was to have all known documents declaring King Edward's sons illegitimate destroyed. Perhaps it was because his own right of descent began in bastardy from the union of John of Gaunt and Katherine Swynford.

Walking back through streets that were rapidly becoming dark, Rob was thoughtful. His father had left him a fine estate. Now he had Melissa's lands and manors and those of Gifford. It made him a rich and powerful man, as befitted the new title he had been given.

He was not sure what he ought to do, for Gifford was in the north and his own lands lay on the borders of England and Wales. He might sell Gifford for he did not wish to live there— and perhaps he should do something for the widowed Lady Gifford and her young son.

Rob had acted according to the King's wish in subduing Gifford. He had not planned or wished to benefit from his actions, other than to find Melissa and marry her. Gifford had betrayed his promise by stealing Melissa from him and had paid the price for his treachery at the hands of Leominster's bullies.

He owed him nothing and would not have given him his lands had he lived—but perhaps he should help Lady Gifford.

He was frowning as he approached the house he had taken for a few weeks. He need make no decision as yet. Lady Gifford had retired to her own small manor and might be content as she was. He would think about it when he had time.

The frown left his face as he went into the house. He had good news for Melissa. He would take her to buy the clothes befitting her new rank tomorrow and perhaps visit the goldsmiths to buy her some jewels—the kind of thing that he could only have dreamed of giving her before this day.

It was only a few weeks to the King's coronation, and after that they could go home.

Melissa started up from her dream. She had been dreaming such terrible things! She blinked as someone struck a tinder, lighting a candle and she saw Rob. He had pulled on a robe, but had obviously just risen from his bed in the next chamber.

'I heard you cry out,' he said. 'Are you ill?'

'It was a dream,' Melissa said. She shuddered and then Rob was there beside her on the bed, his arm about her shoulders. 'I was so afraid…please do not leave me. Stay with me…the monster comes…the monster comes…' She caught back a sob. 'Oh, what is it? What happened to me that haunts me still?'

Rob caught hold of her, pressing her to him, stroking her head while she wept against his shoulder. 'Hush, my love,' he said. 'I am here. There is nothing to harm you.'

'Oh, Rob,' she said on a sobbing breath. 'It was such a terrible dream. I was in a black cavern and there were the bones of men who had died there. I called out for you but you did not come and then I saw it…the black-winged monster of death. It came for me.' She gazed up at him, her eyes wide and frightened. 'It was so real. I was cold and hungry and the candles had burned down and…' She stopped as the mists in her mind finally cleared and she remembered. 'But it wasn't a dream, was it? I *was* there in that terrible place. The marquis said that he did not need me for I was his wife by law and that he would claim my lands by force if need be…' Another shudder ran through her. 'I am not dreaming now—am I?'

'No, my love,' Rob said, and held her all the tighter. 'It must seem like a nightmare, but it did happen. I did not know what that monster Leominster had done to you until I entered the castle.' He groaned aloud, because he knew that if the siege had been prolonged into weeks or months, as it might have been, he would surely have been too late. 'I am sorry for what happened to you. I cursed myself for not coming to you earlier that night at Gifford, Melissa. Forgive me for not protecting you as I ought.'

'Oh, Rob,' she said, and now the tears ran down her cheeks for with the return of her memory had come release from the hidden shadows in her mind. 'It was not your fault. My kinsman used a secret way to enter the castle. Agnes knew he was there but she did not warn me. I believe she thought that I would report her to the Bishop for killing my aunt. I have not told you, but she gave the Abbess her medicine the night she died. The dose was too strong and it killed her. I am not sure if she knew what would happen before she gave it, but I think she may have been carrying out my father's orders.'

'She has been sent away,' Rob said. 'You need never see her again.' He smiled and touched her cheek. 'Has it all come back to you now, my love?'

'Yes, I think so,' Melissa said, and looked at him. 'It has been coming back little by little, and now I think I remember everything. I know that I sent you away the night we were wed, but then I came to you in your bed, because I wanted to be your true wife and you were ill. You told me that you would set me free, but I came to you again because I did not wish to be free of my vows and…' Her cheeks were tinged with rose as she recalled the passion of their loving that night. 'You must have thought me shameless.'

'I thought you warm, giving and lovely in every way,' he said, 'but never shameless, my sweet. I would have you no other way.'

'Then you have forgiven me for what I did—for all the things that were done to you in my name?'

'Long ago,' he said, and smiled at her.

'Then why did you not come to me?'

'Because you were so ill. I feared to touch you for I was afraid that you might become ill again.'

'Oh, Rob,' Melissa said as she nestled against his strong body, her hands moving over his chest, her fingers pushing in between the sprinkling of dark hairs that arrowed down to his navel. 'I am so lucky. If you had not seen me that day by the stream, I should have been wed to the marquis now and desperately unhappy.'

'It was a fortunate day for us both,' Rob said. 'We must put all the rest behind us, forget it as if it had never been, for both our sakes.' His arms surrounded her, pulling her to him as they lay together, kissing her with all the hunger and need such a desperate thought had aroused in them both.

They made love then, and it was a slow, sweet coupling that became a conflagration at the last, consuming them both so that they lay together, satiated and completely as one.

The streets of London were filled with people who had come out to see the new King on his way to be crowned. It was a great occasion for no expense had been spared, for the Steward of the Royal Household had sent his minions flying all over London to purchase cloth of gold, ermine for trimmings, ostrich feathers, silk fringes for the banners that would hang from arches and poles and all manner of costly things. Now that the day had come it was an array of glittering pomp and magnificence that had the people gasping.

Melissa and Rob were amongst the many nobles who attended the ceremony and the feast afterwards, for Henry Tudor knew how to gain the respect of those about him. Melissa was wearing a gown of green silk velvet braided with gold. She wore Rob's wedding gift about her throat and a cap of gold set with more emeralds and pearls on her head.

Watching her as she enjoyed the spectacle, Rob thought that she was as regal as any queen. Her proud spirit had been restored and she was once again the fiery beauty that had stolen his heart.

He longed to take her home, to show her the house and lands he loved, and to live with her in peace and happiness. She turned her head and smiled at him, and he felt the last vestige of bitterness fade away. If Melissa could forgive and be happy again then he could do no less.

Chapter Ten

'Come, Melissa, we are home at last,' Rob said as he lifted her down from her palfrey, holding her in his arms to kiss her briefly before letting her go. 'This is my house—pray, tell me if you think it will suit you to live here, my dearest.'

Melissa looked at the vista before her. They had stopped a little distance from the house for Rob had told her that this was the best place to see it, and, she suspected, he had wanted to be alone with her before they arrived. They were standing on a slope looking down at the valley, which was just now bathed in a rare moment of winter sunshine. The house and surrounding walls were built of a yellowish stone in the midst of rolling parklands, with a dense wood to the east. On the horizon far beyond lay a dark smudge, which she knew were ridges of mountains in Wales.

There was a gatehouse with two towers arching over the entrance to the courtyard. Beyond that she could see the roof of a fine hall, which consisted of one long structure facing the south and another wing to the west. It had arched windows and had been designed in the modern way for living rather than as a fortress, though the walls were stout and would withstand anything but a determined assault.

'It is beautiful,' Melissa told Rob with a smile, for she had seldom seen a finer hall. 'I like it very well.'

'It has replaced a much older hall that once stood here,' Rob said, and she could hear the pride in his voice. 'My father had the old building pulled down when he inherited Melford from his father. He built the main hall first and then added the west wing. It was his intention to add another when he could, but he never did it. I shall finish what he began.'

'It will be a grand house then,' Melissa said, and smiled up at him. 'We shall need a big family to fill it, Rob.'

'Yes, perhaps,' he agreed, and stroked her cheek with his fingertips, sending a tingle of pleasure down her spine. 'But we shall have our friends to stay and you have Alanna to be your companion. There may be others you would wish to live with us.'

'I do not think so…unless…' She sighed for there had been no word from Owain and she was afraid that his search would come to nothing. She lifted her head, refusing to dwell on something that could only spoil the happiness she felt in coming to her home at last. 'Shall we go now, Rob? I am longing to see what it looks like inside.'

'You will wish to make changes I daresay,' Rob told her with an indulgent look. 'My mother died too soon, Melissa, and my father lost interest in the house. I believe that there is much a woman might do to make it more comfortable.'

'That will be my pleasure,' Melissa told him. 'It will be exciting to have the ordering of a house for I was never allowed my way in my father's house.'

'Now you have your own home,' Rob said. 'One day we shall ride over to visit your own estate for it lies only twenty leagues to the west and is, as you know, in Wales.'

'My mother came from there,' Melissa said. 'Owain told me tales of her so that I felt I knew her, but I have always wished that I might have known her.'

'It is sad that you lost her so early in life,' Rob said. 'I can remember my mother when I was a lad and those memories are happy ones.'

'It was generous of Owain to go in search of her,' Melissa said, and frowned. 'He has always been so kind to me. I have often wondered why he was content to stay in my service when he might have returned to his own estates.'

'No doubt he has his reasons,' Rob said. He had his suspicions, but Owain had not confided in him and he could not be certain. He would say nothing for it was Owain's secret to tell, not his.

Owain looked at the Abbey that stood just a little distance ahead. He had that morning come from the Isle of Ely, his inquiries there having been of little help. No one had heard of the lady Elspeth of Whitbread—nor yet of Elspeth Davies. He had been on the verge of giving up his quest when one elderly woman had told him that some twenty leagues farther on there was an Abbey, which took in homeless women and cared for them in a hostel.

'Some years ago I remember a woman who came to pray at the shrine of Saint Ethelreda,' the woman said. 'She was sitting in the road and begging for food. I gave her a coin and directed her to the Abbey for I felt pity for her, but I do not know her name. Many pilgrims come to pray at the Cathedral, but there are so many sick and weary and the miracles do not happen for all. They travel elsewhere looking for shrines where their prayers may be answered.'

Owain thanked her and set out for the Abbey. It was a small chance but he had nothing more to guide him. As the old crone had said, pilgrims came and went to all the important shrines and churches. He had passed several on the roads on his way here. Many went to foreign lands in search of forgiveness for sins or a cure that might come from a powerful saint.

Approaching the Abbey, Owain dismounted and went to ring the bell for admittance. A monk came in answer to his summons, unlocking the heavy oak gate before asking his business.

'I would have shelter for the night, brother,' Owain said. 'I have been searching for a lady and I was told that there is a hostel that cares for the homeless here.'

'That is run by the Abbess,' the monk said. 'Come in, traveller, and we shall give you food and a pallet for the night. In the morning you may ask if the Abbess will see you. I know that many women have received her care. Some stay but a night, others remain for some days or months—some have died here.'

'Thank you for your kindness,' Owain said. He was feeling weary for he had not spared himself on his journey here. He had set out full of hope, but that flame had died and now he believed that his search might well be in vain, though he would go on searching. If Elspeth had come here to pray for help, she might have visited the many shrines up and down the country. He would keep searching until he found her or heard news of her death.

'It is good to meet you at last,' Megan said to her new mistress as she took her upstairs to her chamber. Her eyes went over Melissa, warm with approval. 'I hoped that Rob would find a lady who would love him. I thank God that he has found her, my lady.'

'I believe it was you who nursed my husband when he was so badly hurt,' Melissa said. 'I must thank you for all that you have done for him, for without your care he might have died.'

'I use only simple cures, my lady,' Megan replied. 'I do not have any of the special skills that are granted to some. But I knew that he would live despite his hurts, for none has a braver heart or a stronger will.'

'He is brave and strong,' Melissa agreed, but smiled because it was the tender, gentle side of Rob that made her love him. 'This is a fine house,' she said as they went up the grand stairway. 'I have never seen so much beautiful carving in the woodwork—and the panelled walls must make the house so much the warmer in the winter.'

'We are sheltered in this valley,' Megan told her. 'The house is solid and withstands even the worst storms, but when it is cold we have fires in all the chambers. You will want to see the rest of the house, my lady—though perhaps my lord will wish to show you himself?'

'Yes, perhaps,' Melissa said, and looked thoughtful. 'Can you tell me where the nursery is situated? I should like to see that now if I may?'

'Before your own chamber?' Megan looked at her intently and then smiled and nodded. 'Yes, I see it. Does my lord know that you are carrying his child?'

Melissa flushed a delicate pink. 'I am not yet sure for we have been travelling and I thought it might have been some of the rich food we were given that made me a little queasy of late.'

'You have not been sick?'

'No, though once or twice I felt as if I might be,' Melissa said. 'Are women always sick when they carry a child?'

'It is usually the case,' Megan said, 'though I have heard of cases where it is not so very bad. It may be that you will carry your babe easily—or the sickness may come upon you at any moment.'

Melissa nodded and smiled. 'I have hoped that it might be so for my courses have not come this month. Though I was ill, and they might have been delayed because of my illness.'

'Yes, it is possible,' Megan said. 'But I have seen the signs many times, and now I look at you I see them in your face. I think there will be a child.'

'I shall pray that you are right,' Melissa said. 'I would give my husband many sons—but I would like a daughter, as well. It is my hope that we shall have a large family.'

Megan's knowing eyes went over her slender form. 'It may not be easy for you to give birth, my lady, but I shall be with you when the time comes. As for how many children you will bear, that is in God's hands.'

'Yes, I know it,' Melissa said. 'But if my prayers are answered we shall have at least four children.'

Megan laughed. 'I see that you are as brave as you are beautiful, my lady. I think that Lord Melford has chosen well.'

'Pray, do not call him by that title if you do not wish to see him frown,' Melissa said. 'Rob is new to his honours and prefers to answer to his name or sir.' Her laughter rang out for she was feeling happy. 'As for me, I want no more than to be the wife of Robert of Melford.'

'Did I hear someone call my name?' Rob asked, coming up behind them at that moment. 'You dawdle on the stairs, Melissa. Come, I would show you the rest of the house…' He took hold of her arm, taking her with him. Melissa looked back at her housekeeper and made a face.

'I shall see you later, Megan,' she said. 'I must go with Rob now.'

'What were you talking about so earnestly?' Rob asked as he took her along the gallery to a room at the far end. 'These are your chambers and mine are beyond them, though actually in the west wing. We are connected through a room where clothes are stored on shelves, which means I can come to you at night in private whenever I wish.'

'I like you to stay with me all night,' Melissa told him. 'I want to wake with you beside me.'

'As I shall for most of our lives, my love,' Rob said, and smiled. 'But there may be times when you need to be alone or to rest and then I shall leave you to sleep in peace.'

'I can think of no reason why you should not be with me,' Melissa said as he opened the door and drew her inside. 'Oh, Rob, this is so lovely…the colours are so bright…'

'I had it refurbished for you,' he said. 'Green is the colour of your eyes, and they range from light to dark with your moods. Sometimes they are almost blue but they can be as green as emeralds.'

She laughed, for he looked at her as if he would like to devour her and she knew that his hunger for their loving had grown stronger with the days and weeks.

'Tell me,' he said, because it had puzzled him 'why did you keep that fairing. You wear it sometimes still…'

Melissa smiled and drew the tiny jade heart from inside her gown. 'I keep it to remind me that love is fragile, as fragile as this trinket that you gave me long ago, Rob. It is as precious to me as the emeralds you gave me on our wedding night.'

'You say that love is fragile, but our love was surely put to a harsh test…and in the end we found happiness.'

'Yes, we found happiness,' Melissa said, and smiled. 'And now we have so much—but still I shall keep my trinket.'

She looked at the silken drapes about the bed, which were sea-green and shot through with silver. The coverlet was a slightly deeper shade and matched the drapes at the window, which were looped back with cords of silver thread. A stool had been covered in a deeper green and looped about with silver braid and the coffer on a stand that would be used to hold her combs and brushes had a cloth of green and silver to soften its hard lines. There was an embroidery frame of twisted wood that had a stand formed like an *X* and two hutches with carved panels to hold her possessions. Also a chair with a high back, which was carved with a religious scene, and smooth arms, and since it was new, must have been commissioned for her. Above the bed were draped more silken swathes and a large silver cross was fastened to the wall.

'This is perfect, just perfect,' she said. 'thank you so much for having it done for me, Rob.'

'It is not finished,' he told her with a smile. 'You have enough to make you comfortable, but you will want your own things about you. You must tell me what you need for your pleasure, Melissa, and it shall be ordered.'

'I shall make cushions for the chair,' Melissa said, 'and hangings for the wall, but there is little else I need to order. I have my harp and my writing materials and all the trinkets you have bought for me in London, Rob. Once they are unpacked I shall have all I need here.'

'I am glad you are content, but I fear that the rest of the house may need your touch, Melissa. My father built it but left many rooms unfurnished. You must tell me what you think we need and I shall send to town for them.'

'Yes, of course,' she said. 'If it pleases you, I should like to see the nursery next....'

'The nursery?' Rob was surprised, his gaze narrowing as he looked at her. 'Are you telling me...you carry my child?'

'I am not certain,' Melissa told him, laying her hand on his arm. 'You must not hope for too much just yet, my love—but I think I may have conceived your son as we journeyed here.'

'Beloved,' Rob said, and caught her to him, holding her pressed close to his chest. 'It is wonderful news if it be true— and if it is not, it will happen soon for why should it not?'

'I do not know,' Melissa said. 'I have thought—and Megan says that she can see the signs.'

'If Megan says it is so I think you may rest easy, my heart,' Rob said. 'For there are few wiser.

'She will take care of you,' Rob said. 'And you have Alanna and Rhona to bear you company. I do not think you need to fear it when the time comes.'

'I do not fear it,' Melissa said, smiling up at him. 'I want to have at least four children, perhaps more if God wills it.'

'Whether it be one or six, I shall be content, as long as I have you,' Rob said, and drew her to him, kissing her long and sweet before releasing her. 'And now I shall show you the nursery and the rest of the house before we dine....'

Owain rose early the next morning, breakfasting simply on bread and water as the monks did and joining them for prayers. Afterwards, he went out into the gardens, which were divided into squares. Some had beds of herbs that the monks used for making the cures they sold to support their way of life. In other squares they grew food and others were the home for various flowers, which gave food for the bees that provided honey. The monks made wine from the honey and other ingredients, most of which was sold and the money used for charitable purposes.

The Abbey was like a small hamlet, providing work for all kinds of trades and making the monks completely independent. Next to the infirmary, where the sick were tended was a wall and a gate. It was through this gate that Owain was taken the next morning by one of the monks. A nun, who greeted him with a nod of the head but did not speak, led the way to the small, dark room where he was to have his meeting with the Abbess.

Owain stood looking out of a narrow window at the garden. It was very much like the one the monks tended, but there were no hives. The nuns grew food and made ale for their own use, but did not have all the skills of the monks.

'How may I help you, sir?' A woman's voice made him turn suddenly. His heart leaped as he looked into her face, a finger of ice trickling down his spine for despite the years he knew her. 'Owain…' The colour faded from Mother Abbess's face and she seemed to sag for a moment, though as he would have moved closer to her she held up her hand to ward him off. 'No, do not try to touch me. I am no longer of your world. My life is given to God.'

'Elspeth,' he cried, his voice hoarse with emotion. 'All these years I believed you dead. Why did you not come to me when you ran away that night? Why did you not tell us that you were alive? Melissa has grieved for you these many years.…'

'Do not reproach me, Owain. You do not know my story.'

'Will you tell me?' he asked. Again he moved towards her, but she held up her hand to ward him off once more. 'Forgive me. It is seeing you so unexpectedly…'

'I have seen you since that night,' Elspeth said. 'I saw you with her…my daughter…and I knew that she was safe. I would have come to her if I dared but he would have killed me had he found me. He beat me that night for I would not tell him the name of my lover. I was left for dead, but I still lived and I recovered my senses. I sneaked away under cover of darkness and I ran until I could run no more. Then I became ill and I wandered for a long time…'

'You should have come to me, Elspeth.'

'I am Mother Abbess now,' she said. 'I could not come to you, Owain, for I was too ill to know what I did. I should have died had a good woman not found me. She took me in and nursed me back to life.…'

'But why did you not send word to me then?'

'Because when I was well enough to understand, I knew that she had taken me to join a leper colony in her house. She was a woman of some wealth and she cared for twenty poor souls. She was in the early stages of the disease, but she knew that by taking me to her home she might have given me her disease.'

'A leper…' Owain looked at her face. She was standing in shadows and he could see no sign of the dread disease. 'Are you telling me that you…'

'I did not take it from her,' Elspeth said, 'though I stayed there for two years until she died and I nursed her. She was the last and after she was buried, I left her house. I thought that I might have taken the sickness and I made a pilgrimage to various shrines praying for a cure.'

'But still you did not come to me—to your daughter?'

'At one of the shrines I visited I had a vision,' Mother Abbess told him. 'A voice came to me out of a bright light and said that I had been given a gift, but must use it for the good of others. I was directed to this place, where I have lived ever since. You see, I am able to nurse the lepers who come to us— and by helping them I do God's work and atone for my sins.'

'Your sins?' Owain frowned. 'Do you speak of the love we

had for each other? I do not think of it as a sin. You were un-happy and I sought to comfort you.'

'But it was a sin,' Elspeth said. 'I was married and I made my husband angry, that is why he beat me. He had the right and I forgave him when I took my vows here as a novice. I have no bitterness in my heart, Owain, and nor should you. I am content. You must forget me. It was so many years ago. I had thought you would have found someone else to marry long ago.'

'I gave my service to our daughter,' Owain said. She had moved closer and he could see the serenity in her face. He was aware of anger. For years he had grieved for her and he knew that Melissa longed to see her. 'Have you no thought for her, Elspeth? Do you never think of the child you bore?'

'She is dead to me as I was to you,' Elspeth said. 'It is a pity that you came here, Owain. If I had known it was you, I should not have given you this time. You must leave here at once and forget me. I am the bride of God and can never live outside these walls again.'

'Your sister was an Abbess but she loved Melissa. She saw her as often as she could. Do you not want to at least see your daughter?'

'It would bring her only sadness,' Elspeth said, and for a mo-ment there was uncertainty and a hint of pain in her voice. 'If you ever loved me, Owain, I beg you to tell her that I am dead. Do not bring her more grief.'

'You are cruel and selfish,' Owain said, and moved towards her, intending he knew not what, but she gave a cry and moved back.

'Stop! Do not touch me unless you wish to become a leper.'

'You said that you did not take it from her?'

'I did not then, but it has begun to show in me now,' Elspeth said. 'I do not know if my vision was false, but I have the early signs of the disease. I think it was not caught from my bene-factor, but here, working amongst the sick. As yet I can continue my life here for no one knows, but soon it will begin to show and I shall be forced to live as a hermit in my quarters.'

'Leave here and come with me now,' Owain urged. 'I will tend you until you die. I still care for you, Elspeth.'

'Do you think that I would give you this evil sickness?' she asked. 'I shall come near neither you nor my daughter, Owain, for it might seal your own deaths. Do as I bid you. Tell her I am dead, for it will soon be the truth.'

Owain heard her words and something seemed to die in him. She was not the woman he had loved so long ago and revered in his thoughts: that woman had died the night her husband beat her or somewhere on the road she travelled. This woman was someone else. She might truly have the terrible sickness she claimed, or she might be lying to force him to leave her, but it did not matter.

'Very well, Mother Abbess,' he said. 'Since that is your wish I must accept it. God be with you.' He walked past her, going out of the room without a glance in her direction, never seeing the tears that had slowly begun to trickle down her cheeks.

Melissa had been sick for the past five mornings. She was certain now that she was carrying Rob's child and the knowledge made her smile despite the physical discomfort she was feeling. He had bid her stay in bed until she felt better but after an hour she had become restless and felt that she needed a little air to refresh her.

She went down to the great hall, which was empty for the moment. The servants had done their work here and were busy elsewhere. Melissa had brought her cloak down with her, and she put it about her shoulders intending to go for a short walk.

However, when she went outside, she discovered that it was a pleasant day, much warmer than usual for the time of year, and decided she would go a little farther than she had intended. It seemed an age since she had been free to walk as she pleased, and she wandered through the courtyard gate into the parkland, thinking that she might climb the hill that would allow her to look down at it. The first time she had not truly appreciated it, for she now realised that it was bigger than she had imagined.

She was frowning as she thought about her mother, as she often did, remembering her in her prayers each night. Owain had been gone some weeks now. She wondered if he had found any trace of her mother. For some reason her hope had begun to fade of late. Alanna said that she thought she must have misled her, because there was no true reason to believe the lily had come from Elspeth.

She must not dwell on thoughts of disappointment, Melissa decided as she realised that she had walked far enough. She was married to the man she loved and expecting her first child, which Megan had predicted, would be a son, because of the way she was carrying. It was not always possible to have everything in life. Even if her mother had left Meresham alive, she might have died long ago.

'Why so pensive, sister?'

Melissa was startled from her reverie by the voice, which came from behind her. Turning, she found herself staring into the hostile eyes of her half brother and a shiver of fear ran through her for she knew that he hated her.

'What are you doing here?' she asked, proud and unsmiling. 'This is my husband's manor and you are not welcome here, Harold.'

'Where should I be since you have stolen the lands that should have been mine?' Harold demanded, his thick lips curved in a sneer of derision. 'Did you think I would take no revenge, sister?'

'I do not know what you mean,' Melissa said, determined to show no fear, though she knew that alone outside the walls of the courtyard she was vulnerable. 'We have made no claim upon your estate, sir, nor do we wish to. The matter is in the King's hands.'

'Do you expect me to believe that when I have been told that I am to inherit nothing?' He moved closer to her, a look of menace in his eyes. 'You think that you have everything, sister—but it will gain you little pleasure in the grave…' With a snarl of hatred, he sprung on her, his hands reaching for her throat.

Melissa screamed as she felt his hands begin to squeeze, struggling against him. Harold had always been a strong man, a huge brute with coarse features and a cunning mind. He had waited his moment to find her alone and now he meant to kill her. She knew even as she tried to pull his hands from her throat that she was not strong enough to resist him.

She was gasping as he forced the breath from her throat, her eyes misting as the darkness descended. She did not see the man who came running to her aid, though she felt the force as Harold's hands were torn from her and she sank to the ground, her head bent and gasping for breath. She was aware that two men were fighting but it was a few moments before she could open her eyes to see what was going on.

Harold was fighting with someone. It was Owain, and they were locked in a desperate struggle for neither was using a weapon. It was a test of strength and she feared that Harold must win for he was the younger man, but even as she wondered whether to run for help, she saw that others were coming to aid Owain and one of them was her husband.

Just as they drew near, she heard the sound of something cracking and then Harold shouted with pain, dropping to his knees. His arm was hanging at an odd angle and she knew that it had been broken. He was cursing and shouting threats of revenge, but Rob had reached her, taking her into his arms.

'I never dreamed that he would dare to come here,' he said, holding her as if he feared that she might break. 'I had vowed revenge on him but thought that he would never bother us again. Forgive me for neglecting my duty.' He looked at her pale face. 'My poor darling, has he hurt you?'

'A little,' she whispered for her throat felt bruised and sore. 'But Owain came…he saved me.'

'I thank God for it that he was in time. You were seen to leave, Melissa, and one of the men sought me to ask if he should follow—and then we saw what happened. We were too far away. If Owain had not been near…' He shuddered for he knew that she might have died. His eyes glinted as he looked at her half brother. 'Take him to Shrewsbury,' he said. 'Let him be tried for murder as he deserves.'

Harold was on his knees, holding the arm that had been snapped in the struggle with Owain. It was his sword arm and he knew that he would never be able to wield it as he once had, his bitterness welling up inside him.

He turned his wrathful gaze on Melissa. 'You think that you are secure and protected now, sister. But I know a secret that will destroy you and everything you have.'

'Be quiet, you wretch,' Rob said, his arm about her. 'Nothing you can do can harm my wife.'

'But you break the laws of God and man each time you take her to your bed,' Harold cried. 'Oswald Melford was your father, Melissa, for he raped your mother and left his seed in her belly—and the child you carry is your half brother's.'

'Damn you,' Rob cried furiously. 'You decry my father's name and shall die for it!' He lunged at him, but Owain held him back.

Melissa watched in horror, her hand to her throat. 'It cannot be…' she whispered. 'Please tell me it cannot be…'

'Melissa, my father was a man of honour and he would never do such a thing, believe me. He lies.'

'He lies, Melissa,' Owain said. 'I think Rob has guessed my secret, though I have never told anyone—but I am your father. Elspeth and I were lovers. It was my child she carried. You are my daughter.'

'You are my father?' Melissa stared at him, the tears slipping from her cheeks. 'Why did you never tell me?'

'I have often longed to tell you,' Owain said, and smiled at her. 'You have been very dear to me, Melissa. I loved your mother and I have loved you—but I could give you nothing else and you were a great heiress. Lord Whitbread would have laid claim to you and I had no proof—or none that would have stood up in a court of law.'

'It is true,' Rob said. 'I have seen the likeness many times. I suspected it when I first saw Owain, but I could not be sure.'

'My father…' Melissa's face lit with happiness. 'I am so glad for you have always been kind to me…' She broke off as Harold broke free of his captors and made a lunge in her direction, but in a second he was secured again.

'Take him away and keep him bound hand and foot,' Rob commanded. 'Make sure that he cannot escape.'

'You had best see me hanged, Robert of Melford,' Harold cried in a rage. 'If I live I shall have my revenge though it takes me the rest of my life.'

'You are a knave and a fool,' Rob said scornfully. He looked at the men who served him. 'Take him to the shire reeve in Shrewsbury. He will know how to deal with the rogue.'

Owain turned to Melissa as Harold was dragged away, still vowing revenge. 'You are not harmed, my child?'

'No, you came in time.' Melissa smiled and held out her hand to him. 'You saved me from certain death,' she said. 'Welcome home, Father.'

'You do not mind?'

'I am glad,' Melissa said, her voice hoarse for she found it difficult to talk. 'I have ever loved you, Owain…my most constant friend.'

Owain smiled and moved closer, bending his head to kiss her cheek. 'I have loved you, daughter, though I dared not claim you.'

Melissa nodded for she understood his difficulty. Had Lord Whitbread known that he was her father, he would have been tortured and killed. 'I was thinking of you earlier and your quest. Have you news of my mother?'

'None that will please you,' Owain said. He reached out and took her hand. 'Your mother cannot be found. I looked for her in many places but found her not. The woman I loved died the night her husband beat her because she would not give him the name of her lover.'

'Yes,' Melissa said, and tears glistened in her eyes but did not fall. 'I have suspected that it was a false hope.' She raised her head, pride mixing with the pleasure she felt at discovering her father. 'But I have my father and my husband and I carry my first child—what more could I want?'

'Melissa must never know the truth,' Rob said, his expression grim as he heard the true story from Owain's lips later that day. 'She has accepted that her mother is dead—and thanks to you suffered no lasting harm. She has her father and that must be enough.'

'You are asking me to make my home here?'

'Yes, if you will stay. We have room enough, Owain, and it is my intention to build onto Melford Hall to make it worthy of my wife and the sons that will follow us. I shall need good men about me and I have met none better.'

Owain smiled at him. 'My brother has cared for my small house and the few acres I own for years. It would be a pity to take it from him now for he has a large family. Yes, I shall stay, Rob, and be glad of it.'

'Then I am satisfied,' Rob said. 'Henry made me an earl though I never sought such an honour, but I must rise to the challenge he has set me. In return for favours given, Melissa's own lands and Gifford's, I have promised to serve him when he sends for me. I shall need someone here at those times. David is a good steward, but you will be my right-hand man, my wife's father.'

'You have my loyalty always.' Owain offered Rob his hand.

'It will be good to know that I have a family of my own in the autumn of my life.'

'You have years enough,' Rob said with a grin and clapped him on the shoulder. 'I am not sure that I could have broken Harold's arm as easily.'

'It was a knack I learned when young. I wrestled often at the fairs until…' He shook his head. 'It does not do to dwell on the past and I shall not. Elspeth is dead and shall be allowed to rest in peace.'

'Amen to that,' Rob said. 'Now I would ask your advice on another matter, Owain. Henry gave me the manors and lands of Gifford, but the earl left a widow and a son—what should I do about them? She has her own dower lands, and I allowed her to leave Gifford—but ought I make some recompense? I know I have no obligation, but I would treat her fairly.'

'You cannot return the manors or the title to her,' Owain said, 'for it would offend the King and might bring his wrath on your head. But you could make a recompense of money—perhaps a tenth of its worth?'

'Yes, that is what I thought,' Rob said. 'I shall send her five hundred gold marks and consider the matter ended.'

'You both look serious,' Melissa said, entering the small room where they were talking at that moment. 'David said you were both here—do I interrupt you?'

'No, of course not,' Rob said, and went to put his arms about her. 'I have good news for you, my love. Your father has promised to make his home with us.'

'Have you, Father?' Melissa's face lit up with pleasure as he inclined his head. 'That is the best news I could wish for.' She smiled at Rob. 'My throat is a little sore but I do not wish to remain in my rooms—may I walk outside if I do not leave the courtyard?'

'You may walk where you wish,' Rob told her. 'But in future I shall send one of my men to follow you and watch over you, though I do not believe Harold will trouble us again. The shire reeve will know how to deal with him.'

Melissa gazed up into her husband's eyes, smiling softly. 'I do not fear to walk alone, Rob. I have faced worse than Harold's attack on me and lived. I merely wanted to ease your mind for I knew that you were anxious for me.'

Rob nodded as he met her bright gaze. The woman he loved so dearly had been restored to him and he was content. The future was filled with promise, for what could harm them now? They had wealth and power, and the lands to support it. Melissa was carrying their first child easily and she would undoubtedly have more, though whether God would send the three sons and a daughter she longed for none could say.

'I shall always be anxious for your safety, because I love you,' Rob told her, taking her hand to kiss the palm. 'But the shadows have gone, my love. We have our whole lives before us and, hopefully, years of happiness to enjoy....'

'Yes,' Melissa agreed, and reached up to kiss the scar that was beginning to fade a little now, though she knew it would always be there as a reminder of the pain he had suffered for her sake. 'We have each other, Rob—and we have my father. Soon we shall have our first child. I think that the future is ours to make what we will of it, and I believe that it will be good....'

She had a vision of the golden years stretching far ahead, of the children who would play happily in the meadowlands and bring their house to life with the sound of laughter. Who knew what lay ahead for them? No one knew, but the richness of their love would surely give them the courage to face whatever might come.

* * * * *

HISTORICAL

Novels coming in April 2010

PRACTICAL WIDOW
TO PASSIONATE MISTRESS
Louise Allen

Desperate to reunite with her sisters, Meg finds passage to
England as injured soldier Major Ross Brandon's temporary
housekeeper. Dangerously irresistible, Ross's dark, searching
eyes warn Meg that it would be wrong to fall for him…
But soon sensible Meg is tempted to move from servants'
quarters to the master's bedroom!

MAJOR WESTHAVEN'S UNWILLING
WARD
Emily Bascom

Spirited Lily is horrified by her reaction to her new guardian,
Major Daniel Westhaven. He's insufferably arrogant – yet she can't
help longing for his touch! Brooding Daniel intends to swiftly
fulfil his promise and find troublesome Lily a husband. Yet she
brings light into his dark life – and into his even darker heart…

HER BANISHED LORD
Carol Townend

Hugh Duclair, Count de Freyncourt, has been accused of
sedition, stripped of his title and banished. Proud Hugh vows to
clear his name! Childhood friend Lady Aude de Crèvecoeur offers
her help – after all, turbulent times call for passionate measures…

™ MILLS & BOON®

HISTORICAL

**Another exciting novel available
this month:**

THE VISCOUNT'S UNCONVENTIONAL BRIDE

Mary Nichols

As a member of the renowned Piccadilly Gentlemen's Club, Jonathan Leinster has been instructed to ensure the return of a runaway. Little does he realise that meeting spirited Louise Vail will change his life for ever…

Having discovered she was adopted, Louise has fled to her birthplace, hoping to find her family – but handsome, charming Jonathan stops her in her tracks! His task is simple: escort Louise promptly home. Yet all he wants to do is claim her as his own!

**The Piccadilly Gentlemen's Club
Seeking justice, finding love**

 MILLS & BOON®